ABOUT THE AUTHOR

Tabitha Bree is an author, crafter, and sometimes yoga instructor based in Melbourne, Australia. A long-time fan of chick lit and romantic comedies, she is happiest when creating worlds for her fictional lovers to frolic in. *The Last Take* is Tabitha's fifth book and the first in her new series *Hollywood Heartthrobs,* each installment depicting a new couple. Check out the *Seeking* trilogy if you're interested in novella-length rom-coms or *Rules of a Breakup* for a stand-alone with all the feels. Visit Tabitha's website to receive a free short story and hear the latest books news!

tabithabree.com

facebook.com/tabithabreeauthor

instagram.com/tabitha_bree

ALSO BY TABITHA BREE

THE LAST TAKE

TABITHA BREE

First published in December 2021

Printed and bound by Kindle Direct Publishing Print

ISBN: 979-8-778-08350-9

Also available as an eBook

Cover design by Tabitha Bree

For Billeye

1

EVIE

I slowly push my front door open and cringe as it creaks, the same way all doors creak when you're trying to be quiet. Poking my head into the hallway, I look both ways to check for other forms of life. The coast is clear.

I slide to the other side of the threshold and gently pull the door closed behind me, careful to turn the doorknob so the latch doesn't make a sound. Turning the key in the lock, I immediately regret the amount of key chains I have as they jingle in response. Like a cat being sold out by the tiny bell around its neck while stalking its lunch.

But I am still the only person in the hallway. Exhaling the breath caught in my throat, I tiptoe toward the elevator, nearly home free.

"Evie, just the person I wanted to see."

If only nearly were enough.

I un-scrunch my face before turning to my landlord. He is standing in front of his own apartment, his beady eyes watching me like I might try to make a run for it.

Which I absolutely consider for a hot second.

"Ron, hi," I say, plastering a smile across my mouth. "You're looking very dapper today. Is that a new shirt?"

Ron stares at me unblinking, not even looking at his khaki green button-down. Which I have seen him wear at least twenty times.

"Your rent is three weeks overdue."

He crosses his arms over his chest and looks at me expectantly, like I might have a handy one thousand dollars hiding in my polka dot blazer.

"I know, I'm so sorry. Since this internship started, it's taken up a lot of time, and I had to cut my hours at the café..."

I let the words trail off, as it's obvious Ron gives zero hoots about my crazy schedule or my unpaid internship. So I go with an alternative.

"You know, I have a batch of oatmeal raisin in my apartment. Should I box you up a couple?"

Ron drops his head with exasperation. A clear signal that I'm making his morning more difficult than he would like it to be.

"I don't want cookies. I don't want cupcakes. I want my money." He circles his hand in my direction. "This little act with the Bambi eyes and the baked goods won't cut it now, kid. I need the three weeks you owe me, plus next week by the end of the month. Otherwise, you're out."

I knew I should've gone with chocolate chip. Who likes oatmeal raisin?

"Please, Ron. I need more time," I say, stepping toward him with my hands in actual prayer position. "We can work something out. Maybe I could help around here? Vacuum the hallway? Or... hey, do any of your clothes need fixing? I'm a whiz on the sewing machine."

As I ramble on, Ron looks down at my light sweater,

which I have embellished myself with tiny bows. He's doing that unblinking thing again.

"I think I'm all good for shirt ribbons."

My eyes dart around the walls as I search for another solution. Four weeks' rent by the end of the month? It's impossible. I'd have to pull double shifts at the café. Which *might* be fine. If I could survive off one hour of sleep every night.

"I just don't know how I'll get the money in time," I say, more to myself than to Ron, who has already lost interest.

"Look, I don't care how you get it. As long as it's under my door by the end of the month. This is Hollywood, kid. If you can't keep up, there's always someone else happy to take your place."

And with those final pearls of wisdom, he disappears behind his door. Where he was probably lurking and waiting to pounce all morning.

I groan and press the down arrow next to the elevator, waiting for it to arrive at a glacial pace, as always. I don't even know why Ron lives in the building. If I owned every apartment on the floor, I certainly wouldn't live here. I'd be sunning myself on the balcony of a condo in West Hollywood. But then again, if Ron didn't live in the building, he wouldn't be able to trap his tenants on their way out.

I sit in my old Volvo, dwelling on my predicament while I wait for the engine to warm. Poor Ron, it's not his fault I have no money and no spare time to *get* more money. He's just trying to pay his bills like the rest of us poor chumps.

I knew leaving boxes of buttery treats outside his door could only last so long.

I drive down Santa Monica Boulevard until the sidewalks are less stained and more rainbow, and eventually I pull up beside a Spanish bungalow-turned-production studio. It's only my second month of interning at Guerilla Productions, but I'm learning a lot. Especially how Mr. Jacobs likes his coffee—piping hot with a shot of vanilla. I try not to get hung up on how much actual production experience I get. Because if I've learned anything since dropping out of medicine to pursue work in the film industry, it's this: What I know doesn't really matter.

But *who* I know is going to make or break my career.

Unlike traditional career paths, where you emerge from your college degree and land on a clear trajectory to a stable salary and 401(k), there are no promises for film graduates. In fact, one particularly jaded professor told our class that only fourteen percent of us would find work in Hollywood.

I can almost hear the *I told you so*'s from my parents' house.

But I won't let myself get deterred that easily. If I have to work my way up from the unpaid bottom, so be it. I can fetch lunch and run errands as good as the next desperate millennial. And most importantly, I'm making connections.

I scramble to answer my phone as it buzzes inside my handbag.

"Evie, where are you?" Caroline squawks into my ear before I can even say hello.

"Yes, I'm here, I'm here. I'm just out the front."

"Great, don't bother coming in. Lyle needs his coffee. Get me a green juice while you're out."

I push the door open with my elbow, balancing the drink tray on one hand like it holds a precious vase from the 1800s. I don't need another green-juice-down-the-crotch situation. Like last week.

"Evie, did you buy more storyboard glue? This one is almost empty," Lyle says without looking up from the large board on the table.

"I did. It's in the second drawer."

He retrieves the full bottle and begins shaking it, frowning as his eyes finally land on me.

"You look like Pippi Longstocking."

I run my hand down my long, light-red braid. "Um, thanks?"

He continues to frown through his thick, black-rimmed glasses before returning to his board, trailing the glue around the edges of a piece of card and sticking it to the top right corner.

"What are we making?" I ask, peering over his shoulder. "Is this for the indie film at Venice Beach? I'm so excited for that to start!"

"The Venice project is on hold," he replies, with the opposite amount of enthusiasm. "They've run out of cash. This is for a lotion commercial."

"Oh." I try to sound interested, but I'd be lying if I said jobs like these inspire me.

When I applied for the internship, Guerilla Productions claimed to specialize in feature films. But so far, I've only seen them working on commercials and the odd social media promotional video. But I don't want to seem ungrateful. At least I'm meeting the right people. Lyle Jacobs built the company from scratch after many years of working as a cameraman. I would kill to have a job on the sets he'd been on, brushing shoulders with the heavyweights of the industry, eating lunch next to A-list actors.

"Ugh, thank God." Caroline bustles in and heads straight for the green juice, taking a big slurp through the biodegradable straw. "It's warm. Did you come straight from the juice bar?"

"Of course."

"Hm." She takes another sip and turns toward Lyle. "Is that the mood board?"

"Impossible client. They expect us to have the whole commercial turned around in two weeks. Can you believe it?"

"We need this job," Caroline says, lowering her voice and turning away from me. "Now that they've pushed the Venice project back, we don't have any incoming work."

"I'm aware of that, Caroline," Lyle says, scratching the top of his dark, balding head of hair. "But we don't have the capacity to turn this around in their timeframe. I think we're just wasting our time."

"I'm sure Evie can help."

I straighten up at the mention of my name, like a well-trained dog. "Me?"

"It'll be great experience, being out on location instead of in the studio," Caroline goes on. "And it would only be a few extra days over the next couple of weeks. You would be compensated, of course."

My eyes light up. "That would be amazing! Being a production assistant is the next step in my plan, so I'd love to be involved in the shoot."

There's a funny tickling feeling in my stomach. I can almost see myself there on the sand, clipboard in hand, ready to tackle any task thrown my way. A real, paid job that doesn't involve fetching juice or taking people's coffee orders. Who said changing my life plan was a colossal mistake? Everything is going to be fine. I don't know why I let myself get so worried.

"Perfect. We'll just have you sign a waiver and at the end of each week, you'll be reimbursed for gas."

"Okay," I say, thinking the free gas is a nice little perk. "And if you don't mind my asking. What would the hourly rate be?"

"Hourly rate?" Caroline looks at me, forehead creasing.

"I mean, I'm guessing minimum, which is totally fine! I was just curious because you see my landlord is chasing me up for—"

"We can't pay you for your time there." Caroline looks at me like I might have an undiagnosed head injury.

"Oh? I thought you said something about compensation."

"For your gas, yes. And you'll get lunch every day on set."

"Right," I say, the tickling feeling in my stomach turning to nausea. I can't afford to take time off for my internship as it is, let alone sacrifice more shifts at the café. But passing up extra production work feels like a cardinal sin.

"We will pay you in experience," Caroline continues, like she's reading my mind. "And you can't put a price on that. Not in such a competitive field."

I chew on my bottom lip, nodding. "I agree, it's just... I don't think I can swing extra days away from my job at the café if I'm not getting paid."

I know that logically, this is quite reasonable. But I can't help the nagging guilt rippling through my brain. And the brief look that passes between Caroline and Lyle doesn't help either.

"That's why we usually get film students who still live at home to intern for us," Lyle says, leaving the unfinished mood board. "More flexibility. Fewer bills to pay. Caroline, let's leave the board until we know what's happening. I'm going to make a call."

As Lyle walks out the front door, Caroline sighs, running a finger over the pictures that are yet to be glued on.

"I'm really sorry I can't help. I'm in a money bind at the moment, that's all."

"Someday, you will understand the financial strains behind a production," Caroline says, draining what's left in her glass jar. "We simply don't have the margin to pay our interns."

They clearly have the margin for her thirteen-dollar organic juices, but I decide not to point that out.

"That is, if you ever make it in the film business."

As the ominous undertones of her last comment sink into my pores, I nod and turn toward my desk. "Right. Well, I better start renaming that footage from last week's shoot."

Maybe I won't be able to go on set. But I'm still getting valuable insight into how a production company runs. I open the computer folder containing last week's raw footage, armed with the printed naming convention document Lyle left on my desk.

"Hold off on that. I'm starved," Caroline says, looking at her rose gold watch. "It's nearly noon. Can you fetch us some lunch?"

2

If I've learned anything from my years in the film business, it's that you don't say no to Nolan Smith. As far as executive producers go, he's the top dog. Which explains why I'm schlepping along the sidewalk toward an obnoxious fancy restaurant for lunch, and not to my favorite sandwich place. I told myself it was worth going, if only because I could walk to the fancy restaurant from my house—a rarity in LA. But as the midday sun assaults my squinting eyes, I'm having second thoughts.

The heat bears down on my head, and I feel a trickle of sweat making its way toward the band of my shorts, destined for my buttcrack. Perfect.

I turn the corner and further up the path sits a homeless man, his scraggly gray beard glistening in the light of day. As I get closer, I can read his 'I'm With Stupid' t-shirt and see the lines that cover his face, shaded by a trucker cap.

"Hey, Bob. What are you sitting here for?"

A low motorcycle-like grumble rolls out of his throat. "Some young kids have taken my usual spot around the corner. Yahooing until all hours every night." He scratches his leathery cheek. "I'm too old for that."

"Yeah, I hear ya."

He cranes his head, shielding his eyes from the sun, and looks me up and down. "What's with the hoity toity clothes?"

I look at my button-down shirt and shorts. "I have a meeting. On my way now."

"Ahh, another one of those action man movies."

"I don't think so. I'm just going to show my face."

Another deep grumble escapes Bob's throat. "I don't know why everyone is obsessed with their iron hulks and their spider girls. It's all a bunch of boloney."

This is what I like about Bob. No bullshit. It's hard to come by in LA.

I shrug. "Beats me. I better get going. Have you got lunch?"

He waves his hand dismissively.

I pull out a ten-dollar bill from my wallet. "Go to the sandwich shop on Melrose. Ask for the pimento cheese with pastrami. You won't regret it."

He accepts the money and tips his head.

"See you round, Bob."

"Take it easy."

I make my way to the restaurant and soon I'm standing outside the front door. As I'm ushered in by the host wearing a suit, I look back to see Bob turning the corner toward Melrose and know who I'd rather be eating lunch with.

≈

I drum my knuckles on the white tablecloth and check the time on my phone. Again.

"Nolan should be here any minute," Eric assures me, taking a sip of his kombucha. "Are you sure I can't order you a drink?"

"Water's fine," I reply, sitting back in my chair and observing the other patrons on the patio. Business meetings, work lunches, and a sprinkling of tourists hoping to glimpse Hollywood's rich and famous. And I'm sitting here with two of the biggest bozos of all.

"Did you catch the last episode of *The Walking Dead*?" Eric says, grinning at Simon.

"Epic!"

"So epic!"

"What about you, Adam? Did you catch it?" Eric looks at me excitedly.

There are few things in life I hate more than small talk. Is it so hard for people to just sit back and enjoy the silence? The need to fill any quiet moment with shallow chit chat is a testament to how insecure and self-conscious society is these days.

"I don't watch a lot of TV."

Eric laughs. "Right, an action director who doesn't watch a lot of TV." They chuckle together like it's the funniest thing in the world.

"I'm not an *action director*," I say, trying not to grit my teeth. "I've just done a lot of action films. It's not my *thing*. I have other things."

"Right, right," Eric says, now distracted by a leggy blonde who just walked in with a man much older than her. And by the way he rubs her lower back, I'm guessing it's not her grandpa. "Ah, here he is!"

Eric and Simon both stand, and I turn to see Nolan

Smith. Finally gracing us with his presence. I get up, shaking his hand with a tight jaw.

"Adam, good to see you," Nolan says, his easy smile blinding me. "Sorry, my meeting ran over. You weren't waiting long, were you?"

Before I can answer, he waves over the server and orders an Old Fashioned. He leans back in his seat, nodding at a few people around the patio. Unlike his right-hand man, Eric, Nolan doesn't need to leer at the ladies. They are already leering at him. From his shaved head to his dark skin to his Lamborghini parked out front, Nolan Smith is the most eligible bachelor in the restaurant.

But his eyes are now trained on me.

"Let's just cut to the chase," he says, ignoring the waitress as she sets down his drink. "The director just backed out of my film. We start shooting in three weeks. I need someone to step in, and I know just the man for the job."

I take a sip of water to buy myself more time before responding. "I'm flattered that you thought of me, Nolan. But the thing is—"

"Let me walk you through it," he jumps in, rubbing his hands together. "It's a sci-fi action comedy. Think *Doctor Dolittle* meets *Planet of the Apes*. A young veterinarian who can talk to animals must expose his powers when all the animals in New York City revolt against humans for reasons unknown."

Eric and Simon are grinning at Nolan, clearly excited about the movie—or at least how much money it's going to make them.

"He discovers there's something in the water, and it's a race against time to find the antidote and save the city. Lots of mayhem, lots of laughs. We've already got Damon Reeves signed on for the lead. Eric is producing and Simon's on the script. We just need someone to bring it home."

I watch Simon, who looks pretty smug after the big spiel Nolan gave his story. I try not to openly grimace. It sounds like the worst movie ever.

"I think that someone is you," Nolan finishes, in case that whole sales pitch didn't make his intentions clear. "Action and sci-fi is your forte, after all. You could do it with your eyes closed."

I feel a knot forming in my stomach. "The thing is, I'm not sure that's the direction I want to keep going in," I reply, contemplating the quickest way to shut this whole thing down. "I want to pursue something with a little more substance. No disrespect."

"More substance than the millions we'll make on opening weekend?" Eric says, pumping fists with Simon. "It's going to be next summer's blockbuster."

Jesus, he is such a douche.

Nolan leans forward, lowering his voice. "Look, I get it. You're going through a weird time right now. I was sorry to hear about your father."

My shoulders seize up at the mention of it. "It was months ago now. I'm fine."

"What a legend, am I right?" Eric chimes in.

"I still have an autographed copy of one of his books," Simon adds. "I went to a signing when I was thirteen. Stood in line for an hour. He was my first favorite author."

I swish the water around in my glass. "Yes, the great William Thorne. Literary genius."

Nolan is still watching me, like he's trying to analyze his next best angle.

"The thing is, I think it's time to move on to something new," I continue, moving back to the main subject.

"What do you have lined up?" Nolan asks.

"Well... nothing yet."

"I see." Nolan smiles to himself, checking his phone. "Let me put it this way. It's harder than ever to make a box office hit. These days, with your streaming and your on-demand, if you want your films in movie theaters, you've got to stick with the big leagues. And to stick with the big leagues, you've got to keep playing the game. When was your last film? A year ago?"

"Something like that," I reply, scratching the back of my head. I've heard about Nolan's hard sell, but I've never experienced it like this.

He sucks air through his teeth. "You don't want to stay away from the game too long, my friend. I know some ballers who took a break and never got back up."

He picks up his cocktail and finishes it in one long gulp. "Look, you've heard my pitch. Now I've got to be somewhere, so I'll leave you with Eric to discuss details." He leans across the table to shake my hand. "But I'm sure you'll make the right decision."

Eric and Simon watch him leave in awe while I feel the knot tightening in my stomach. It hasn't been *that* long since I did a film.

Eric motions toward the empty Old Fashioned glass to order one for himself, before picking up where Nolan left off. "We obviously want you on board. *Galactic Man*? My youngest LOVES that movie. I can't get him to take the helmet off." He laughs and I suppress a groan, knowing my name will be forever attached to such garbage.

"Nolan is right," he goes on. "You could do this with your eyes closed. What's the big deal? You come in, you direct, you take home a big check. Everyone wins."

"It's just not what I want to do anymore."

"Make this your last action movie?" Simon suggests.

"I said that last time, and the time before that," I mumble. Being a director in Hollywood, you get type cast just like everyone else. You do one goofy action sci-fi, and then another, and the next minute, you're the goofy action sci-fi guy. No one wants to be that guy.

"So make this one different," Eric says, reading my mind. "How's this—you'll have full creative control. Whatever your vision is, it's our vision, too. We just want you on the team."

"Full creative control?" I ask, narrowing my eyes.

"Within the parameters of the script, yeah," Simon jumps in, a flicker of concern in his eyes.

"This isn't just some funny, outlandish action story," Eric says. "This is a story about humanity, and our role in the animal kingdom. This is a story about understanding, and communication, and fear of the unknown. And in this social climate?" He makes a whistling sound. "What could be more relevant?"

"And you're saying I'd have full creative control? I can set the tone, the style?"

"Within the parameters of the script," Simon parrots before Eric places a hand on his arm to silence him.

"Full creative control. And this is what we're offering, plus ten percent of the film's gross." Eric writes on a napkin before sliding it over to me. I look at the obscene amount before turning it over.

"I need to bring my own first and second assistant directors," I say, still unsure if I'm making the right decision.

"I don't see why that would be a problem." Eric nods.

"And I need my team to pick the production assistants. The last lot I got were basically teenagers and I don't need people dicking around on set."

"You got it."

I frown, watching Eric flinch as he sips the Old Fashioned.

"So," he splutters. "Can I tell Nolan we have a deal?"

I look at his outstretched hand. I guess it's truer now more than ever.

"We have a deal," I say, shaking his hand.

You don't say no to Nolan Smith.

3

EVIE

"Let me get a small double shot cappuccino with soy milk, a regular almond milk skinny latte, and a gluten-free blueberry muffin."

I nod my head, tapping the customer's order on the iPad. "Sure, do you want whipped butter with the muffin? It really takes it to the next level."

She looks at me like I've just asked her if she wants a mammogram with that. "Like... real butter?"

"As real as the cow it came from."

"Ew, that's disgusting. No."

She taps her card to pay with her face scrunched up and I head to my rightful position at the espresso machine. "I think I offended that girl. Have people always been like this about dairy?"

Sylvia looks up from the sandwich she's making as my customer walks toward a table, where another pretty young blonde is sitting.

"Ignore her. She's an idiot."

"You don't know that," I say, paranoid they can hear from their window seats. "She's probably lovely."

"I *do* know that. I've seen her at a casting before. She was abusing the assistant for spelling her name wrong."

Sylvia goes back to making her turkey on rye, her long nails nearly poking holes in the plastic gloves. With her long black hair and olive skin, she looks like she should be in an exotic razor commercial, not working with cold cuts. She's the only real friend I've made since moving to Los Angeles. My first day at the café, I dropped an entire tray of iced coffees, and as my manager Glen was about to send me packing, she told him it was her fault. Just like that, took the blame for me. I suppose it helped that Sylvia is a gorgeous model and Glen has a crush on her. But I knew I had found a true pal.

"Maybe you could join one of those medical trials to get some extra cash?"

I've spent the morning filling Sylvia in on my money issues, but so far, none of the solutions are very appealing.

"You realize I come from a family of doctors, right?" I say, twisting the portafilter into the espresso machine. "I don't want to be a lab rat. Surely there are other options."

"I know some gigs the girls at the agency do when modeling work isn't coming through. But I don't think it's up your alley."

"Hit me with it."

Sylvia sighs. "I don't know, like one girl did lingerie waitressing for some rich guy's business dinner. Just handed out drinks and laughed at their gross old white man jokes. She took home like five hundred bucks."

"Five hundred dollars for one night of waitressing?" My eyes widen as I watch the coffee trickle into the cup. "I could do that."

"Sweetie, you wear a t-shirt over your bathing suit at the beach."

I bunch my shoulders. "I get cold easily."

Once I've made the coffees, I call out the name and the two blonde girls collect their order.

"Have a great day," I call after them, which they completely ignore.

"Excuse me, Miss?" A man from earlier is standing at the other end of the counter. "I found a hair in my muffin bag."

I close the distance between us, and he pulls out a long red strand from the brown Kraft bag.

"You got the lucky bag," I say with a light chuckle, but then register his expression. "I'm so sorry. I tie it back and wear this little cap, but it still somehow wiggles free. I always say it's my confetti. I'm a par-tay." As I sing-song the last sentence with jazz hands, I know it's a mistake.

We're cast into silence.

"Um, how about I refund your muffin and get you another, on the house?"

He pushes the bag closer to me. "It's the least you could do."

"Again, I'm so sorry."

"Just make sure you keep your head away from this one, will you?"

My face falls, but before I know it, Sylvia is next to me.

"Listen, buddy. She said she was sorry. Now how about you go sit on that stool over there and we'll bring it over when it's ready. Okay?"

The man opens his mouth to respond, but is taken aback. By her abruptness or her beauty, I'm not sure. But he does as he is told and disappears from the counter.

"What are you doing?" I whisper, pulling her aside. "You could get fired for talking to the customers like that."

"You're too nice," she replies, returning to wrap another

sandwich and placing it in the display cabinet. "So, what are you going to do about this rent thing?"

I groan, grabbing another muffin from the cake stand with tongs and keeping it at arm's length as I slide it into a hair-free bag. "I don't know."

"I know you don't want to hear this, but have you thought about calling—"

"Nope."

"You're not even going to consider it?"

"Going to them for help is not an option," I say, twisting the bag closed so that no hairs can sneak in before I deliver it to the angry man. But before I can leave, Glen pops his head out from the side office.

"Evie, did I hear you say that muffin is on the house?"

"Um... sort of?"

He puts his hands on his hips. "You know, muffins don't come free. We don't have a nice little muffin tree out the back." He laughs at his own joke. Sylvia rolls her eyes. Meanwhile, I feel the familiar dread of making yet another mistake, curdling in my stomach.

"I know, I'm sorry. It's just a hair got in his bag and... customer is always right and all that..."

"I see. Well, I have to dock it from your pay. Maybe you could consider a hairnet."

He disappears back into the office, and I look at Sylvia with rounded eyes.

"I know you don't want to call them," Sylvia says, putting a hand on my shoulder. "But it kind of looks like you don't have a choice."

～

I wind some blue yarn into a soft ball, tucking the tail inside to keep it from unraveling, and place it in the box. I've been wanting to color coordinate my collection for weeks now, and it's nice to get around to it.

I've finally gotten used to the sound of sirens and shouting from the streets of LA outside my window, and no longer need to have my TV on level forty volume. I flick through the channels and land on a cooking show, which reminds me I will need to feed myself at some point this evening.

I look around my little studio. It's not the biggest or the fanciest apartment I've ever had, but it's all mine. And it's in a great location, right between the café and Guerilla Productions. I glance at the note that was left under my door, waiting for me when I got home.

$1,350 by the end of the month. No excuses. - Ron

I push the note off my coffee table so I don't have to look at it. I did a thorough analysis of my finances and the findings were not promising. With my current schedule of work and interning, even if I live off ramen noodles, I will only have about half of that by Ron's deadline. Caroline already told me that if I cut down my hours at the studio, they would have to give my spot to someone else. And I can't walk away now, not when I've only just got my foot in the door.

I grab another ball of yarn, this time lime green, and start winding forcefully. My phone buzzes on the floor.

Sylvia: Have you called them yet?

I huff, throwing the ball into the box and typing.

Evie: No, getting a few things done first.

Before I can put my phone down, I get a reply.

Sylvia: Stop stalling.

I pick at my nail as another comes through.

Sylvia: Just do it.

Ugh. I know she's right. If I want to keep my internship and my apartment, I need help. I just have to rip the Band-Aid off. I launch myself off the floor and pace, staring at the number I've brought up on my phone screen.

My heart races as the phone rings in my ear.

"Hello?"

"Dad... hi. It's Evie."

"Yes, I know the sound of my own daughter's voice. I may be getting older but I'm not hard of hearing just yet."

I smile to myself as he talks. At least he answered, and not Mom. If there is an easier parent to talk to, it's definitely not Diane Miller.

"How are you?" I ask, desperate to buy myself a little time.

"Is something wrong?"

"What?"

"I just can't remember the last time you called us. Something must be wrong. Did you get mugged on the filthy streets of Hollywood?"

"Nothing is wrong," I say, immediately feeling exhausted. "I just thought I would check in."

I can tell by my dad's silence that he's not buying it, so I inhale before diving right in. "Well, actually. There is something I wanted to talk to you about—"

"Sorry Evie, my pager's going off. I'm on call tonight. Let me pass you through to your mother."

Before I can beg, plead or protest at the offer, another person picks up the line.

"Well, isn't this a surprise?"

I squeeze my eyes shut. "Hi, Mom."

"Is it my birthday?"

"Huh?"

"It's been a long time since you called, so it must be my birthday."

"It hasn't been *that* long," I mumble. "How are you?"

"I'm doing quite well, thank you," she chirps down the line. "Your father and I have both been busy at the hospital. Your sister has been coming to dinner every week. Of course, that probably doesn't excite you like the glitz of LA."

Again, with the exhausting.

"You know it's not like that," I say, knowing it's pointless to explain myself for the hundredth time. "How is Sarah doing?"

"She's wonderful. She just got an attending position."

"Wow... that happened fast," I say, remembering a time when that was my career goal, too.

Mum makes a funny noise. "Yes, well... good things happen when you stick to the plan."

I close my eyes, psyching myself up to ask what I called to ask. Even though my mother is making it increasingly impossible to get the words out.

Taking a deep breath, I say, "So, there was another reason I called."

"You need money."

"What? No, hang on a second."

"You don't need money?"

I chew on my lip. "Well, yes. But it's a bit more complicated than that."

"Evie, if you need money from us, just come out and say it." She sounds exasperated, which is shocking to me, as she is the one making this much more difficult than it needs to be. "We knew it was a huge mistake, you taking off to Hollywood. So it doesn't exactly come as a surprise that you're broke."

I go to respond, but words don't come out of my mouth. How can she say that to me? Is it so hard for them to support my ambition, the way they supported Sarah through years of med school? Is it such a joke that I want to do something creative with my life? If they don't understand, fine. But it's like they get satisfaction out of watching me fail.

Which is how I feel in this moment.

A failure.

I knew this was going to be horrendous, but sometimes, just sometimes, it would be nice if my parents surprised me. I take a shaky breath, ready to swallow my pride. But an incoming call interrupts me.

"Mom, this might be my boss. I'll have to call you back."

I hang up without hearing her response and try to regain my composure. I'm already dreading picking up where we left off.

Lingerie waitressing would be a walk in the park compared to this.

I clear my throat, answering the unknown call. "Hello, this is Evie?"

"Evie Miller? Hi, this is Delilah. I'm calling on behalf of Vanguard."

I shake off my mother's words to focus on the woman who is clearly not my boss. "Err, sorry... Vanguard?"

"Productions. I got your details from the Screen Jobs website?"

My brain seems to be stuck in idle. Screen Jobs? That random website I added a profile to? I didn't even know if it was a legit register. I was almost sure I'd surrendered my details to an elaborate scam and I'd wake up one day in a bathtub without a kidney.

"Listen, we're down to the wire and need to get our crew together quickly for a feature. I'm just gathering the PAs," she goes on. "Are you available?"

My heart is leaping from my chest. Did I pass out during my conversation with Mom? Did I hit my head, and this is all a hallucination? I scramble for a response.

"Y... you're offering me a production assistant position?"

"That depends," she replies. "Can you start Monday?"

4

ADAM

There is always a certain buzz on the first day of shooting. The sets are built; the cast are excited, and the crew aren't yet exhausted by fourteen-hour days filming. And as I drive into the studio lot, I almost share the same enthusiasm.

I've spent the last three weeks trying to pick up where the last director left off—which was a dumpster fire. The storyboard was garbage, the shot list was trash, and I have no idea what they had been doing in rehearsals. The cast were as prepared for principal photography as they were to pilot a mission to Mars.

But after many late nights, cups of coffee, and some gentle bullying aimed at Simon the Scriptwriter, I feel we have an okay movie on our hands. Previously titled *The Worst Film of All Time*. And let me tell you, it was no easy feat. I mean, turning a story about a vet reasoning with animals as they scale the buildings of New York City into something of substance? I'm surprised I even pulled it off.

What I have now is a critical look into the minds of mankind and our relationship to living things around us. A commentary on the obvious superiority complex most people have. Is it Oscar worthy? Fuck no. But at least I can look in the mirror without wanting to punch myself in the face.

"Brian is at it again," Delilah says, greeting me as I pull into my designated car space. "I swear to God if he comments on my ass again, I'm going to shove his boom mic some place where only his digestive noises can be recorded."

"And you have my full support with that."

There are very few people in the world who don't annoy me. Dee is one of those people. Which is why I insisted on bringing in my own assistant directors. She is my second AD.

"Damon is waiting for you inside," she says as we make our way to stage three. "He has concerns about the scene in the vet clinic. Says he can't emotionally connect with the CGI prop."

"It's a tennis ball on a stick. What does he expect? It's called acting. He should be familiar with it."

"He's asking for a stand-in with a green suit to take its place."

We enter through the side door into the darkness. "Well, I'm glad he's bringing it up now. Rather than say, during rehearsal when we had time to arrange that."

Dee gives me a wry smile, before speaking into her shoulder mic and heading in the other direction.

It takes a few seconds for my eyes to adjust, but then I can see stage three clearly. It houses all of our smaller sets for the film—the veterinary clinic, the protagonist's living room, kitchen, and a small cupboard space where he hides from a sadistic raccoon (I wasn't able to remove *all* the ridiculous scenes). The place is swarming with crew members getting ready to shoot our first scene of the day.

The art department, camera and lighting, sound, and the video village; all bustling around their sections. I have to admit, I missed this.

"Adam, I've been looking everywhere for you. We've got a problem."

And then there are things I didn't miss.

Divas.

"Damon, what's the problem?"

"It's this scene in the clinic," Damon says, ruffling a hand through his blond hair despite just being in the hair trailer for the past twenty minutes. "I can't talk to that tennis ball. It's giving me nothing."

I blink at him. "It's a tennis ball."

"And this line here about me being afraid," he continues, pulling a script from his back pocket. "I don't think it's going to work."

"Why?"

"Well, look at me." He gestures toward his chiseled torso, which is currently clothed in an extremely tight V-neck. "I just don't look like the kind of guy who gets afraid."

I rub my eyes with my thumb and index finger. "This isn't one of those macho, 'nothing scares me', action films," I say, though I'm pretty sure I've said it multiple times already. "And as for the tennis ball, you've got to make it work. We're only using creature performers in action scenes. We can't get someone in just to sit there and look at you."

But Damon appears not to be listening anymore. Instead, he's watching a young costume assistant walk by. He gives her a wink, and she giggles into her coffee cup.

Sickening.

"Anyway, I have to go talk to Joel. I'll see you on set."

I leave Damon before he can think of something else to

complain about and head toward the camera department, passing sound as I go.

"Hey, Brian. If you make any more inappropriate comments to members of the crew or cast, I'll boot your ass off the set. Got it?"

I glimpse Brian's moronic expression before I reach Joel. "Can you keep an eye on Damon? I have a feeling he's going to be a pain in the ass the whole shoot," I say, sitting in my director's chair. "Casting really screwed us on this one."

"Roger," Joel replies.

We sit there in a comfortable silence, which is the main thing I like about Joel and the reason he is my first assistant director. He is a man of few words. His big bear-like exterior, combined with his quietness, seems to have a calming effect on the talent as well.

"Here." Dee joins us, handing us each a disposable cup.

"Aren't you a little far up the food chain to be fetching coffee?" I say, accepting it regardless.

"The production assistants haven't arrived yet." She takes a long sip from her own cup. "But they should be here any minute."

"Remember to tell them no selfies on set, no scrolling on social media, and no—"

"No asking the cast for autographs," she finishes my sentence. "How long have I worked with you now? I think I have a handle on your neuroses."

"I wouldn't call them neuroses."

"Fine. Your grumpy old man-erisms then. Better?" She laughs at her own hilarity. "Sometimes I wonder what you would do without me and Joel. We're the only ones who can put up with your shit. Right, Joel?"

"Sure," Joel replies, more interested in the shot list than in our conversation.

"Just wait till you're a director one day," I say, watching the craft service guy load up a table with muffins. "Then you'll see what *I* have to put up with."

"That'll be the day." Dee rolls her eyes.

I have to give her credit—she's a trooper for sticking it out in an industry dominated by men. And men like Brian, for that matter. Not that I ever question her gumption. She could take on any guy in this sound stage.

"It'll happen," I say, draining the rest of my coffee. "A smart ass like you? Who would be brave enough to say no?"

"That's easy for you to say, Mr. Son of William Thorne. That connection alone could get you work in any creative field."

I smile tightly and take out my copy of the shot list.

"I mean... fuck. Sorry, I didn't mean to bring him up," she scratches at her thick brown curly hair. "I'm a dumbass."

"It's fine," I say. "I'm not going to have a breakdown at the mention of his name."

She scrunches up her face. "Muffin to make up for it?"

I scoff. "Only if it's chocolate chip, none of that blueberry crap."

"You really need to eat a vegetable."

As Dee leaves, I see a girl come into the building. She's wearing a bright red outfit with yellow rain boots. I've never seen her before, and by what she is wearing, I'm guessing she's an extra who got lost from the flock. She looks around the room with big, bright eyes.

"There he is!"

Eric strides over to me, a stupid grin on his face. Simon hurries behind him.

"Day one of shooting. How good is this?!"

"Pretty standard," I say, hating how extra he is. People who are always 'on' are exhausting.

"Ha! Love it, love it. So listen, you know that scene we cut, with the Mexican walking fish jumping out in the classroom and attacking the teacher? We wanted to explore bringing that back in."

"And why would we do that?"

"Because it's entertaining," Simon says, still salty on me for changing so much of his script. Honestly, he should be kissing the ground I walk on. That pile of scrap paper was terrible.

"We've gone over this. It doesn't even make sense," I reply, standing up. "Mexican walking fish don't even survive out of water, let alone have the energy to terrorize a bunch of kids during a math class."

"We're just spit balling here," Eric jumps in, the goofy grin still on his face.

"Look, you said full creative control. I don't want to make some bozo spoof with murderous fish and monkeys climbing buildings. I've got to set up my first shot. Are we good here?"

Eric and Simon share a look before they're interrupted by Dee.

"I got you raspberry white chocolate, and I don't want to hear you bitch about the fruit." She sets the muffin in my hand and then notices Eric leering at her.

"It's great to see you, Delilah. You got one of those for me?"

She looks at him like he's something stuck to the bottom of her shoe and then notices the same girl I did from before. "I better go wrangle the newbies."

"Yeah, I think you've got a lost extra over there," I say, taking a tentative bite out of the muffin.

"She's not an extra. That's one of your production assistants. I recognize her from her profile on Screen Jobs." Dee hooks a walkie talkie into her belt and picks up her clipboard. "The others must be here somewhere, too. I'd better go warn them about their grump of a director."

"You're hilarious," I say, watching the rain boots girl again with a big smile spread across her face.

5

EVIE

I can't believe I'm here.

It's like a dream. I literally think I might be dreaming. I pinch my skin between my fingertips and instantly regret it, rubbing my arm.

The sound stage is exactly how I imagined it. There are guys walking around with trolleys, carting expensive-looking equipment across the room. People bustle around with scripts and clipboards, talking and writing notes. Lights are being arranged on one of the sets—the one that looks like a doctor's office. And the entire ceiling is covered in lights too, just waiting to be arranged into the perfect formation. In one corner, I can see a guy leaning against the pole of his mic, talking to another guy who is sitting behind a sound board. And in another corner, a few people are sitting around in those chairs that have names on them. One of them has 'Director' written on it, but the person sitting in it only looks a few years older than me. He glances over and frowns, and I quickly avert my gaze so he doesn't think I'm staring.

"Evie?"

I turn to see another person not much older than me, with bright green eyes that stand out from her light brown skin.

"I'm Delilah Moore. The one who called you last week?"

"You're so pretty," I gush, before remembering I'm supposed to be professional. "It's nice to meet you."

She looks at me curiously and laughs. "Thank you. It's nice to meet you too. Did you find the studio okay?"

"I've been wanting to come here for years. I did once, actually. But that was for a tour on one of those little shuttles that runs around the sound stages. So it doesn't really count. I can't believe I'm here!"

I inhale deeply and remind myself to breathe. I don't want to start freaking people out too early. But Delilah just laughs again.

"I love the enthusiasm. Just remember this feeling when you've been on your feet for twelve hours, and the actors keep forgetting their lines and we can't go home before the take is finished."

I nod my head, scribbling in my notepad. I knew it would come in handy.

"Are you writing that down?" Delilah asks, cocking her head.

"I'm a note taker." I smile, tucking a stray piece of hair behind my ear.

"In that case, let's go find the others and I can give you the proper introduction to the job."

I follow Delilah outside and my eyes take a moment to adjust to the bright sunshine. Trucks are being unloaded with more equipment, and extras are coming in and out of the costume trailer. Further up the lot is the production office, with a couple of people standing out the front watching everyone else go about their work day. We walk toward them, and I soon realize they are both in their twenties, like me.

"You must be Jackson and Kylie. This is Evie, another PA," Delilah says.

"Hi." I wave.

Jackson gives me a succinct nod and Kylie gives me a dazzling smile, but her face instantly resumes a neutral position.

"All right, now that introductions are out of the way, let's get to the real fun." Delilah turns so that she's facing the three of us. "My name's Delilah, but most people call me Dee. I'm the second AD."

"That means assistant director," Jackson whispers. It's hard to see in the brightness, but I can just make out Kylie rolling her eyes.

"Being the second AD means that if a job needs doing, and no one puts their hand up, it comes to me. Which is why I've got you. So I need you to listen up and pay attention, because I don't want to repeat any of this twice."

I fumble with my notepad, turning to a fresh page with my pen at the ready.

"You are production assistants, which means any area of production might ask you for help at any given time. This is okay, but know the main people you will report to are myself and Joel, the first AD. I know for some of you, this is your first time on a major film set. And for all of you, this is your first time on Adam Thorne's film set. So it's imperative that you follow the rules I'm about to tell you... if you ever want to work in the industry again."

I share a nervous glance with Jackson. Kylie, however, still looks as confident as ever, with her all-business pixie cut and all-black ensemble.

"Rule number one, always be on time. Rule number two,

don't touch anything unless you know how to use it. Rule number three, turn your phones off and put them away. Actually turn them off, because silent mode messes with the radio mics. Rule number four, when the first AD calls action, do not move. Even the tiniest sound can mess up a take. And trust me, you don't want to be the one to mess up one of Adam's takes."

I'm writing furiously when my ink fades out. I scribble to make it work, but nothing happens.

"Don't take pictures, don't be noisy, even in-between takes. And for the love of God, don't ask anyone for an autograph."

I flip to a new page and draw big circles, but still nothing. *Why the heck didn't I bring a spare pen?*

"If you need to go to the bathroom, say ten-one for a quick break and ten-two for a longer break. I won't go into detail there. At all other times, you must have your walkie on and be available. The jobs you do will vary day-by-day. The most important thing is you are ready and willing to help at the drop of a hat."

I give up, and slide the notepad into my back pocket just as Delilah is wrapping up her speech. I guess my memory will have to do.

"So, are we all ready to meet the director?"

I soon realize the young guy sitting in the director chair was, in fact, the director. We wait with Dee in a little huddle as he talks with the cinematographer, which gives us time to go over the walkie talkie basics and some of the common lingo used on set.

"We're ready for our first shot." A tall, bearded man joins our group.

"Joel, these are the PAs. Guys, this is Joel, your first AD. Ahh, and here is the man we've all been waiting for. Adam, here are your PAs, Jackson, Kylie and Evie."

Adam makes his way to the group and looks at each of us, but his eyes rest on me for the longest. I panic and decide to do a curtsey.

Which I regret immediately.

Oh my God, kill me.

Dee conceals a laugh behind her hand and looks at Joel. Adam just stares... a crease forming between his eyebrows.

"You're wearing rain boots."

I look down at my bright yellow boots, one of my favorite things that I own. "I know. Aren't they fun?" I do a little heel-toe dance move so he can see them from all angles.

"Why are you wearing rain boots? You're in LA. It literally never rains here."

"I just think they're cute. Don't you think they're cute?"

Adam keeps staring with his dark brown eyes, like he's trying to decipher what planet I come from. His brown hair is tousled—a just-got-out-of-bed look, though I suspect he's been here for hours. And he's wearing a flannel shirt with the sleeves rolled up, like he's ready to do some manual labor.

"Well I hope they're comfortable, because you're going to be on your feet all day," he says, before turning his attention to the set. "Dee, we're about to do our first shot. Can you get everyone stationed?"

Adam and Joel walk back to set, resuming their conversation with the cinematographer.

"Okay. First shot. Everyone feeling ready?"

Before any of us can answer, Dee goes on.

"Well, if you're not, you better get ready, and fast. Jackson, I'm going to put you on set. Kylie, you will circulate the sound stage. Evie, you're going to be on the stage door. All right, break a leg!" And with that, she joins Adam and Joel on the set, leaving the PAs to look at each other.

"I have hot bricks, if anyone is looking for them," Kylie says, unclipping her walkie from her belt.

"Um... hot bricks? Don't burn your hands," I say, laughing to myself and managing a weak smile from Jackson.

Kylie narrows her eyes. "A hot brick is a fully charged walkie battery. Is this the first time you've been on a set?"

I feel my cheeks flush and am grateful for the dark lighting. "I've been on sets before, just nothing that required radio communications." I grab my own walkie and talk out the side of my mouth in an old timey voice. "Echo two, this is Sierra one. The eagle has landed, and the horse is in the barn. Copy that. Roger Roger."

Jackson scratches the back of his head. "I'm going to go to set."

He leaves me there with Kylie, who is still smiling at me like she just figured something out that makes her really happy.

"Right... well, you should get outside. I'll see you later."

She flounces across the room, greeting people as she goes like a seasoned professional. I fumble with my walkie, shoving the earpiece in place, the mic on my shoulder, and the walkie on my belt, before heading to my post at the stage door. The second I'm standing outside, I realize all the fun happens on the other side of the wall, and feel sad I can't watch the first shot being filmed. After a few minutes, I hear a small voice in my ear.

"Quiet on set."

I get a little tingle down my spine. It's officially starting; my first day on a real film set. After I got the call from Delilah, it didn't take me two seconds to call Glen at the café and tell him I wouldn't be coming back. I also called Lyle and Caroline, who were less than impressed that I was leaving my internship. But I don't have time to feel guilty about that. I have an actual job in the industry now. A *paid* job. And I'm not going to do anything to stuff it up. If I can make this work, not only will all my dreams come true, but I can afford to stay in my apartment without going to my parents for help. The day Dee called me was the best day of my life.

"Rolling." Joel's voice comes through the earpiece.

"ROLLING," I call to everyone outside, keeping my position in front of the door so no one can sneak in.

I wish I could see what's happening inside. The next thirty minutes go on like this as they redo takes—me parroting everything Joel says to the rest of the film crew who are stuck outside like I am. But it doesn't curb my excitement. Whether I'm a big-time film producer or a lowly production assistant, I can still say the same thing.

Hi, I'm Evie, and I work in the movie industry.

In fact, my excitement is so pronounced that I can feel a familiar pressure in my bladder. Darn it, I knew I shouldn't have downed that large coffee before I got here. What is the code for the bathroom again? I pull out my notepad, which is entirely unhelpful since my pen stopped working.

I shuffle on the spot, bending my knees and trying to convince myself that I don't really need to go that much. I can hold on till lunch.

I look at my watch and see that it's barely past nine o'clock.

Nope, I absolutely can't wait till lunch.

"Evie for Kylie," I say into my shoulder mic.

"Go for Kylie."

"Hey, um... I need to go to the bathroom."

"That's fine. I'll come out and take your spot."

"You will? Oh, thank God! I'm dying."

"I'll be right there. You go now," she assures me.

Without further prompting, I run to the closest bathroom outside, careful to turn my walkie off before I pee. I don't trust myself not to be heard by the entire studio.

I take a moment to gather myself in front of the mirror before I walk back out to everyone. A piece of hair has fallen out of my ponytail again, but at least it doesn't matter now. No more serving muffins for me. I turn my walkie back on and a voice is barking through.

"Evie?! Does anyone have eyes on Evie?"

I jerk my shoulder towards my mouth so fast I look like I'm auditioning for the 'Thriller' dance. "Go for Evie."

"Evie!" It's Dee. "Where the he—"

The earpiece crackles and then goes silent. I pull out my walkie, turning it off and on again, but it doesn't come back to life.

"Shoot," I hiss, running out to the tent that has the batteries on chargers. But they are all gone. "Did Kylie take all of them?" I say to myself, as one of the craft service people watches me with concern.

I run back to the door, where Jackson now stands on guard.

"Are they rolling?"

"No, you can go in. Delilah is looking for you," he says, before talking to his shoulder. "Eyes on Evie. She's coming in now."

I go through the door, making sure not to get in anyone's way while I power-walk to set.

"There you are!" Dee is looking at me wild-eyed, her smile long gone. "Where the hell were you? Where is your walkie?"

"I'm so sorry, I got a dead battery," I say, looking over at Adam, who has a stormy expression on his face.

"You left the door and someone came in while we were rolling," she says. "Where did you go?"

I rack my brain for the right code word. I've already stuffed up, I can at least try to talk with the proper lingo. "I was, um... I was... ten? Two?"

The boom mic guy and camera assistant snigger at each other while Dee brings her hand to her face.

Adam walks toward me. "I don't need to know about your bowel movements. I just need you to stay in your post so my take isn't ruined."

"My bowel...?" I look between him and Dee, and then it clicks. "Oh, God! I wasn't pooping!"

There is more laughter now. Even Joel, who has barely spoken a word, is giggling into his beard.

"I don't care what you were doing. But if you fuck up another shot, you'll be off my set. Got it?" Adam storms back to the fake clinic, muttering to Joel as he passes. Joel speaks into his shoulder mic, and of course I can't hear because my walkie is still dead.

"Resetting!"

I turn toward the booming voice and see Kylie.

"Hot brick?" she asks, smiling sweetly and holding out a fresh battery.

6

"Cut!"

I lean forward in my chair, rubbing my hands against my face.

"This just isn't working for me," Damon says, gesturing at the CGI prop. "I don't know how to perform under these conditions."

"And I don't know how else to help you," I say. "Did we not go over this enough in rehearsal?" Obviously this is a rhetorical question, because we went over this scene in rehearsals a thousand times.

"That was different. I didn't have this *thing* throwing me off."

To make the tennis ball on a stick more animal-like, the special effects department added green hair, a green nose, and little googly eyes. It now resembles a cheap *Sesame Street* puppet. The kind that only appear in your nightmares.

"Look, we just have to go with what we have. Take ten to pull yourself together and we'll try again."

Damon stalks off to his trailer, his personal assistant and

acting coach rushing behind him. I don't envy them. But then again, I don't envy me either. I walk over to where George is operating the camera. "This is horrible."

"It's these hot-shot actors, coming in here with their Hollywood good looks and full head of hair," George says, repositioning his flat cap against his balding head. "They don't know how to suck it up and get on with it."

"You're telling me."

I look around as the rest of the crew start talking among themselves. What a waste of valuable filming time. Evie walks tentatively onto the set, whispering something to the wardrobe assistant. They giggle, but then Evie sees me watching and quickly goes about her business.

"What else is new, George? How's Elsa doing?" I say, turning back to my cameraman.

George lets out a deep sigh. "She's doing okay, you know... considering." He leans back in his seat, folding his arms together.

"I heard she was sick again... I'm sorry to hear that," I say, already regretting bringing it up. Feelings are not my forte.

"These things happen."

Brian taps him on the shoulder, asking him a question about the frame, and our conversation is over.

That's the thing about the older generation. Something terrible could be happening and they just pick up their socks and keep moving.

"All right, let's go again. Dee, can we get Damon back?" I ask.

Dee speaks into her shoulder mic. "Fly in Damon."

I rub my hands together, psyching myself up for more diva antics. I need this scene to work. Not only is it the most emotional scene of the film, but it conveys a powerful message. The only problem is that Damon can only convey how in love with himself he is.

"Okay, let's do this." Our leading man appears on set, crouching down to his position in front of the prop. I make eyes with George before the usual commands are called out. Evie repeats her prompts so everyone can hear, and by the look on her face, she even finds that exciting. Rookie.

"All right, quiet on set."

"QUIET ON SET."

"Picture's up."

"PICTURE'S UP."

"Roll sound"

"ROLLING"

"Sound speeds."

"Camera speeds."

"Two apple. Take fourteen. Mark."

"Set."

I take a deep breath and hope that Damon's acting coach worked a miracle in the last ten minutes. "Action."

Off screen, the actor who is going to voice the dog says his lines, and we all wait with bated breath for Damon to respond.

"I don't know what to do," Damon says, running a hand through his sandy blond hair. "The truth is, I don't have any faith in mankind anymore."

I rub my knuckles into the palm of my hand, praying that Damon can just make it through one successful take. So far, so good.

"All you have to do is walk out your front door to see it— people only thinking about themselves. Judging each other. And God forbid you have a different opinion. Gone are the days where altered perspectives are valued. No one *listens* to each other anymore, they're just waiting to throw their own opinions out there."

He looks up at the prop.

"And I don't know what that means for you. I don't know how to help you if people won't listen to me. How do I make them *listen*?"

He looks into its beady, glued-on eyes.

I can see Damon's face slipping, losing its composure. And then there is one unmistakable flinch.

"I can't do this."

"Cut!"

"CUT," Evie parrots.

There's an audible groan throughout the crew as Damon stands up straight.

"That thing is terrifying," he says, placing his hands on his hips. "I can't work with it."

"Fine," I reply, trying not to growl like an actual bear. "We'll just go back to the original prop."

On command, the special effects assistant appears with the original tennis ball on a stick, without the freakish add-ons.

"That's not going to work for me either."

I clamp my eyes and mouth shut to stop the rage from spilling out.

"I just can't perform with balls in my face," Damon continues.

Brian and the camera assistant turn to each other and stifle a laugh. Even Dee has a smirk on her face. But I'm too angry to find it amusing. I'm going to lose it.

"Maybe one of the stand-ins can sit where the dog will be?" Dee suggests.

I shrug and turn away. We will never get this scene done.

"Does anyone have a call sheet?" Dee asks.

"Here!"

Evie comes stumbling onto the set, tripping on her yellow rain boots. I knew they were a bad idea. Those ridiculous things are anything but practical.

She hands a folder to Dee.

"It's bright pink," I say, intercepting as she passes it.

"With sticker tabs for each day," Evie adds proudly.

I flip through the call sheet, which has been embellished with more stickers and drawings of small animals. "You like your colors, don't you?"

Evie just smiles in return, and it goes all the way to her big brown eyes. It's only now I notice the smattering of freckles over her nose and cheeks, blending out to her copper hair. But it seems I'm not the only one noticing her.

"Now *you* I could look at." Damon walks over to our group, regarding Evie up and down. "I could look at you all day."

Evie turns a deep shade of red and looks at the ground, tucking her hair behind her ear.

"We'll get you a stand-in or an extra," Dee confirms, taking the call sheet from me. "Evie is a PA. She's needed elsewhere."

But Damon isn't listening. He's still eyeing Evie like she's about to give him a lap dance.

"I don't believe anyone has introduced us," he says, holding out his hand. "I'm Damon. Evie, is it?"

"I know who you are." She smiles. "Nice to meet you."

She goes in for a shake, but instead, Damon brings her hand to his mouth, kissing the tops of her fingers. "The pleasure's all mine."

"All right, we need to move on," I interrupt. If Damon was as talented an actor as he is a slimy Romeo, maybe this scene would be wrapped already.

It's nearly ten by the time I get home. The place is dark as I push the front door open, and right on cue, something smooth and furry circles my ankles.

"Hey Rufus," I say, crouching down to give the cat a quick scratch behind the ears. He enjoys it for two seconds before he shakes me off, and we separate amicably. Neither of us have the desire for prolonged displays of affection.

"Come on, I'll get your dinner."

He follows me into the kitchen, and soon enough the downlights brighten up the room. I pour the tiny fish-shaped pellets into his bowl on the floor and grab myself a beer from my bare fridge. Who needs groceries when you have Astro Burger?

Three nights in a row of Astro Burger.

I move some dirty laundry off the couch, tossed there yesterday after another long day, and slump down for the evening. I know other directors have personal assistants to do things like go shop for groceries and keep the laundry under control. But I don't like the idea of a stranger poking around in my things. Especially in my dirty underwear.

Done with his meal, Rufus comes in silently, jumping up on the foot stool a comfortable distance away from me. I never considered myself a cat guy, or an animal guy, for that matter. But our cohabitation works. Which is lucky, because after the woman who took him in decided *our* relationship wasn't going anywhere and moved out, Rufus had nowhere else to go.

I watch as his stomach rises and falls, remembering a time when there were three of us in the house. Not that we were here together very often.

Let's be honest, she was probably right to leave.

I rifle through my backpack to go over the shot list for tomorrow, but pull out something I'm not expecting. The bright pink folder. It must have gotten mixed up in my stuff on set.

I turn it over in my hands and shake my head. Who has the time or energy to decorate their call sheets with sparkles and tiny unicorns? Evie was an interesting choice from Dee.

I didn't have the same conventional film school, then internship, then assistant gig on a set experience like most people breaking into the industry. My first time on a film was when one of my dad's novels got picked up by a huge production company, and he brought me along. I knew the second I saw the cameras rolling, that was what I wanted to do for the rest of my life. Make meaningful stories. Make films that *mattered*.

Maybe I'd gotten sidetracked. Caught up in the next job and the next job and lost sight of what I wanted. I look up at my bookshelf, at the rows upon rows of novels by the great William Thorne. Some people don't have to choose between doing something meaningful and important, and doing something that makes them money. Some people get both. Some people, like my dad. At least, he did while he was alive.

I flip open the folder and see that handwritten, in fancy handwriting, is a name on the inside.

EVIE MILLER.

Even her boring paperwork is bubbly. I wonder if Evie Miller knows what she's in for—that Hollywood has the habit of dangling your most cherished dreams in front of your face, and then laughing as it hides them behind its back and flips you off.

Judging by the tiny unicorn doodles, I'm going to say no.

If I'm going to be stuck on stage door watch, at least it's always sunny in Burbank. I lean on the side of the building. Imagine doing this in New York? Or London, where it's always cold and raining? Though I suppose then I'd have a proper use for my rain boots. I kick a stone across the ground, listening to it click against other rocks.

Another pro to being on stage door watch is that it means Dee has forgiven my mistake from a couple of weeks ago, and trusts me with the task. I have a feeling you aren't allowed too many mistakes on this set. And you aren't forgiven easily.

"Can I go in?"

Damon's stunt double stands in front of me, his Australian accent taking me by surprise. Almost as much as his insane uncanniness to the leading man himself.

"Holy moly, I can see why *you* got the job."

"Sorry?" He squints at me, shielding his eyes from the sun.

"You could be Damon's twin. If I saw you on the street, I'd ask for an autograph. But definitely not here, because that's against the rules." I shake my finger in the air, teacher-style.

"You can have my autograph if you want," he laughs. "So, can I go in?"

"Oh... absolutely not. Not a chance."

"So that's a no then?"

He leans next to me on the wall, unscrewing the cap of his water and downing half the bottle.

"How do you like being a stunt guy?" I ask.

"It's all right. I like to stay active, so the training is fun. And the pay is decent."

"Is that why you moved to LA then?"

He looks at me sideways. "You're the chatty one, aren't you?"

"I'm not sure I'm *the* chatty one. Usually people call me Evie. You're Gus, right? My dad used to say I could talk underwater. Have you ever tried that? Going underwater and trying to figure out what the other person is saying? It's actually really funny."

"I can't say I've ever thought about it." He smiles.

"So, did you? Move to LA to be a stunt guy?"

We are joined by a makeup assistant, a bag of tools strapped to her hip. "Can I sneak in?"

"Nope, sorry. No one is getting past me."

"Not even if we're really quiet?" Gus says. "I'm pretty limber, you know. I can move easily in confined spaces."

"I don't care if you can turn into liquid and slide under the door," I say, bracing in a karate position. "Neither of you is getting past until I say. Consider me Gandalf."

The MA raises her eyebrows. "Gandalf?"

"Yeah, with the big old staff." I hear them call cut through my earpiece, but I'm so engrossed in my reenactment that I can't back out now. I put on my best booming wizard voice - "YOU SHALL NOT PASS" - and bang my imaginary staff on the ground. Gus laughs, but not before the stage door flings open and Adam walks through, seeing my Gandalf impression from start to finish.

I can't figure out the look on his face, caught somewhere between amusement and judgment. I figure I may as well loop him in on the joke.

"So what do you say? Do I have a role in your next film?" I ask, completing the whole thing with a superman pose.

Adam opens his mouth to speak, but then closes it again. He turns to Gus instead. "We're setting up for the next scene. You can go through. I'll be back in five."

Adam walks off toward the production office as Dee's voice comes through my ear piece.

"Evie, Jackson is taking over the door. You can come in now."

Before I leave my post, I see Adam look back in my direction, do a sort of confused smile, shake his head, and keep walking.

"Action!"

Gus runs across the set roof, leaping into the air at the building's edge. He waves his arms and legs around as the wires sling him across to the other roof, where he lands gracefully.

"Cut!"

"CUT," I repeat, giving Gus the thumbs up from my position in the corner. He grins and starts chatting to the stunt coordinator.

"I think we got it that time," Adam says to the cinematographer. "All right, let's set up for the next shot."

The crew starts packing equipment to bring it down to the ground, and they fly back Gus to my rooftop.

"What do I need to do to get a turn on that thing?" I say as he lands a few feet away from me.

"About six months of general stunt training, for a start."

"Evie, can you fly in Damon?" Dee calls out to me. "We're moving on."

"Copy." I shrug at Gus. "Looks like this is the only flying I'm allowed to do."

Gus scrunches his face. "That's a terrible joke."

"He's right. Truly terrible."

I turn to see Adam beside us.

"Aw, come on, boss. I know you like me."

Adam winces before clearing his throat. "What I'd like is for you to fly in Damon."

"Oh, right. On it!"

I power walk through the sound stage and back to the outside world, making my way to Damon's trailer. Which, from the exterior, looks like an intergalactic luxury bus.

"Damon?" I knock lightly on the door. "They're ready for you on set."

"I can't," he replies, muffled and higher pitched than usual.

"Are you okay?"

"Go away."

"Can I come in?"

"That is the opposite of going away."

"Okay, I'm coming in. I hope you're decent."

I walk up the small steps and into the trailer, the cool air immediately refreshing me.

"Jesus," he says, rubbing his hands over his face. "You really don't know the meaning of go away, do you?"

Every flirtatious vibe he's been sending my way has

vanished, and he's sitting in a chair with a glass of either water or straight vodka.

"Is something wrong?"

"I just need a few more minutes," Damon says, downing the rest of his drink. By the way his face flinches, I'm thinking it isn't water.

"Um... Adam says they need you now."

"I just need a minute, okay?"

He looks at me with huge hazel eyes, which I'm now noticing are a little red and puffy.

"Are you sure you're okay?"

He huffs and buries his face in his hands again.

"Right. A minute. Got it." I step out of the trailer and wait in the heat of the sun. A minute goes by, and then another minute, and then five more. I know my walkie is going to go off any second. Might as well beat them to the punch.

"Evie for Delilah."

It's quiet on the other end for a moment before, "Dee's gone ten-one. You've got Kylie."

"Oh... okay. Well, can you just tell them we'll be a couple more minutes? Damon's just having a..." I look back at the trailer door for signs of life "...moment."

"Is everything okay?"

"It's fine, he said he just needs some time."

It's quiet on the other end. I try to look through the trailer window, but can't see anything.

"If Damon's having issues, you can just send him to lunch early."

"Um... really?" I try to scratch an itchy spot at the back of my head, but my braid is in the way. "Are you sure? Adam said they need him."

"He does this all the time," Kylie says. "They usually just take a break and pick up when Damon's had a breather."

I chew on my lip. After the stage door fiasco, I'd prefer to hear this guidance from the horse's mouth.

"I can check with Adam if you want," she continues, reading my mind.

"Actually, I do."

A few moments of silence follow, and there is still no sign of Damon emerging.

"It's fine. Tell him to go to lunch," Kylie's voice comes back through the earpiece.

"Oh, okay great. I'll let him know."

I step back into the trailer, where Damon has made no progress in the moving department. "Good news, you can go to lunch."

"Really?" He looks up, already grabbing his car keys.

"You're not eating lunch here?"

"Nope. I'm going to get sushi."

He's out the door before I can say California Roll. Instead of staying in his holding space like a weirdo, I head back to set.

"Gosh, actors, am I right?" I say to Dee, who is back from her bathroom break.

"Ugh, what is it now?"

"Just Damon, being Damon." I wave my hand. "But don't worry, I sent him to lunch."

"Huh?"

"We're ready to go. Where's Damon?" Adam joins us, looking at me.

"He's gone to lunch?"

"He can't go to fricking lunch. We're about to shoot. I told you to fly him in. Go and get him."

My stomach drops. I look around, trying to spot Kylie. "But you... you said he could go to lunch?"

"Why would I say that? Look, I don't have time for this. Just get him." Adam stalks back to the camera guys and I have to stop myself from throwing up. I follow Adam to meet my doom.

"He's like... *gone* to lunch, though. Like, he left the lot... in his car..."

Adam turns around at a pace so slow it's unnerving.

"You've got to be joking."

"Ha ha?" I bring my hands up next to my shoulders, but my attempt to lighten the mood falls flatter than gaffer tape.

"What part of *fly in Damon* means let him get in his fucking car and drive away?" Adam's face has turned red now. "What is wrong with you?"

"But you said—"

"Do you have any idea how far behind we are already?" He is almost shouting now, and the entire sound stage is silent, listening in. It feels like not a single person is breathing. Except for Adam, whose chest is rising and falling like he's about to morph into the Incredible Hulk.

"This is going to screw up the entire schedule."

"I'm sorry, I really thought—"

"Just get out of my sound stage." He points toward the door, not making eye contact.

"Adam, I..."

"Seriously, leave."

I will not cry at work. I will not cry at work.

I look at Dee, whose mouth is in a hard line. In fact, everyone either looks angry or as uncomfortable as I am.

I speed walk out of the building before anyone can see me get upset. It's not until I'm closing the door behind me I see Kylie skulking in the corner with a huge grin on her face.

I was nine the first time someone called me a snitch. It was during math, and I saw Jimmie Morris defacing his desk with tiny penis drawings. The school had only just received new desks to replace our old ones, and I couldn't believe someone was making them ugly already. At least draw something nice. But *penises*? Nobody wanted to see that. I raised my hand and told the teacher.

For the next two years, they called me Snitchy Miller, and I vowed never to be a tattletale again. But I'm having a real hard time keeping that promise to myself now. Especially with Dee in front of me, holding a hand in the air and waiting for an answer.

"Seriously, what the hell happened?"

"I guess I just... relayed the wrong message," I reply, watching as the crew spill out of the sound stage to go on early lunch.

"I just don't get it." Dee's not giving up. "Why would you think it was okay to tell him to leave?"

I know I don't owe Kylie anything. But Dee would probably just question why I listened to her anyway. Say that I'm not meant to take orders from other PAs about these things.

And what I really can't figure out is why Kylie set me up in the first place. What have I ever done to her? I'm always nice, always friendly. I just want us all to get along, but it's like she has it in for me.

"Well?"

I exhale and meet Dee's eyes. "I was trying to reach you,

but you'd stepped out, so I had to go to someone else. And I guess the message got mixed up or something."

"Someone else who?" Dee's eyes narrow.

"Kylie."

Dee's shoulders melt away from her ears and she nods, putting an arm around me. "Okay, I think I know what's going on here."

We start walking toward the lunch tents.

"Listen, Evie. You seem like a nice girl, so can I give you some advice?"

I nod.

"This is a dog-eat-dog industry. Sure, it's great to make friends and I love your energy, don't get me wrong. But some people will not be your friend. Take it from someone who's spent years trying to get her big break."

She stops and faces me.

"There are only so many spaces at the top, and everyone is trying to claw their way there."

So that's what this is about? Kylie trying to take out the competition? We pick up trash for God's sake. It's a bit early for her to see me as a threat.

I smile weakly. "Thanks."

She squeezes my arm and walks away.

I turn around and look at the sound stages spread across the studio lot. Each housing incredible sets, gorgeous costumes, talented artists. Dee was right. I'm in now, this is my foot in the door. And if I want to make this work, I have to wise up. I like to see the best in people, but I've waited too long to be taken down by some psycho with a pixie cut. It's time to step up and start facing this with a bit more gumption.

But I have to talk to someone first.

8

ADAM

"What about the scene where he's driving across the city?"

I tear a piece off my dinner roll with my teeth. "What about it?"

Eric rests on his elbows, putting big hand movements into the pitch I know I'm about to get. "I say we add a lion there, maybe a few chimps. More animals getting in his way, destroying his car—"

"I swear we've had this conversation already."

Eric huffs and leans back in his seat, making eyes at Simon across the table. Simon rubs his jaw and goes in for a shot. "I think what Eric's trying to say is, we're veering too far away from the integrity of the script."

"Integrity?" I laugh and then see the look on Simon's face. "No offense."

"How is that not offensive?"

"All right, all right, let's not get off track," Eric says, placing a hand on my arm. He must catch my vibe because he quickly removes it. "The thing is, we still need to make the film we set out to make."

"This will be *better* than the film you set out to make.

Plus, cutting most of the cheesy CGI animal fight scenes is saving millions," I point out.

"I think we all know money isn't an issue for Nolan." Eric smirks.

"Excuse me, Adam?"

I look up to see Evie chewing on her lip.

"I hope I'm not interrupting."

Before Eric can answer, I cut in. "You're not."

"Great. I was hoping we could have a quick chat?"

Despite the fact this girl completely fucked up my morning, I would rather be anywhere than having this conversation for the millionth time with Eric and Simon.

"Guys, could you give us a minute?"

Eric and Simon both look at Evie, like it's unfathomable that a young PA could have anything more important to say than them. But on request, they push out their chairs and take their plates to another table. Evie sits down opposite me, her gaze darting around. Seeing her big brown eyes, I have a flashback to shouting at her in the sound stage and feel a pang in my side.

She clears her throat and finally faces me with a determined expression. "I wanted to apologize for earlier. I took directions from the wrong person and... I don't want to make excuses. But it will never happen again. I'm sorry for spoiling your schedule."

I can tell by the way she speaks she's been rehearsing this for the last twenty minutes.

"Look... I didn't mean to yell at you in front of everyone," I say, wanting her to learn from this but also not liking the way she seems so... *nervous* around me. I'm not that scary, am I? "But you can't just come in here with your yellow rain boots and your hair ropes and treat this place like a playground. It's really important you know that."

"My hair ropes?" She looks at me, tilting her head.

"Yeah," I reply, bunching my eyebrows together. "Those... ropey things in your hair."

"You mean my braids?"

She pulls one rope to the side, sliding it through her hand.

"I'm not hair and makeup. I don't know the technical term."

She's smiling now, trying to conceal a giggle behind her hand. The way her nose scrunches makes her freckles stand out more.

"Anyway, I just need you to know this is serious. We don't have much room for screw ups like that. There's a lot at stake."

That's the thing about these PAs. They have zero understanding of what it's like to have a position at the top. People depending on you. Great power equals great responsibility and all that crap.

She nods. "Sure. You must be under a lot of pressure to get it right."

"Err... yeah. Exactly."

She shrugs. "And you don't need me and my hair ropes coming in here and making it harder for you."

I'm distracted by her face. When she smiles, the way she's smiling now, with her mouth closed, her lips look smooth and soft. Not huge and uncomfortable, like many people I see around these parts. But sweet... and approachable. Her eyes float down to the table.

Fuck.

Did she see me staring at her lips?

"Um, yeah. You get my point. But we're good now, so don't worry about it."

"Thanks." She stands up. "And this job is really important to me, too. I won't let you down."

I watch as she walks away, only dropping my stare when she turns around and flashes one final smile.

Whatever tantrum Damon pulled earlier to be sent to lunch, he's back on set now, being his usual broody, obnoxious self.

"Why does he keep pulling that face?" I whisper to Joel as we play back the last take. "Let's do one more. I feel like he's trying to impregnate me with his eyes."

Joel laughs gruffly before speaking into his shoulder mic. "We're going to do that one more time."

"Hey Damon." I motion with my hand so I can speak with him privately. "Let's try it again. Do less of the eye thing and more... I don't know, like you're trying to stop a car hitting your best friend. Remember, it's a dog, not your love interest."

"It's these hazel eyes." He smiles out the side of his mouth. "What can I say? I can't help what they do." He finds the petite blonde extra behind me and winks, and she titters in response. I have to actively stop myself from gagging.

"Just try to tone it down."

We end up doing five more takes, but we finally get something I can work with. At least we're making progress. Actually, considering we factored Damon's habit of slowing things down into the schedule, we're making good time. I'm starting to feel like this film won't be the death of me.

"Let's reset for the car crash," Joel says into his mic, with Evie repeating it loudly to the crew. I catch her eye and she gives me a huge, bright smile. Not one of those fake ones you see everyone in LA do, but one that reaches her eyes. I nod to her and turn to the cinematographer to discuss the angles for the next shot.

Much to Damon's relief, we have a creature performer playing the dog in this scene, so he doesn't have to fret about having balls in his face. The performer walks onto set, thick metal stilt legs attached to his own so he can walk and move like a German Sheppard. We rehearse the scene a few times before we start rolling, just to go over the choreography.

"I need you to jump in a second earlier," I instruct Damon, who is running his hands through his hair and nodding. "And remember you move into the car sideways, like you're blocking it with your shoulder to protect Max."

"Ooh, like *Twilight*!"

We both turn in the voice's direction, but I already know whom it belongs to.

"*Twilight*?"

"Yeah, when Edward stops the car from hitting Bella," Evie says, before crouching down and reenacting the scene herself, shooting her arm out to the side and stiff-arming the air. "God, what a classic. Am I right?"

I hear some muffled sniggers from the crew and the makeup artists whispering to each other.

"I can't say I've had the pleasure of watching *Twilight*, but I'll take your word for it," I reply, amused at her complete lack of fucks given about how ridiculous she looks.

Her mouth drops open. "*Haven't watched Twilight*—"

"Let's get this show on the road." Dee smirks between me and Evie.

I refocus on the task at hand. "Agreed, let's shoot this one."

It takes Damon a few tries to get the timing and movements right, stopping the imaginary car on cue, but eventually he gets it and we're able to wrap for the day. As everyone is packing up, I can't help but think the mood has shifted. The entire crew feels lighter—more optimistic about the work ahead.

Or maybe it's just me.

"Today was good," Dee says, walking with me to the production office. "Seems like the crew has found its rhythm."

"You know, I don't want to jinx it. But I think you're right."

Dee scoffs. "Like you believe in jinxing and all that woo woo stuff. You almost had a stroke when the production coordinator wanted to burn sage on our last film together."

"That production coordinator was insane."

We both laugh.

"But you're right. We have a good team here... if you ignore Damon, Eric and Simon," I say.

Dee grimaces. "Well, you seem to be making it work. And how about that Evie, huh?"

"What do you mean?" I stop walking. "What about her?"

"She's a fire cracker, right?"

I scratch the back of my head, trying to act more casual. "Or maybe just cracked."

Dee nudges me in the ribs. "She's a *little* extra."

I raise my eyebrows at her.

"Okay, she's a lot extra. But I like her. She's made a couple of stumbles, yeah. But who didn't when they were new?"

"I'm not going to fire her, if that's what you're worried about." Do people really think I'm that big of a jerk?

"Good," Dee replies. "Because I think she brings a good energy to the team. That's why I got her in. Even her profile was bubbly."

We walk along for a few more steps in silence, and I replay Evie's strange *Twilight* reenactment in my head.

"Yep, she definitely brings something."

9

EVIE

It seems like the crew call is getting earlier and earlier. First it was eight am, then seven, and now it's before six in the morning, and I'm creeping out of my apartment like I'm about to commence a walk of shame.

I'm hit with a pang of disappointment when I remember my love life is completely barren. A walk of shame would be an exciting change.

It's been a while.

I gently pull my front door closed and make my way toward the elevator. At least now I'm sneaking around because I don't want to wake up my neighbors, and not because I'm avoiding my landlord. Which is a good thing, as he's standing by the elevator door, smoothing plaster over a dent in the wall.

"You're up early, Ron."

He jumps at the sound of my voice, making a ripple in the plaster. "Jesus, kid. You scared the life out of me. Don't you make sounds when you walk?"

"I was doing my best Pink Panther impression."

He looks at me, puzzled.

"You know. Da-na, da-na, da-na da-na da-na da-na da-naaaaaaa. DANANANA." I circle in front of him with long, sneaking strides.

"Yeah... I don't do impressions before I've had my morning coffee."

"Oh." I hold out my reusable cup. "Here, why don't you take mine? I'll get another on set."

Ron hesitates for a second but then shrugs, accepting my gesture and taking a long sip. "That seems to be going well. The movie thing?"

"Well enough for me to keep sliding envelopes of cash under your door, at least. Sorry I'm still a little short. Just playing catch up on what I owe you."

Ron waves me off. "Don't worry about it. Now that I know you're working for actual money and not interning, I trust you."

I tilt my head sideways. "Aw, Ron. You were listening when I told you what I was doing."

"Get going before they fire you and I have to reconsider."

I salute him and board the elevator, not needing to be told twice.

On the drive to Burbank I think about the last few weeks, and how the call from Dee was like a call from God herself. To think I was just moments from begging my parents to pay my rent. On a scale of one to getting in trouble in front of the entire film crew, going to my mom with my tail between my legs is top-of-the-list mortifying.

I think about my conversation with Adam at lunch. He seemed different alone compared to when he's trying to wrangle a crew. Softer, maybe. Under all the gruff bravado, I suspect there's a kind soul. I'm just one over-the-top impression away from cracking a smile. Maybe one day we will actually be friends.

I roll down the window as the early morning sun breaks through the sky.

Damon walks out onto a makeshift cliff, gazing out onto a land of green screen. The camera crane soars through the air behind him, filming what will be the last shot of the movie. It's funny seeing this stuff from behind the curtain. I can just imagine when it's done, with its impressive CGI landscapes and booming orchestra soundtrack, it will be one of those blockbuster scenes that appear larger than life. But here on the ground level, it's just a man sitting on a fake rock staring at a green wall.

It's still the best job in the world though. I grin to myself.

"Cut!"

"CUT," I repeat, just in time for Jackson to sidle up next to me. Kylie is on stage door duty, and I'm glad to be standing here with him instead of her. Even if it means listening to his commentary.

"This is going to be epic," he whispers, watching Damon stand there triumphantly.

"I think we need to do that again," Adam says, motioning to the camera guys to reset.

"What was wrong that time?" Damon's eyebrows bunch as he turns to face Adam, still in his valiant final pose.

"You look too victorious," Adam replies. "Remember, this isn't a happy ending. Yes, you saved the dog, but the entire city has descended into chaos. The human tendency to react instead of understand has resulted in a war between men and beasts. You failed to get anyone to listen. Didn't we go over this?"

"Yes, but what's wrong with what *I'm* doing?"

Adam rubs his forehead. "I just need you to look less heroic, more troubled. More like you've failed."

Damon rolls his eyes and goes back to his starting position as they prepare for another take.

"I think we're going to be here for a while," Dee murmurs to us, before walking over to Joel.

"Did you know *Jaws* had all kinds of problems on set?" Jackson says to me. "The script wasn't even finished when they began principal photography. They were re-writing it throughout the shoot."

"You don't say."

"That's not even the half of it," he goes on. "The shark? They hadn't tested it in salt water, and when they used it out at sea, it sank! Right to the bottom of the ocean!"

"I think I have heard that one."

I have definitely heard that one. Twice, in fact. Jackson is one of those newly graduated film nerds who knows everything about every film ever made. He's full of 'fun' facts, and he loves to share them with anyone willing to listen. Anyone unfortunately meaning me, because everyone else is too busy to let him go on and on.

Come to think if it, I'm too busy to let him go on and on as well. But I don't have the heart to cut him off. Unlike Kylie, who met his latest fact with a snappy "what are you, like, a film encyclopedia?"

Eventually we're shooting the last take (while Jackson ranks every Steven Spielberg film in order of lowest to highest grossing) and it seems like Damon is finally doing it right. But before Adam can call 'cut', a loud bang reverberates from the back of the sound stage and everyone turns to see who is responsible.

"Are you fucking *kidding*?" Adam turns around, removing his headphones. "Who is on the stage door and why is my take ruined, again?!" But before he can keep yelling, he sees the person marching toward the set and his face falls.

From my extensive research prior to my first day (always be prepared), I know every name and every face of the top dogs on this film. And as the man traipses toward us, I know this face belongs to Nolan Smith. Billionaire and executive producer. AKA, the boss of everyone here.

He reaches the set, his expensive suit standing out against the typical cargo-pants and t-shirt uniform of most of the crew, and all eyes are on him. He is the kind of man who commands the attention of a room. And by that, I mean he is very attractive and powerful-looking. I can't help but notice a few women, mainly the makeup team, making eyes at each other.

"I'm sorry to interrupt," Nolan says, with a confidence that suggests he doesn't care an iota about interrupting. "So I'll make this quick." He deadpans Adam. "What the hell is going on with my film?"

Adam clamps his eyes shut, holding his palms up. "Nolan, you hired me, remember?"

It only takes me two seconds to realize Adam isn't intimidated by Nolan at all, unlike everyone else in the room.

"I'm the director, so I think you'll find it's *my* film," Adam continues.

A few sounds are made around the room, and one audible "damn" from Dee. Everyone looks back at Nolan.

"As the executive producer and the man paying your income, I think most people would disagree." He walks into the set so that he's standing next to the makeshift cliff, his fancy shoes clopping as he goes. "I was hoping the reports were exaggerated. But no, it seems you've completely obliterated my movie."

Nolan nods to the side of the room, where Eric and Simon come slinking out. "But at least I was brought up to speed before it was too late."

"We tried to handle it ourselves," Eric starts toward Nolan. "But—you know what he's like…"

Eric tilts his head at our director and Adam glares back, before returning his attention to Nolan. "Before it's too late? What are you talking about?"

"Before there's no going back. We need to get this film back on track, back to the vision we originally had."

"What, with cats attacking their owners and apes climbing buildings?" Adam laughs. "The original vision was ridiculous."

"That's not really your call to make now, is it?"

"Ah, again. As the director, it kind of is."

There's an uncomfortable silence, and I'm not sure who's about to pop. But Nolan just smiles, like he knows something Adam doesn't. Like he has the answer to the magic riddle and Adam's an idiot.

"Your stubbornness may work on these two," Nolan says. Eric and Simon both look sheepishly to the side. "But you're dealing with me now. All right? You've had your fun, now it's time to get back to business."

"Fun?" Adam balks. "I've had my *fun*? For weeks we've been working our asses off shooting this film. We're not changing anything now."

"Yes, you are."

"Then good luck finding another director."

The breath catches in my throat. And by the looks on other people's faces, they are just as concerned as me.

He wouldn't walk now.

Would he?

"Easy, Thorne. Remember, you're under contract."

Adam stares him down, a fire in his eyes I've never seen before.

"For what it's worth, I liked the original script better, too."

Everyone looks up at Damon standing on his fake rock.

"No one's asking you, Reeves," Adam says through clenched teeth. "Maybe it's time you learned how to act when you're not playing a big macho hero." He turns to Nolan, shaking the script in the air. "I turned this garbage into something meaningful. Something with substance. Not something people will mindlessly watch for ninety minutes and never think of again. I won't put my name next to another joke."

"Well then finance your own film." Nolan opens his arms out wide. "Make a little indie drama that no one will ever see. I don't care. But take it off my set."

"I was promised full creative control!"

For the first time, Simon pipes up from the back. "Within the parameters of the script."

"Shut up, Simon!" Adam growls.

The whole sound stage is swallowed in awkwardness so thick you could swim through it. I look over at Dee, who is hiding her face behind a clipboard. And then it dawns on me. What will happen to us all if Adam leaves? Production will stop, that's for sure. It would have to until they find a new director. But Dee is on Adam's team and she's the one who hired me.

Will I even have a job if Adam walks?

My stomach drops, and this time, not just because I hate watching confrontations. But because I'm realizing now, this could be the end of my dream job.

It could be all over.

Nolan takes a few steps towards Adam so that they're

only a couple of feet apart. I'm frozen, waiting for one of them to knock the other one out. Nolan looks down at him, a comfortable three inches taller.

"I don't care what Eric promised you to get you on the film. I don't care about your vision. I don't care about your juvenile need to prove you're a serious director. What I care about is the bottom line."

His voice is just above a whisper now, but the room is so quiet, you could hear a pin drop.

"What matters now is that I'm here, and I'm telling you we're going back to how it was. I don't care what you have to do. Just get it done."

Adam's jaw flinches under his facial hair as Nolan takes a step closer.

"I don't care who your father was, or what you usually get away with on set. But you're in Nolan's land now. And you're playing by Nolan's rules."

10

ADAM

It takes a specific type of douchebag to talk in third person. And apparently Nolan Smith fits the bill.

I grimace when he brings up my dad. "You mind telling me what that's supposed to mean?"

"I think you know," he replies with a smirk, before backing away. Which is lucky because I'm about three seconds away from lodging my fist into his eye socket. I glower after him.

"All those scenes you cut? Consider them added back in," he says, walking off the set. "Eric will go over the details."

I look at Eric, whose expression is caught between frightened and smug. Simon, however, looks quite pleased with himself. His embarrassment of a film will get made after all.

But I won't be a part of it.

"Good luck with that. I'm out."

Nolan stops walking and turns around slowly. "Excuse me?"

"I'm out. Find someone else who will direct your stupid film."

Nolan chuckles to himself, rubbing his jaw. "You might want to think carefully about this, Thorne. Remember who you're dealing with."

I tilt my chin up to the ceiling mockingly, pretending to ponder. "Yep. I'm good with that."

The smirk fades from Nolan's face. "You're going to let your arrogance shut down an entire production?"

I cross the space between us. Out of the corner of my eye, I can see Evie watching us like Bambi watching his mother get gunned down by the hunter. When I reach Nolan, I press the script against his Armani-wearing chest.

"You can shove your production up your ass."

And if I had a microphone, now would be the best time to drop it. As I make it to the stage door, I hear what can only be the sound of Nolan throwing the script against the floor.

The production office is empty when I push the door open. I close it firmly behind me, happy to leave the drama outside. Slumping into the chair, I drag my hands through my hair.

It's hard to pinpoint how I feel. Relieved? Disappointed? I should've been more careful getting into business with Nolan Smith. It was a mistake saying yes to the job to begin with.

"Are you out of your fucking mind?" A furious Dee flies through the door.

Well, so much for leaving the drama outside.

"Dee, how lovely of you to join me."

"Shut up. What the hell has gotten into you?"

I look up at her, scrunching my face. "What are you talking about? You heard him in there. 'You've had your fun' and all that 'you're in Nolan land' bullshit. How did you expect me to react?"

"With a bit of self-control for a start!"

"Self-control? Dee, he's lucky I didn't punch him in the face. You saw how he was up in my grill."

"Up in your grill?" She stares at me, wide eyed, like there's someone else she wants to punch in the face. "Jesus, Adam. We were actually getting somewhere."

"We were! But he came and changed the terms on me! I swore to myself I wouldn't do another meaningless—"

"I swear to God if you mention meaningless films or stories without substance one more time, I'm going to stab myself in the eye with this pen." She holds up an actual pen.

"What's your problem?"

"You are. You're being a total asshole."

Well, that's uncalled for. "I am not an asshole," I mumble.

"Really? Then you're doing a very convincing impression of an asshole. Maybe you should cast yourself in one of your own movies?"

Dee stands there with her hands on her hips and I frown at her. "I don't understand why *you're* so mad. I'm the one who's had my entire movie torn apart."

"You just don't get it, do you?" She shakes her head. "This is just a blimp for you. You'll weather some backlash from Nolan and then you'll be onto the next project, Mr. Multi-Million-Dollar Director. But what about the rest of us, huh? Some of us are counting on this film. Some of us are still trying to make it to where we want to be."

"You think this is where I want to be?" I shoot my arm out toward the sound stage. "Directing flying monkeys and talentless actors who only got cast because of their Instagram following? I have goals too, Dee."

"Yeah... it's just easier for you to bide your time in your West Hollywood condo. We're not all in the same position as you."

"Is that what this is about?"

"Of course that's what this is about!" she shouts, the tiny curls around her hairline looking even more frazzled. In all the years I've worked with her, I've never seen Dee so mad. "People are depending on this pay check. We can't afford production to stop and risk not getting hired when it starts back up. The people in there have families to provide for, roofs to put over their heads."

I groan, returning my face to my hands.

"And what about George?" she continues. "His wife's chemo treatments don't just appear out of thin air, you know."

I tilt my head back up to meet her eyes. "That's a low blow."

"Yeah, well, that's reality."

"George is employed by the studio," I say, standing up to regain some kind of higher ground. "He'll get more work by tomorrow."

"And what about the other ninety-nine people in there?"

"It's not that simple!"

"Ugh!" She throws her hands in the air, turning toward the production office door. "You try to talk some sense into him. I'm done."

I jolt my head to see who she's talking to. *Please don't be fucking Eric.* Or worse, Nolan. But the voice that soon follows is much softer than I expected.

"Do you mind if I come in?"

Evie appears through the threshold. Today her hair is tied back, with little messy bits hanging around her face.

"That depends, are you going to lose your shit like Dee?"

She smiles crookedly and walks in, closing the door behind her. I'm hoping that means 'no'.

She walks around the perimeter of the room, looking over the various documents and headshots stuck to the walls.

"I guess my photo got lost in the mail," she says in a deep, joking voice, pointing to the headshots of the main cast. I take her strange stall tactic as an opportunity to think about what Dee said. I know a ton of people on other productions in charge of hiring crew. I could just make a few phone calls and get everyone back on a payroll... then I'd be home free...

"Who's the Trekkie?" Evie scoffs, picking up a Darth Vader paperweight with one hand and muffling her mouth with the other. "Adam," she makes it say in my direction. "I am your father."

"Trekkies like Star Trek, not Star Wars."

She shrugs. "Same thing."

"You are going to tell me why you're here eventually, right?"

She sighs and puts down Darth, taking a seat in one of the chairs. "You don't know much about me, do you?"

I bunch my eyebrows together. "Um... no? I guess I don't?"

"Film school was never part of the plan," she begins, leaning back. "I studied medicine for three years before I realized I never wanted it in the first place. It wasn't until I was twenty-three that I went back to get my film degree."

I do the math in my head. It all makes a lot more sense now. I knew she wasn't as young as the other PAs. Mind you, the hair ropes don't help in the guessing-her-age depart-ment. Most days she comes to the studio looking like an extra out of *Degrassi*. Or whatever show pre-pubescent teens watch these days.

"My parents were furious, of course. I mean, their studious med school daughter, a drop out?" She places her hand against her chest and does a mock posh accent. "Picking up and moving to LA? They thought I was crazy." She laughs to herself. "Everyone thought I was crazy."

She stands up and returns to the wall, looking over a row of call sheets stuck to the paint. "But I knew without any doubt that this is what I wanted to do... work in Holly-wood... be a part of something special... see my name roll up in the credits..." She trails a finger down one of the call sheets until she lands on her name. A small smile appears on her lips. Those smooth lips...

She turns abruptly to face me. "So you can only imagine how excited—no—how *ecstatic* I was to get the call from Dee—that I had a job on an actual movie set. Not a job slinging coffee to people who have meltdowns about foam to liquid ratio, not an unpaid internship shooting commer-cials for ingrown hair removal, but an *actual paid job on a feature film*."

"I think I know where this is going, and—"

"No, you really don't know." She steps toward me. "I made the biggest risk of my life dropping out of medicine. I gave up everything to follow my dreams—my relationship with my family, my friends in San Diego, a pathway to a stable career. But I did it anyway, because I knew that if I worked hard enough, I would make it. Now, I know you don't get it—being a successful director and all—but this assistant job means everything to me. Not only is it a step-ping stone to more work in the film industry, but it's paying for the apartment I live in, and protecting me from going to my parents with my tail between my legs for support."

She is basically on the ground now, hovering in front of me.

"So I'm asking you, Adam. No, I'm *begging* you... please don't quit this film. If you walk, they will have to stop everything. And I was hired as part of your team, so there's a huge chance they won't want me to come back when they replace you."

I feel a stab of guilt in my stomach.

"Stay. Give *Primal Nature* a chance."

I wince. "Geez, even the name is fucking terrible."

She pulls a face and nods. "Look, I know it's not the film you want to make. I know you say you're done with cheesy action sci-fi's. But just the one? Just because we're already started? And then no more. Heck, if you go to sign on to another tacky blockbuster, I'll stop you myself. I'm pretty forceful when I need to be."

"You do a pretty convincing Gandalf impression." I haven't been able to get that ridiculous thing out of my head since I saw her banging her fake staff on the ground.

She grins.

"So? What do you say?"

I look into her brown eyes. What did I say? I have no idea where to even start. This girl just poured her heart out to me. And I have to give her credit. Her tactic is a lot more effective than Dee screaming at me like a sassy banshee. But it doesn't change the way I feel about this moronic movie. Especially now that I have to do it on Nolan's terms. Tacky animal action scenes, cringeworthy jokes, a totally unrealistic ending complete with a happily ever-after kiss. She's right, I'm done with this stuff. My dad was a literary giant, for crying out loud. Talk about big shoes.

But she's looking at me with those pleading eyes again. Something about her hopeful expression... it reminds me of how I felt when I was first getting in the game. So excited to make my mark. So grateful for any opportunity.

Do I really have it in me to take that away from her?

"You won't regret it," she says when I don't respond. "I pinky-promise you won't regret it."

I exhale, letting out a grumble and looking at her bent little finger, held out toward me. The only thing more embarrassing than this film is a grown man doing a pinky promise.

But here I am, hooking her finger with my own.

"I highly doubt that."

There is never a safe assumption to make when it comes to LA traffic. Even at six in the morning. Will it take me an hour to get to work? Will it take me twenty minutes and I'll have to sit in the catering tent for a half hour? Find out on the next episode of I Have No Flipping Idea.

Unfortunately, today is option one, because of an accident on the freeway. Which explains why I'm trying to get out of my car comically fast in the studio parking lot and don't bother to check the caller ID when my phone rings.

"Hello?"

"Well how about that, you answered."

I suppress a groan. "Mom."

"Yes. I'm surprised you remember who I am."

Is it really necessary to start every conversation with some variation of 'I never hear from you'?

"I remember, but I'm also running late to set so—"

"Oh, you're still doing that, are you?" she says, with a tone that suggests I've taken up soap carving or crafting wind chimes out of forks.

"Yes, I'm still doing it. It's my full-time job now."

"I assumed the reason you haven't been in touch was because it fell through."

"Why would you assume that?"

"Well, you never know with these things."

"These *things*?"

"Darling, I've just come off a twenty-two-hour shift. Please don't sass me," she sighs, like I'm the one being insulting.

I take a deep breath. "I've been really busy, too. Which is why I haven't had the chance to call."

"Your father and I were just wondering when you are planning on visiting again," she cuts in. "You are planning on seeing us eventually, right?"

"The road between LA and San Diego goes both ways, you know."

She gives a fluttery laugh. "And battle against the tourists and the homeless people? Besides, your sister would like to see you too."

I chew on my lip. "I wasn't planning on coming back until Thanksgiving. The next couple of months are flat out, and I want to be available when this shoot is done if any other work comes—"

"Hopefully you can find it in your busy schedule to see your family. You only have one."

One too many.

"I'm going to lie down," she goes on. "Let us know when you're coming."

And the line goes dead.

I stuff my phone into my bag, reminding myself to never again answer it without checking who's calling first. If I think that was painful, I can't even imagine what it would have been like to tell them the film had been canceled.

I owe Adam big time.

"Don't shoot!"

Damon is standing at the bottom of a ramp, waving his hands above his head.

"They'll only attack if they feel threatened. Put down your weapons!"

A cluster of creature performers come running out from behind him on all fours. They have little stilts attached to their arms with balls on the ends, so they can run on their hands like gorillas. Three actors in police uniforms stand at the top of the ramp, guns aimed at the fake apes.

"Please! Don't shoot!" Damon cries.

The creature performers charge, gliding up the ramp with rhythmic strides. It's impressive how much they look like actual animals. The cops aim their guns.

"No!"

Just as they tighten their fingers around the triggers, Damon breaks out in a weird monkey language. A strange combination of almost Russian and a lot of grunting. Out of the corner of my eye, I see Adam drop his head into his palm.

On Damon's cue, the creature performers stop and look back at him, returning the strange grunting by way of answering. Damon drops to his knees, his face flush with relief. "And I thought my dog Max was a handful."

"Cut!" Adam calls.

"CUT," I repeat.

We all wait to see if Adam wants to do another take. He looks across at Joel, who just shrugs and nods.

"That was great, right?" Damon asks, a satisfied grin on his face.

"Exactly as Nolan wants it to be," Adam grumbles,

before turning to the camera crew. "Let's set up for the next shot."

Damon does a little air punch and starts chatting with the creature performer, the biggest gorilla of them all.

I hand Adam and Dee a bottle of water each, grimacing. "On a scale of one to ten, how much did that hurt to watch?"

"Remind me again how I won't regret doing this film?" he says, accepting the hydration.

"At least Damon is completely in his element now," Dee says, watching our lead actor as he practices macho poses. "And he's taking half the time to get a scene done."

"Imagine how that thrills me," Adam says in monotone. He looks down at the shot list, his face completely flat. I can't help but feel a little responsible for his low mood. Ever since he agreed to keep going with *Primal Nature*, any tiny spark that he had is gone. He's as grumpy as ever.

But maybe I can do something to make him feel better.

While the crew is setting up to shoot the next scene, I sneak outside to the craft service trailer, knocking on the side. Out pops a guy's head, his hair pushed back in a baseball cap.

"What's up?"

"Hi," I say, putting on my best smile. "Those cupcakes we had yesterday, I wondered if you had any left?"

"I think there's a couple in the back, sure. Go nuts."

"That's the thing, it's not for me," I reply, twisting the hair in my ponytail. "Actually... I was kind of hoping you could do me a favor."

～

The lunch tent is swarming with people. Crew members, cast, extras dressed in dirt-stained clothing after a stampede through the streets of New York City. Gang's all here.

But there's only one person I'm looking for.

"Ooh, I didn't know we were having these again," Brian says, reaching for the treat in my hand before I slap him away.

"Don't even think about it. I'm a girl on a mission. Have you seen Adam?"

But Brian is already grinning at a brunette extra with dirt stains on her face. "After you," he says, motioning to the spot in front of him in the cue. She smiles and takes her place in the line, which weaves its way to the tables running through the middle of the tent. They're packed with steel trays filled with all kinds of food. My stomach rumbles at the smell of it all. Noodles, salads, lasagna, those delicious little dinner rolls warmed in the oven. But I can't get distracted by carbs yet. I have to do something first.

I spot Adam across the tent, sat next to Joel and cameraman George.

"Hello, gents," I say, sliding up next to them. "Mind if I join you?"

"Pull up a chair, sweetheart," George says, nodding at the space across from him. "You can be a rose amongst three thorns."

"Oh stop it." I flap my hand at him. "What are we talking about?"

"We weren't," Adam says without looking up. "Enjoying a rare moment of silence."

"You can have silence when you're dead. I have something for you." I place my gift on the table in front of him and slide it forward. "It's my way of saying thank you. You know, for not bailing on us."

He looks down at it. "A cake from yesterday?"

"Not just any cake," I say, pressing my hand to my chest. "Look at the frosting."

His eyebrows pinch down in confusion.

"Well?!"

"There's a little man on my cake," he says.

"It's not a little man." I roll my eyes. "It's an Academy Award. See the gold sparkles?"

"Well, would you look at that," George says, leaning in closer. "That's a tiny little Oscar, that is."

"I wanted them to write Best Director on it but they said there wasn't enough space," I say, slumping my shoulders.

Joel looks at the cupcake with his mouth downturned and nods, showing his appreciation for my work.

"I'm not sure this film is going to win me an Oscar any time soon," Adam says. He's still frowning, but his lips curve up in an almost smile.

"Maybe not, but you're the best director to me. To all of us, right?" I gesture to Joel and George, who reluctantly agree as Adam smirks at them.

"I'm not much of a sweet tooth," Adam begins as he looks up at me, his eyes lingering for a moment before he goes on. "But that's—"

"—very thoughtful," George finishes for him. "You're a doll."

"I try my best," I flick my hair. "Anyway, I better get some lunch before the hungry crew polish it off."

As I walk away, I'm ninety percent sure Adam will toss the cupcake in the trash.

But it's the thought that counts.

"A yoga instructor?"

"No."

"A professional boardwalk roller-skater?"

"No."

"Um... a fake tan ambassador?"

Gus laughs. "No."

It's another lovely afternoon on stage-door duty, and I'm passing the time with Gus, trying to guess why he moved to LA. Because it wasn't to be a stunt guy.

"I've got it! One of those character impersonators on Hollywood Boulevard."

"Does anyone come to LA wanting to be one of those guys?"

"Okay, I give up. You have to tell me," I say, dropping my arms by my side.

Gus faces the ground, rubbing the back of his neck all bashful-like. "I don't know. It's such a cliché."

"We're in Los Angeles!" I spread my arms out wide. "The City of Dreams! We love clichés."

He snorts. "City of Broken Dreams."

I tilt my head, waiting for him to answer. He lets out a dramatic sigh. "Okay, because you're so relentless."

I grin.

"I wanted to be an actor."

"Is that it?" I squint at him.

"Yes?"

"That's not embarrassing," I say, scrunching my face. "Every second person who moves here wants to be an actor."

"Which is exactly why it's embarrassing. I obviously haven't been successful."

"You get to fly around on wires like a superhero!" I exclaim. "You have the coolest job in the world!"

He smiles crookedly at me. He has a few more freckles, and his hair isn't quite as quaffed, but the uncanniness between him and Damon really is amazing. Chiseled jaw. Defined cheekbones. Hazel eyes. The works.

"Yeah... I can't complain," he says, adjusting his ripped shirt that matches the one Damon is wearing identically, right down to the tiny blood stain on the shoulder. "At least I've got a job in the movies, right?"

"I would pick up trash all day and still love this job," I say, staring dreamily out at the expanse of trailers. "Oh wait, I do pick up trash all day!"

Gus laughs.

We spend the next twenty minutes chatting, covering the basic getting-to-know-you stuff. He likes mountain biking. He's single, but went on a promising date with some guy called Mitch last week. And he's a Gemini. But when we get up to family, the conversation stops flowing as freely. I can't help but feel a little guilty hearing about how much he misses his family, being so far away from them. Especially when mine are just a couple of hours away and I choose not to see them.

"That's a wrap for the day," I say to Gus when I hear Joel through my walkie earpiece. "They're really powering through it now, aren't they?"

The crew spill through the doors, packing up and saying their goodbyes. Which means it's the PAs turn for trash duty. And by the PAs, I mean me and Jackson, because Kylie has come up with an excuse to help in the production office so she doesn't have to spend the next hour sweeping and collecting empty water bottles.

By the time I come back outside with an enormous bag of recyclables, most people are gone, so I'm surprised to see that Adam is still hanging around outside the catering truck.

The door opens, and the chef hands him several containers that I'm assuming are full of food. I watch as Adam nods at him, taking the containers and putting them in his car.

I don't take him as a leftovers kind of guy. He is the kind of guy who could afford fancy restaurant takeout every night. Or maybe he has a girl waiting for him at home, with dinner already on the table. Try as I might, he hasn't told me anything about his personal life.

He is the toughest of nuts to crack.

As he climbs into his car, he sees me looking, and I wave goodbye to cover my creeping. He gives me a tight smile and shuts the door.

12

I pull into my driveway but instead of going inside, I take the containers out of the car and start walking up my street. It's dark but still warm, the late September breeze rippling down the back of my t-shirt.

I turn the corner and emerge where there is a bit more life happening. People going out for dinner, catching up for a drink. But all I can think about is crawling onto my couch with a cold beer and ordering a pizza with extra cheese. There are only so many hours I can spend with other people before I'm tapped out.

"Haven't seen you in a few days," Bob growls from his setup next to the sidewalk. Today he's wearing a Guns N' Roses t-shirt and his trucker cap is sitting next to him. His wispy gray hair flicks around in the balmy air.

"I've been working pretty late most days," I reply, handing him the containers. "Here."

Bob takes the food from me, opening each lid like he always does and sniffing the contents.

"That chicken thing is pretty good," I say, pointing to the biggest container. "And that round container is apple pie."

"I don't get the obsession today with putting nuts in everything," he says, flicking through a salad with a wooden fork. "And these little red things."

"I think it's pomegranate."

He waves me off with another grunt. "How's it going, anyway?"

"Eh... it's fine." I shrug.

"That pretty boy still giving you grief?"

"I haven't met an action hero I can't handle," I laugh, looking down at his arm, which is extra swollen today. "How's that wrist going, Bob?"

Another rumble echoes in his throat. "I'm getting old, that's how it's going."

"I told you I'd pay for you to get it looked at."

"I don't need to see a quack in a white coat to know I'm getting old."

I draw my eyebrows together. For years I've known Bob. Not once has he let me take him to get checked out, or to buy clothes, or to get a sleeping bag, for that matter. He had a fit the time I offered to pay for an apartment. The only thing he ever accepts is catering leftovers, or the odd crumpled bill to go buy some lunch. He's independent, I get it. And he doesn't complain a lot either. Unlike most people these days.

Our conversations never last that long, which is fine by me. We are both about as chatty as a doorknob. And sure enough, he starts investigating the containers again, cuing me to leave so he can eat his dinner in peace.

"What's this about?" he says, opening the brown paper bag and lifting out the cupcake. I forgot I put it in there. "Do they feed you this little girl food at work?"

I smile, looking down at the slightly smudged golden man nestled into the frosting.

"Actually," I lean down, taking it out of his outstretched hand. "I'm going to keep this one."

I walk all the way back to my house holding the cupcake like a complete tool. It's not until I'm fishing around in my pocket for the house keys I notice the front door is already open.

Wide open.

I step through the doorframe, peering into the darkness. I can't hear a thing. Whoever they are, they are the worst burglar alive, because they forgot the television, an expensive watch I got as a gift and never wore, and a MacBook Pro sitting on the counter. I snort to myself.

Unless they're still here.

I stiffen as the thought comes to me. What if there's a burglar rummaging around in my things upstairs? Or a crack head off the boulevard waiting to whack me? Or a disgruntled actor I rejected on a previous film? People get crazy over that kind of stuff. And we all know how *Joker* ended.

I walk slowly into the living room, and there is still no sign of anyone else. But I hear a creak upstairs, and the hairs on the back of my neck stiffen.

"Hello?" I call out, trying to keep my voice even. "Look, I don't want any trouble."

And then I have a thought. What if *they* are looking for trouble? What if this is how I go? Suddenly, it all flashes before me. The slideshow at my funeral, with pictures of me wearing my headset and barking orders at people. Posters of all the terrible movies I've made. People dressing up as action heroes and aliens and rabid monkeys as a tribute *to me*. I can already feel myself rolling in my grave.

"He lived a solitary life," the priest would say during my obituary. "Alone in his West Hollywood condo with his cat Rufus, who ate half his face before neighbors started complaining about a smell and the body was found."

Dee and Joel would sit in the front row, because I have barely any family left. Maybe Bob would come. The wake would be his last free meal from me.

I hear another creak and my heart pounds.

Oh God, I'm not ready to die.

I cannot leave this world as 'that director guy who made all the really bad but popular films and died alone with his cat'. At least my dad left behind a legacy.

There's another creak at the bottom of the stairs, and Rufus comes darting toward me. But he's followed by a much taller specimen, shielded by the darkness. It all happens very fast, and all that I can manage is a jumble of gibberish and growling as I throw the only thing I have as a weapon.

There's a loud shriek as I hit my target.

"What the fuck!?"

If the shriek didn't give it away, the voice does.

It's a woman.

I scramble for the light switch on the wall, flicking it on, although it isn't immediately obvious who the person is because of all the cake and frosting covering her face. She wipes it out of her eyes before shrieking for the second time. "What the fuck?!"

I stare past the crumbs.

"*Kimberly*?"

She flings a chunk of cupcake onto my hardwood floor. "Yes, it's me! What the hell did you do that for?!"

I look at Evie's gift, smothered all over Kim's face.

Well, that's one way to greet your ex.

To say it's an uncomfortable silence is inaccurate. An uncomfortable silence would be correct for two exes sitting in a living room, not speaking. But for two exes sitting in a living room, not speaking, after one of them has hurled a cupcake at the other one's face, I need a new word.

"I'm sorry, I really didn't know it was you."

"Who else has a spare key?" she says indignantly, like it should have been expected that she was creeping around in my house.

"Correct me if I'm wrong, but you don't live here anymore," I say, wanting that beer more than ever.

"I had to collect a few things."

"So you decided to come here when I wasn't home and sneak around?"

"I wasn't sneaking around." She rolls her eyes. "I just finished a shoot not far from here and figured now was a good time." She extends her big giraffe neck, looking around the room. "I see you've done absolutely nothing with the place."

"What I do with the place isn't really your concern anymore."

"I'm not concerned," she says. "It just figures, that's all."

"What does?"

"That everything is exactly the same. That *you're* exactly the same." She shrugs her lean shoulders. "I knew I was right to leave."

"It's funny you mention that, because you never actually

told me why you left. I just got home from work one day, and all your stuff was gone."

"Are you kidding?"

"Do I look like I'm kidding?"

"Adam, I tried to talk to you for weeks. You were never around! And don't act like you were so cut up about me leaving. It was clear this relationship was never going anywhere."

I raise my eyebrows. "You say that like it's my fault."

"Um, it IS your fault. We were together, what, eight months?"

I shrug. To be honest, I have no idea how long we were seeing each other.

"And in all that time, you never let me in. You barely even spoke to me when your dad died."

"It was a weird time," I say, watching Rufus lick the frosting off the floor.

"You never saw a future with us. Just stop pretending. It's not like it matters now, anyway." She flicks her cakey hair over her shoulder nonchalantly.

I stare at her, trying to remember how I felt when we first started dating. Models aren't my usual go-to, but Kim seemed different. She liked foreign films and rescuing animals and she had traveled all over the world. It wasn't like we stayed up all night talking, but she seemed like someone I could spend time with without wanting to jump off a cliff. And that was saying something.

Then somewhere along the way, she wanted more. More dinners out, more vacations, more talking about feelings. *Intimacy*, she called it. Ugh, what a buzzword.

And then she got strange with me, and distant. Like I was always disappointing her. I couldn't keep up. And, although it makes me feel bad to say out loud, I had no interest in keeping up. I let her be distant. It was just... easier that way.

"Anyway, I'm seeing someone else now. I thought it was time to get the rest of my stuff." She pouts her lips.

"That's great, I'm happy for you."

"Yeah, he's into cats too. So I can take Rufus off your hands."

"What?"

"The cat," she points to him like I'm stupid. "I'm taking him home today."

"He is home."

"Adam, please. You never wanted him. You said he would shed fur and make the place smell like tuna."

She is right. I did say that. But... I've gotten used to having him around. I look down at his little furry face, now covered in gold-speckled frosting. A pang grips my stomach as I realize I'll now be here, really alone.

Not that I would ever say that out loud.

"Fine." I stand up from the couch. "Is that all?"

She smiles tightly and follows my lead. It forever shocks me she can stand properly in the enormous heels she wears. And she definitely doesn't need the extra height.

From memory, my five-nine stature was another issue she had with me.

She hooks her handbag over her wrist so her hands are free to scoop up my roommate. "Come on, baby. Mommy's got you now." Rufus licks her cheek, and she giggles, like it's an actual sign of affection and not just because she has a tub of Pillsbury frosting all over her face.

"Dave's going to be so excited to meet him," she says as she puts Rufus in the passenger seat of her car. "He joked about getting us a cat last Christmas, but I told him Rufus doesn't play so well with others." She shuts the door and I look at him through the window, wondering if he feels as crappy as I do.

"Hang on, Christmas?"

"Yeah," she says, smiling at the memory.

"But we were still together last Christmas?"

She sighs, like me pointing that out is ruining her smooth getaway. "Let's not hash out ancient history."

I laugh through my nose, shaking my head at the ground. And to think I actually felt guilty about how everything went down.

Kimberly walks to the driver's door, but stops before getting inside.

"Don't take so long to open up to the next one, okay?"

I clench my teeth. Is she giving me relationship advice when we just established she cheated on me?

But I don't have the energy to bite back. I just give her a thin smile and commit the vision of her with cupcake smooshed all over her face and hair to memory.

I may not have a sweet tooth, but looking at how it all ended up, that cupcake was the nicest gift Evie could have given me.

13

EVIE

The skies are clear and the sun is out for our first day shooting on location. Which isn't exactly uncommon for California. But it's convenient none the less.

We're filming on Big Rock Beach in Malibu. Tucked away off the Pacific Coast Highway, there is only one access point, which makes it easy to control random people coming into the shoot. The only drawback is that the shoreline is very narrow, and disappears during high tide. Which is why we are all standing back, waiting for the water to shrink away from the sand. Luckily, I have some extra company today.

"Okay, give me the rundown on everyone," Sylvia says, looking at the crew over the top of her sunglasses. I managed to get her work as an extra for this scene. It's not her dream job, but it beats making turkey on rye for fifteen dollars an hour.

"That one behind the camera is George, and I also like to think of him as my unofficial uncle," I start, pointing as I go. "The girl with the curly hair is Dee. She's the best. That's Brian with the boom." I look at Sylvia's tiny bikini. "Best to avoid him today. That's Joel, he's very chill. And that one with the brown hair next to him is Adam."

"Ah... so *that's* Adam." She tilts her head back to take a good look. "Interesting."

"Why is that interesting?"

She makes a little high-pitch noise. "No reason."

We have a smaller crew today, which I'm happy to say doesn't include Kylie. Try as I might, she still has no interest in being friends. But at least she's stopped trying to sabotage me at any opportunity. I suspect Dee spoke to her after our conversation. Like I said, Dee is the best.

With the tide low enough, the crew sets up and Damon starts rehearsing. This time, it involves his love interest in the film. A beautiful actress called Emma with tiny pores and an even tinier waist. During this scene in the film, their romantic moment in the water is interrupted when a shark appears out of nowhere and tries to eat them. I watch from the shore as Adam goes through the blocking, his pants rolled up to his calves to reveal surprisingly muscular legs.

When it comes time to shoot, Sylvia walks as instructed across the back of the frame with another model-looking extra. I give them a thumbs up as I watch it on the monitor. Everything goes without a hitch, and the crew starts setting up to shoot from another angle.

"So let me get this straight." I stand next to Adam, watching Damon rehearse. He scoops Emma away from the invisible shark. "The animals in this movie attack the humans because of something they're drinking in the water, right?"

"The more you talk about it, the more I want to kill myself," Adam groans.

"But sharks live in the sea, so why are they affected by the drinking water?"

Adam inhales and bunches his shoulders around his ears.

"And furthermore, sharks are already predators to humans. So why is this scene even relevant to the storyline? It's not out of the ordinary that a shark might try to eat you."

Adam turns to me, placing his hands on my bare shoulders. An unexpected current runs down my arms as he touches my skin. I need to reapply more sunblock—I'm probably getting a sunburn.

"When it comes to working on films as nonsensical as this one, I find it best to just ignore the glaring plot holes and let it kind of," he looks out at the ocean, "wash over you."

I laugh and see Dee behind him, staring at his hands on my shoulders. My laugh is abruptly cut short and Adam drops his arms, turning back to Joel.

Dee wouldn't think I'm trying to *flirt*, would she?

The last thing I need is someone on set getting the wrong idea about me. To think that I'm the kind of girl who would bat her eyelashes to get what she wants.

I pull a tube of sunblock from the supply bag strapped to my hips and squeeze a blob into my hands, rubbing it into the spaces where Adam's hands were just moments ago.

"You don't think I'm a flirt, do you?"

Sylvia snorts. "You? You're practically an elementary school teacher. All buttons and crayons and braids in your hair."

"So... does that mean no?"

"That means no, sweetie."

"Okay good." I relax my shoulders, watching Adam talk angles with the cinematographer.

"Why do you ask?"

I shrug casually. "I just... want to make the right impression here. Especially to my superiors."

"I see." Sylvia nods, following my eyes to where they land. We're quiet for a moment, listening to nothing but the sound of the waves lapping against the sand. That and the sound of Brian's goofy laugh as he annoys Dee.

"But he's been looking at you all day, if that's what you're wondering."

"Who?"

"You know who," Sylvia says with a smirk.

"*Adam*?"

"No, George. Of course Adam!"

"Adam can barely stand to be around me. I exhaust him," I reply, curling my braid into a bun so I can feel the sun on my back. "He said I was like one of those singing Christmas toys that never seem to run out of battery."

"You are like one of those singing Christmas toys that never seem to run out of battery," she confirms. "But he's still been looking at you."

"I'm a PA. He's probably been looking for water because he's thirsty."

"He's thirsty for something."

I pinch her arm skin.

"Ow!"

A few heads turn in our direction, including Adam's.

"Nothing to see here folks," I say, holding a hand in the air. "Just some innocent girl-on-girl play fighting on the beach."

Sylvia drops her head and groans, and I hear a quiet "All right!" from Brian.

It's time to shoot the next scene—the one with Damon and Emma rolling around on the sand together—and it's my job to be on standby with fresh towels to brush the sand off their backs in-between takes.

There is something about watching two very attractive people maul each other for half an hour that makes you think about your own love life.

Or lack thereof, in my case.

It's not like I've never been interested in finding love. It just sort of... never happened for me. And forget love. I've never even had a boyfriend.

I was the girl in school who, despite taking every science class under the sun, spent my free periods in the drama room, watching the theater geeks rehearse. Or sneaking into the media class so I could play with the cameras. And when I wasn't doing that, I was usually found under a tree, by myself, with my nose stuck in the next great adventure novel. I wasn't a girl the boys were interested in. At my first boy-girl party, I got picked for seven minutes in heaven with a guy called Rich. The silence in that wardrobe was so deafening that I decided to entertain him instead with a rendition of 'Hot in Herre' because I thought it would lighten the mood.

It didn't.

I was always the weird girl. The *extra* girl, before it was trendy to be extra. I liked to sing, and I liked to dance, and I liked to dress up as old male characters for Halloween. And none of these things were conducive to being asked out on dates.

But it's not like I haven't had sex. I had sex with my biology partner just after graduation, the softly spoken guy from the movie theater, the tech rental guy from college. But it's not until now that I'm looking down at Emma writhing over Damon with her string-bikini backside mooning the air, that I calculate I haven't had sex for a really, *really* long time.

"Cut!" Adam calls, followed by, "Evie, we need it to be wetter."

"What?" I look up with rounded eyes. Did I recite that last part out loud?

Jesus, take the wheel.

"The ground. It needs to be wetter. The sun's dried them off too much. They're meant to look like they just got out of the water after he saved her."

"Oh... right."

I grab the bucket and march toward the ocean, grateful for it cooling my feet as I scoop up the water. I'm probably just dehydrated. Too many hours in the sun.

"Where do you want it?" I ask, standing there with the full bucket.

"Just all over."

Adam looks like he's had some sun, too. But not in a dehydrated way. In a tanned, sun kissed kind of way. Not that I'm thinking about kissing. I shake my head, returning to the task at hand, and empty the contents of the bucket.

Which is followed by an ear-piercing screech.

Everyone is staring now. At me, holding the empty bucket over Damon and Emma's heads. Who now look like a couple of drowned rats.

"Why did you do that?!" Emma looks up at me, water pouring from her chin.

"I meant on the ground, not on them! We have makeup for that," Adam says, pointing to the makeup girl standing by with a spray bottle.

"I'm so sorry!" I cover my mouth. "I misunderstood."

But Adam's shoulders are shaking, his face muffled into

his hand as he and Joel laugh at Damon and Emma's sounds of distress.

"I'm so sorry," I say, turning back to Emma. "You still look really pretty."

She glares at me, and this seems to make Adam laugh more. As he leans on George's shoulder, I can't help but watch—the sun making his brown hair fleck golden, the crinkles at the corners of his eyes, the huge genuine grin on his face as he tries to compose himself. It's completely refreshing to see after weeks of grump. And completely infectious.

I find myself smiling over at him before I catch Sylvia's eye. She is smiling too, but hers is different—smugger.

I huff, taking my empty bucket back to the ocean and wishing I could dive right in.

I need to cool down more than just my feet.

The tide has risen again, so we are waiting right next to the rocky wall for it to go back down before we can do another take. The sun is lower in the sky, and although we're being held up, the vibe is mellow. Everyone is relaxed, taking a moment to appreciate the serenity. Sylvia has been wrapped for the day, so I take a seat on a rock next to George, who looks like he's enjoying a peaceful moment of his own.

"Whatcha thinking about, George?" I ask, adjusting my shorts to make sure I'm not flashing anyone.

"Oh, you know… this and that."

"There's something about the beach, isn't there?" I say, gazing out at the cloudless sky. "No matter what's happening in your life, it always makes you stop and ponder."

"It sure does."

I look across at him, and can see the afternoon sun reflected in his eyes.

"Do you go swimming much?"

"I'm not into the saltwater," he says, before smiling. "But my wife, Elsa, she loves the ocean. Can't get enough of it."

I grin. "I bet she drags you out here."

"All the time." He pauses for a moment, and his smile slowly disappears. "Though not as much lately."

"How come?"

He picks up a stick from the sand. "Cancer."

I inhale sharply. "Oh George, I'm so sorry."

"She got sick a few years ago. Breast cancer. Beat it like a trooper, too." He fumbles with the stick before snapping it into pieces and throwing them onto the sand. "But we found out a few months ago it's back. She doesn't feel too good with all the chemo. She spends her time indoors, mostly."

"That must be really hard on both of you."

"Oh, I'm all right," he says with a tight smile. "I'm not sick."

"You don't have to do that, George." I place my hand on his wrist. He looks at it and then at my face, his eyebrows curving.

"I'm sure you're a rock for your beautiful wife. But it's just us pals talking," I go on. "You don't have to be tough in front of me." I give his arm a squeeze and take my hand back, following his lead and picking sticks from the sand.

He laughs, looking at me curiously, before taking another stick. "Well, I suppose you're right. It sure has been rough."

I nod, letting him go on.

"And I come to places like this, and it hits me all over again. All the things she is already missing out on."

He is still smiling, but his eyes are glassy when he looks over at me.

"And I don't want to come to beautiful places without her."

I have to hold back my own tears. In any other case, I'd be sobbing like a baby. But if George is holding it together, gosh darn it, so will I.

"You're lucky to have found each other," I say, meaning it with all my heart.

Hearing George talk about his wife the way he does... I can only imagine what it feels like to have that kind of support in my life. Someone who is always in your corner, no matter what. Someone who has your back completely. That kind of unconditional care is foreign to me.

I let the conversation meander to other things. I can tell George isn't the type of man to talk about his feelings often, so I don't want to be a pest. And eventually, the sun's dipping toward the water.

Adam lets out a disheartened sigh. "Looks like we're losing the light. And this tide is going nowhere fast. We'll just have to work with what we have."

The crew doesn't need any more encouragement. We pack up the equipment, walking everything up the narrow steps that lead to where we are all parked. Adam is the first to leave, and I have a flashback to watching him on the beach earlier.

Stupid Sylvia.

It's all her fault for getting in my head.

I've picked up all the trash we left behind when Dee comes running up to me, jingling. "Great! You haven't left," she puffs, handing me a set of keys.

"Adam left his house keys here. Can you drive them to

14

ADAM

Whoever made up the expression 'adding insult to injury' must have been talking about their ex-girlfriend cheating on them, stealing their cat, and then fleeing with their spare key.

Of all fucking times to lose my house keys.

I check underneath the potted cactus for the third time, just in case it has magically materialized since I last looked. It's dark now, and all I can think about is climbing under my showerhead and washing the salt and sweat off my body. Not that it was a terrible day. Actually, as far as ten-hour shoots in the sun go, this one was relatively painless.

Until I lost my fucking house keys.

"Are you a peeping tom?"

I spin around and see no other than Evie Miller, walking up my driveway.

"I should call neighborhood watch on you," she says with a grin.

"Err..." I splutter, trying to make sense of her being here, on my property. Like when you see an old teacher at a supermarket and can't place them away from a classroom. "I lost my house keys."

She opens her palm, revealing three keys on a chain. "Ta-da!"

"How–?"

"You left them at the beach," she says, tossing them to me. "Dee told me to chase after you. It was all very stop them before their plane leaves from the airport, rom-com style."

"Right." I blink, not even beginning to know what she's talking about. "Well, thanks."

I finally step through my front door, relieved that a shower isn't too far in my future.

"Wow, great place!" Evie says, following me inside like I invited her. "Your ceilings are so high, I can hear my echo."

She cups her mouth, and I brace for whatever she is about to do next.

"Hello!" she shouts in a strange low voice, followed by a quieter impression of an echo, "hello... hello... hello..."

"If you can hear your own echo, why do you need to fake an echo?"

"Aw, cute!" she chirps, ignoring my question. "Is this your kitty?"

She picks up a photo of Rufus, the only remaining proof that he ever lived here. Except for the stray hairs that have accumulated under every piece of furniture.

"He was."

She brings the photo to her chest, looking at me like I just told her there is no Santa Claus. "Oh no, I'm so sorry."

"No—he didn't *die*," I jump in, because it looks like she's about to burst into tears. "My ex came and took him a couple of weeks ago."

"She *stole* him?"

"Well, he was technically hers, I guess," I say, feeling like she very much did steal him. "But I'd been looking after him the last few months."

"And she just came and took him back?" Evie puts the photo back on the mantle. "That's awful."

"It's fine, really."

"But you must miss him? His little paws padding across the floor to greet you... his little meows to tell you he's ready for dinner..."

Something unexpected tightens around my chest, and I know she's right. I do miss that stupid cat. The place has been so quiet since he's been gone.

"Yeah... I guess it sucks a bit."

She smiles sympathetically and continues her walk around the living room. It's so strange seeing her here, in my home. Walking around and looking at my stuff. A home is a very private thing, and having her inside is oddly... intimate.

"Jesus, you don't like color, do you?"

"Excuse me?"

"The walls." She points around in case I don't know what walls are. "They're just stark white. Don't you own any other photos? Any artwork?"

"I don't have time to bother with that stuff." I shrug. Kimberly always talked about decorating the condo early on. But when she grew distant, she lost interest in the place. Too busy banging dudes named Dave to care about couch cushions.

"Okay, well, I guess I'll get out of your hair," Evie says, walking toward the door.

"Where did you park?"

"Just over on another side street, around the corner."

"It's sort of a shady area at night," I say, looking out the window. All I can think about is jumping in the shower, but the last thing I need is my PA getting jumped after running an errand for me. "I'll walk you."

Darkness is falling and the air has turned fresh. Evie wraps her arms around herself, her shoulders still bare from a day under the sun. I feel like a jerk for not offering her a jacket, but all I have is my sweaty t-shirt, so giving her that would be inappropriate for many reasons. And also gross.

"Today went well, right?" She looks at me hopefully.

"Every day done is a day closer to me finishing this job. So, yes."

She rolls her eyes. I know that after talking me into staying, all she wants is for me to have fun. But I'd be lying if I said the fact that I'm still directing this movie doesn't stab me in the guts like a kidney stone. Though I have to admit, having a great team makes it more tolerable.

We turn the corner and I see a familiar face further up on the sidewalk. I feel bad that I don't have any leftover catering today, because the crew just got takeout for lunch. As we get closer, my body tightens up. I consider Bob a friend, but you can never predict how people will react around the homeless. Sometimes with disgust or pity. But usually they just pretend they don't exist at all... which is probably the worst. I hate to think of people being like that to Bob. I hate to think of *Evie* being like that to Bob.

We're a few feet away, and I consider just talking to him on the way back so I don't have to find out what Evie will do.

He's right here now.

I'm out of time.

Fuck.

"Beautiful fresh night, isn't it?" Evie says.

Great, so she's just going to do the old talk to me as a cover for ignoring the homeless guy routine. I turn to respond, but she isn't looking at me.

She's looking at Bob.

He growls from his picnic blanket. "They're all the same here. There are no seasons in Los Angeles."

She laughs. "That's true. You can't beat the crisp feeling in the air when it changes to fall."

"Um... Bob, this is Evie. Evie, Bob," I say, running introductions.

"Oh, I didn't realize you were friends!" She leans down and holds out her hand for a shake. "Pleasure to meet you. I hope he's not as grouchy to you as he is to me." She yanks her head toward me.

Bob chuckles, one of the few times I have ever heard him do it. "He can be a bastard, can't he?" Still laughing, Bob looks at me. "But he's a good boy."

Evie is beaming, and I shake my head.

"You had dinner, Bob?" I say quietly, reaching for my pocket. But he waves me off.

"Yeah, yeah. I'm all good. You kids get out of here before someone thinks I'm selling you drugs."

Evie bursts out laughing and quickly covers her mouth, and Bob grins to himself, satisfied with his joke.

"I'll see you tomorrow," I say, continuing down the path.

"Lovely to meet you, Bob!" Evie calls as he nods us away.

We don't talk again until we reach her car—an old clunker that she's done up with bright seat covers and dangling things from her mirror. It somehow suits her.

"Big day tomorrow," she says, climbing into her front seat. "I'm kind of curious to see how you handle it."

And as though the lovely quiet night stroll has been

interrupted by a screeching record player, I'm reminded of the scene we're shooting tomorrow.

"Ugh." I rub at my eyes. "You had to mention it."

It's mayhem. Absolute mayhem.

"Now class, settle down. It's time to move on to your creative writing task," the fake teacher says, pointing at the chalkboard behind her. The kids are throwing things at each other across the set, giggling and yelling the whole time. Yes, this is part of the scene. But do they settle down in between takes?

No.

They do not.

I make a mental note to get the old snip snip at the earliest convenience.

"Now remember," the teacher continues. "Your writing assignment is to be about Scratchy."

She points to a small enclosure where the class rat is kept. The rat that is soon to turn homicidal and escape the tank after a drink of water.

"Cut!" I call. "Let's set up for the next angle."

As George and his team move the camera equipment, the kids descend into more chaos, screaming and laughing and making a lot of fucking noise in general.

"I knew this was a mistake." I turn to Dee. "I should've never let you talk me into getting an actual classroom of kids and not actors."

"Aw, come on now, Mr. Grinch. They're from a low-income area. Can you imagine how much this means to them?" Dee looks over the chaos with tender eyes. "Look how excited they are."

"Yes, I can see that. They're excitedly ruining my set."

"It's sweet. Isn't it, Evie?" Dee says, bringing a third into the conversation.

"Oh yeah, kids are the best." Evie shrugs.

I roll my eyes. "You *would* say that because you're basically a seven-year-old trapped in a grown-up's body."

Evie scoffs. "If you're still using the term grown-ups to describe adults, then I'm not the only child here."

Dee smirks at us and walks over to the wild kids, trying to calm them down.

Three hours later and we have just one shot left before we can send them all away forever. It's a tracking shot from behind the rat as it runs down the center of the classroom, kids diving out of the way like shrapnel. Except after the first take, one kid at the back won't stop crying. I growl in my throat and throw Dee the side eye. She tries to console the kid, but her efforts fall flat. He sits at his desk, wiping his red eyes, his mouth downturned.

"We'll have to sit the sad sack out," I say when Dee returns. "We're wasting time here."

"You can't do that!" Evie jumps in. "Think of how sad he'll be when he's the only kid in his class not in the movie."

"What am I supposed to do?" I gesture wildly to the kid, who is snorting boogers.

"Let me give it a try."

I huff, but sweep my hand out to give her the okay.

Evie crouches down beside the sad kid, holding onto the desk where he sits. "Hey, I'm Evie. What's your name?"

"Billy," he stutters.

"Why are you crying, Billy?"

"The rat." He points to Scratchy, who is waiting in the animal trainer's hands, waiting for his next take. "We're scaring him."

"And that's why you're sad?" she coos. "Oh sweetie, he's okay. I promise. Scratchy is a professional. He's been trained around people screaming and explosions and all kinds of scary sounds. So you don't have to worry about him, okay?"

She places a gentle hand on his shoulder and he nods.

"The only thing I need you to worry about is doing your best yell. Can you do that?"

Billy shakes his head.

Ugh.

"Aw, yes you can. Here, I'll go first. Have you seen the movie *Home Alone*? Put your hands up to your face, and go like this." She opens her eyes and mouth wide, followed by a rough "Ahhhh!"

Billy giggles and surprisingly follows her lead.

"That was great! Now how about this one?" She sticks out her tongue, and her neck disappears into her shoulders, a noise following out of her mouth that sounds like a large bird being strangled.

All the kids are laughing now. Out of the corner of my eye I see the wardrobe assistants whispering, and I look back at Evie. If it wasn't obvious before, it's obvious now— Evie gives absolutely zero fucks what people think about her.

She continues making ridiculous sounds and faces to match until Billy's red eyes have cleared up and his down-turned mouth is replaced with a huge grin. The students hop back into their starting positions, and within a couple of takes, we have the shot we need, every kid diving and screaming to perfection.

I look over at Evie and give her a nod, which she returns with one of those smiles that reaches her eyes.

And a wink that gives me a weird tingle.

15

I may be a positive, bubbly person, but that doesn't mean I don't know when somebody is being a jerk. People assume that when you smile a lot, or don't cuss, or like to see the best in your fellow human beings, that you are rendered incapable of identifying jerky behavior. On the contrary, I know exactly when people are being jerks. I just choose not to react most of the time.

Which is why I know what Kylie means when she picks up one of my braids, smiles like Professor Umbridge, and says, "You really love your ribbons, don't you?"

"I think they're highly underrated," I reply, taking my braid back and returning her smile with the same amount of sincerity. Which is zero.

"The children seemed to like them the other day," she says, in a tone that suggests ONLY children appreciate my fashion choices. I don't want to stoop to her level, but she has been testing my patience for weeks. I can't understand how someone could have it in for me from the moment they laid eyes on me.

"At least you know if film work doesn't pan out, you have

a fallback. You could be a babysitter. Or one of those people who supervise the ball pits at play centers."

I don't know much, but I *do* know that if I fail in the film industry, there's a ninety-nine percent chance she is involved somehow.

"Aw, don't be so hard on yourself. I'm sure the kids like your hair too. It reminds me of a Disney character," I say, flicking the edges of her pixie cut. "Prince Phillip, maybe."

Her fake smile descends into a scowl, and I'm saved by the bell when Dee calls me over.

"You look like you needed saving," she says under her breath.

"Just Kylie and her famous compliments."

"I didn't know she was such a twerp. If I did, I never would've brought her in. And now I need a reason to send her ass packing."

"It's fine." I wave her off. "Nothing I didn't deal with in high school."

"Oh God, don't remind me."

I look at Dee, with her striking green eyes and pretty curly hair. I can't imagine her being anything but popular and awesome in high school. Way too cool for me, of course.

"I wasted a lot of time trying to fit in with girls like Kylie," she continues, like she's reading my mind. "Until I realized they weren't worth shit, and it wasn't getting me anywhere. The sooner you can figure that out, the sooner you can get on the right path."

"I wasn't cool enough to even try to fit in," I chuckle. "The cheerleaders weren't interested in the girl who still rocked a Care Bears backpack."

Dee laughs, shaking her head. "And I bet they didn't know what they were missing. You know, we should get to know each other better. Why don't you come out tonight? A couple of us are getting drinks once we wrap."

"Sure, that sounds great!"

I can't stop smiling as Dee is called to the other side of the set. My first social gathering with the film crew.

Who needs cheerleaders?

After lunch, we set up for a scene where Damon is doing research on the strange animal behavior in an old library. It doesn't make any sense, because nobody does research in libraries anymore. Everything is on the internet. But like Adam suggested, I've stopped asking questions about the plot holes and just enjoy the crazy ride.

Another thing that doesn't make sense is why the library needs a huge wrought iron chandelier with massive candles when a library in the twenty-first century would have working electricity. But again, I let the prop guy do his thing, helping him light the candles before the chandelier is drawn up toward the sound stage ceiling.

I do my usual routine while everything is getting set up —fetch waters, exchange cold bricks for hot bricks, hand out gaffer tape—and then I settle in at the side, ready to repeat after Joel when the camera's start to roll.

I feel like I have a handle on everything now. I got off to a shaky start (and Kylie the Sociopath didn't help there), but now I really feel like a contributing, valuable member of the team.

I watch Adam in between takes, discussing camera angles with the cinematographer, directing Damon as he flicks through books. He might find this movie idiotic, but I can tell he's totally in his element here. I just wish he could see it.

I feel a funny sense of familiarity when I remember being in his house the other day, walking around his things, hearing his anecdotes.

Anecdotes about his ex.

It's difficult to imagine him with a girlfriend, sharing a cat, snuggling up on the couch together. He's always so gruff and dry on set. Not exactly someone I would describe as *affectionate*.

And yet, I've been seeing a different side of Adam. Between forgiving me for my dumb mistakes in the beginning, his friendship with dear old Bob, the way he walked me to my car even though the streets were brightly lit and plenty of people were still around...

"Sometime this century would be great," he says to the gaffer, who is trying to adjust a difficult light while Adam watches with his hands on his hips.

And then there is *that* side to him. The grouchy, sarcastic, cynical side. The one that seems to dominate his brain most of the time.

On the bright side, at least he doesn't yell at me in front of the crew anymore.

There's a weird screeching sound, followed by someone in the upper scaffolding of the set shouting "duck!"

I look up just in time to see the chandelier lurch threateningly many feet above my head, followed by toppling cream candles. The ones I just set on fire.

Before I can react, the floor goes out from underneath me and I'm on my back. Somewhere a few feet away, I hear the candles smack hard against the floor, splatters of hot wax going everywhere. But what I am more focused on is the weight on top of me.

I look up to see Adam.

His face is so close, I can feel his breath on my neck. My heart is beating out of my chest as I try to process what just happened, but I find myself intoxicated by the subtle scent of some kind of man shampoo and the gum he's been chewing. His eyes meet mine, and something flickers behind them. He's looking at me. *Really* looking. I let out a shaky exhale, trembling from the close call, the feeling of arms around me and being scooped into the air, and the sensation of a man's body against mine... I can't tell if it's been one, two, or twenty seconds, but the moment is gone when Adam gets up, pulling me to my feet.

"What the fuck happened?!" he shouts, looking between the guy in the scaffolding and the props assistant who set up the chandelier.

"The rope slipped," the guy above says. I can tell by the look on his face he's glad to have about twelve feet between himself and the seething man below.

"Well how the fuck did the rope slip?" Adam asks. "One of those candles could've hit Evie in the head and killed her! She could've got hot wax in her eye!"

Jesus. I'm suddenly extra appreciative that Adam intervened when he did.

"It was an accident," the man squeaks.

"Don't fucking make me come up there." Adam points a finger at the scaffolding.

"I'm so sorry. It won't happen again."

"You better hope it doesn't happen again. I can't have Ev—" Adam looks at me, still frowning, his chest moving up and down "—my crew getting hurt on set. Another fuck up like that and you'll never work on a film again. Got it?"

The shivering man nods his head. Adam brushes a hand

through his hair, face still flushed, before turning to me. "Are you okay?"

For some stupid reason, I'm still trembling. "I'm fine, thanks to your superhero antics." I laugh weakly, but I'm not up to my usual standard of cheesy jokes. I can barely concentrate.

What is wrong with me?

Adam nods and turns back to the camera team as the props assistant jumps in to clean the wax and candles off the floor.

And I try to ignore the intense tingling feeling south of my navel.

"But seriously, that was some Clark Kent shit." Dee is laughing over her bourbon. "I half expected him to rip off his shirt and reveal the big red S on his chest."

I flush at the memory of Adam saving me, taking a large sip of my rosé.

He didn't join us at the bar. Which is awkward, because I overheard him telling Joel earlier that he would be there. It was only when he realized I was going too that he went straight home.

I get it. I wasn't born yesterday. It's one thing for the director to drink with the ADs. It's another for him to drink with the production assistants.

And to be honest, I'm kind of relieved he didn't come. I can't help but feel embarrassed about what happened. He was teased all afternoon about swooping in the way he did. And I feel kind of dumb for needing saving in the first place. I mean, I know the candles falling wasn't my fault. But

Adam definitely seemed uncomfortable about the whole thing.

And the other thing I can't get out of my head is the weird expression on his face when he was lying on top of me.

"Another round, ladies?"

Brian appears next to us, a lazy arm draped around each of our shoulders.

"All the drinks in the world wouldn't make either of us go home with you," Dee says, removing his hand. "And yes, another round."

Brian grins and nods, completely missing the rejection part of her response, and disappears toward the bar. The only other person here is Joel, but he's a man of few words, which leaves me and Dee free to chat.

"Do you have a guy, or girl, in your life?" she asks, finishing her first drink.

"Neither," I admit. "Although a nice guy wouldn't go astray. Not that I'm looking," I add quickly.

"I hear that. I'm way too busy for a man. Right now, I'm focused on my career. Once that is on track, then maybe I'll try dating again."

"You seem to be pretty on track to me," I say brightly.

She shrugs. "I'd love to direct one day. But I'm having trouble getting past second AD gigs. Once I get to where Joel is, I'll be on the right track. You know he gets to direct some of the second unit scenes on *Primal Nature*?"

I shake my head. It's dawning on me now that getting anywhere in this industry is such a long process, and mine is only just starting. It's lucky I got in when I did. I certainly have a long way to go. Dee's right—a man is the last thing I need right now.

I let my mind wander back to the idea of dating.

"So, did you know Adam's ex?"

The words are out of my mouth before I can think better, and Dee looks at me curiously. "He told you about her?"

"Just that she took his cat," I rush, clasping my hands around my glass. "When I dropped his keys back."

She sits back in her chair, blowing air out of her mouth. "Kimberly. She was a piece of work. High maintenance type. To be honest, I never got what he saw in her. I mean, she's gorgeous and everything..."

I feel an uncomfortable twinge in my stomach.

"But they were never compatible. And if I'm being honest, Adam never seemed excited about her. You know what I mean?" She scrunches up her face. "Don't you want to be with someone who *excites* you?"

Brian places our drinks on the table with a wink, and Dee rolls her eyes.

I think about the guys I've dated, the guys I've slept with, and try to conjure up a feeling of excitement. But nothing's there. I know I've never been in love, but I'm realizing now I've also never really *liked* anyone.

My thoughts then trail to a feeling I had earlier... to that strange tingling in my stomach.

"I know what you mean," I say, taking the fresh glass of wine to my lips.

16

ADAM

We have a night shoot later, and the crew call isn't until after lunch. I take the opportunity to come to the studio and get some work done while no one is here. I find an empty office and pull out the shot list for the next few days, cringing at what is ahead.

Despite Nolan coming in and turning everything on its ass, we're still surprisingly on schedule. We only need to cut a few scenes that we already shot to fit in with the revised story. And unsurprisingly, Damon is much more efficient at being the cheesy, manly action hero than he is the pensive, complex male protagonist.

Shocking, I know.

I keep reminding myself this is the last one. I just have to deliver something Nolan is happy with so he doesn't blacklist me across Hollywood and keep my crew in a job. And then it'll be over.

I take a sip of my coffee, wishing there was a splash of whiskey in there. Maybe when all this is done and dusted, I can become one of those tortured artist types. The ones who roll out of bed at noon and start their day with a scotch neat.

"Oh, you're here!"

I spit my coffee over the shot list, a few drops trickling down my chin. "Jesus, fuck!"

"That's no way to speak to our long-haired pal upstairs," Evie quips, edging through the door with a large rectangle board in her arms. "I didn't think you'd be here today?"

I wipe the coffee from my chin. "I just came in to get— I'm the director, I'm always here. Why are *you* here?"

"I wanted to bring something in before heading to location later." She sets the board down, leaning it against the wall. Today she has swapped out her yellow rain boots for converse, which she has decorated herself with tiny flowers. When she turns around, I busy myself picking up the shot list and sponging the coffee from it with a tissue.

"That should go with the other props. It might just get lost in here," I say, nodding toward the board.

"It isn't for props," she says, a grin spreading across her face. "I sort of did a thing."

"Well, don't hold out on me, Miller. The suspense is killing me."

If she detects my sarcasm, she doesn't care, picking up the board and spinning it around so that I can see the other side.

"What the—?"

"A present. You know, for saving me the other day," she announces.

"We don't need to bring that up again."

"I know." A piece of hair falls from behind her ear, and I have the bizarre urge to tuck it back where it belongs. "But I still wanted to show my appreciation."

I nod, looking back at the canvas, which displays a large painted cat face. "Well... it sure is something."

It suddenly clicks that this is not just any cat. This is

Rufus. Up close and personal. The likeness is impressive, don't get me wrong. I've just never seen a cat's face quite so zoomed in and... large.

"How did you...?"

"Yeah... I kind of stole your photo of Rufus," she admits, making a 'my bad' sort of face. "Originally, I planned to get it framed, so you'd have something to hang on the wall. But after the chandelier thing..." Her freckled cheeks have touches of pink in them as she sets the painting back down. "I just thought this would be cooler."

"You painted a portrait of my cat?"

"Of course!" she chirps, like it's the natural reaction to someone saving you from a bunch of falling four-pound candles. "I thought it would brighten up the place. You're in desperate need of color."

"It will definitely be a focal point." I look at Rufus's huge face, captured in bright colors and thick brush strokes.

I'm never getting laid again. At least, not with that in my house.

She bounces on the spot, waiting for my official reaction. I can't exactly tell her what I really think—that I find it slightly terrifying and creepy—so I nod my head and do my best impression of stoked.

"It's great. Thanks."

She smiles. "I knew you'd like it. Now you can see his face every single day."

I look at the cat's intense gaze. Seeing it in my condo late at night will take some getting used to.

"Well, I'm going to head to location. I'll see you there," she says, bouncing out of the office.

But then again, I'm sure it will grow on me.

The drive to location takes longer than I expect, but it gives me a chance to think. Not about the movie, and not about my dad, but about something I haven't allowed myself to think about.

The weird incident on set the other day.

I can't get it out of my head, as much as I've tried. And trust me, I've tried. But there's only so many times you can scold yourself to *stop fucking thinking about it* before you give up and try a new tactic.

It's not just the intense instinct to protect Evie that caught me off guard. I'm sure all bosses want to protect their team from getting fucking maimed. No... it's the weird feeling I got when I was lying on top of her, and our eyes met...

I can still see them now, deep brown and gazing intently back at me. I can still feel her chest rising and falling under mine. I can still smell her sweet vanilla-y perfume as my nose sat inches from her creamy neck.

Creamy neck?

What the fuck is happening to me?

And this is why I have to sort my head out. It's been months since Kimberly and I broke up, and I still haven't got back out there. Dating is exhausting, and I just don't have it in me right now. But if the incident proved anything, it's that I'm starved of female interaction. Why else would my brain be hovering around this memory like a dumb, love-struck teenager? I just have to admit it to myself.

I find Evie very attractive.

And I haven't had sex in a long time.

There, that's it. That's the uncomfortable truth behind my distracted mind. I had a physically close encounter with an attractive girl and my muscle memory isn't ready to let it go.

Especially the muscle memory in certain parts of my body.

But admitting it is the first step, and now I can move on. The last thing I need is to be distracted by something shiny at work. And the last thing Evie needs is her director getting close-call hard-ons at the slightest touch.

Okay, being pressed on top of her wasn't exactly a *slight* touch. It was more insanely intense and even thinking about it now...

Fuck.

Okay. That's enough. I'm moving on.

I pull into an empty space near the beach access and make my way down to the sand, where most of the crew are already waiting.

"Sorry I'm late. Traffic was a bitch."

"No worries," Dee says. "Can I go over something with you?" She flicks to the next page of her script and starts circling dialogue, talking as she goes, but something has caught my attention across the shoreline. Damon, with his shirt off, being oiled up by the makeup team. Talking to Evie.

I can't make out what they're saying, but the way he puffs out his bare chest makes me want to puke. It's like he is perpetually peacocking, trying to appeal to anything with two legs and boobs.

Oh my God, why would you bring up boobs?

I clear my throat and force my brain to return its focus to Dee.

But I can't help one ear pricking up, tuning in to the sound of Evie's laughter across the sand.

~

"You've got to be joking."

We're standing at the access point for our second beach location, one that has a rocky cliff face. And we're staring at a thick iron chain blocking our way.

"Falling boulders, use alternate access," Brian reads off the sign. "But we can't get the equipment down the other access point. You have to climb over rocks."

"Thank you, captain of the fucking obviou—"

"We know that, Brian," Dee cuts me off.

"How did this happen?" I spin around until I can find the location scout hiding at the back of the group. "You literally had one job?"

"It wasn't closed off when I scouted it a few weeks ago," he says, quivering in the October sun.

"And you didn't think to check it, I don't know, before we got here?"

"It's going to be okay," Evie says, stepping tentatively through the group. "We'll just look for a bigger access point further up the path. One we can get the camera down. Won't we?" She looks at Brian and the scout, who nod obediently.

I let her pacify me, mainly because I want the others out of my face. I wave them away and sit down on the wooden fence, watching as Evie bounces after them, her signature hair ropes swinging behind her.

"What do you think about Evie?" I say to Dee as she perches beside me.

"What do I think of her?"

"Yeah, like... as a fellow woman."

"You mean, as the enigmatic species that is the human female, what's my opinion of her?" Dee smirks at me.

"You know what I mean," I sigh.

She pinches her shoulders upward. "I think... she's great."

I pick some leaves off a nearby shrub as she elaborates.

"She's crazy, but not put your rabbit on the stove crazy. She doesn't give a shit what anyone thinks about her. Yet she's very considerate and sweet. And those two things rarely go hand in hand."

I frown at her to prompt an explanation.

"Most people I know who care a lot about other people's feelings often care too much what people think of them. And the people who don't give a shit about the opinions of others tend to not give a shit about anyone," she finishes, taking a sip from her bottled water. "You know, kind of like you."

"Well that's a bit of a drive by. I'm not that bad!"

She just laughs. "You know I love you, but you don't have time for most people. Evie cares about everyone, big and small. She rescued a beetle from being squashed on the path on the way over here."

I laugh out my nose. "That checks out."

"She's pretty much sunshine in human form. It rubs off on people."

A pause.

"You've been *way* less of a jerk since she's been around," Dee continues.

"*Pardon*?"

She laughs and nudges me in the ribs. "You know it's true."

We fall into silence and proceed to pick leaves off the shrub and throw them onto the ground.

"Why do you ask?" Dee finally says, raising an eyebrow at me.

I curve my mouth downwards. "I just... can't get a good read on her. I'm trying to figure out her game."

"Not everyone in LA is playing a game, you know." She rolls her eyes. "Some people are actually genuine."

"Yeah. Right."

Our conversation is brought to an end as the group appears up the path.

"There are no other access points," Brian says, holding his side like he has a stitch.

"Why are you puffing?" Dee grimaces.

"We went all the way to the cliff!"

"He's right." Evie scrunches her face, disappointed that her hopeful plan didn't pan out. "There's nothing."

Brian tries to stand up straight. "We even tried carrying the camera between us down the narrow trail before—"

"—before you remembered that camera is worth over three times your annual salary?" I finish, horrified at the thought of that oaf hauling our expensive gear over sharp boulders.

I groan, linking my fingers behind my head. "We're going to have to scout a new shooting location for the cliff scene."

"First thing tomorrow, I will go," the scout says.

"Seeing as you obviously don't know how to do your job, I'll go." I huff, turning to Joel. "I know a few places toward San Diego."

"You don't want to go all that way on your own," Dee jumps in.

"That's very nice of you, but I'm a big boy. I think I'll be fine."

She narrows her eyes. "No, smart ass. I mean, you'll need someone to help take photos, write notes, apply for permits, that sort of thing?"

Hmm. Dee has a point. I hate that admin-type stuff.

"Take Evie with you." She puts her hand on Evie's shoulder, who suddenly looks very alert.

"Me?"

"Evie doesn't want to come to San Diego," I say, because I can already tell Evie has been put on the spot.

"Well, maybe we can hear that from her," Dee says, raising her eyebrows and turning to my PA. "Evie, do you mind accompanying Adam to San Diego?"

Evie looks between her and me. "Um... sure. On one condition..."

I inhale sharply, wondering where this is going. The last thing I want to do is drag a PA along with me who doesn't really want to be there.

A grin spreads across her lips.

"I get to play road trip DJ."

"You can't be serious."

I look across at Adam innocently. "What?"

"*Journey*? Really?"

"What's wrong with Journey?" I say, turning up the volume on his fancy car stereo. "'Don't Stop Believing' is the ultimate driving track."

The breeze streams through the window, rippling my hair out behind the car seat. It took about twenty minutes to convince him that, no, air conditioning is not the same as natural air, and for him to let me have the window down.

"Just a small-town girl, livin' in a looonnely world!"

"Jesus," he mutters, rubbing his forehead. Though if I'm not mistaken, I swear there's a twentieth of a smile on his lips.

"Don't worry, I'll let you do the next verse."

"I think I'll be okay, thanks." He laughs. "I bet you only know about this band because of *Glee*."

I arch my eyebrow at him. "You would only know about that if you *also* watched *Glee*."

He has the decency to let me belt out the rest of the

song, sighing as he rests his head in his palm. When it's over, I sneak a look at him. Suddenly I'm reminded of him at the beach, looking all relaxed and happy. He's got one hand on the steering wheel, the other weaved through his thick brown hair. The blowing wind makes it flick around.

What is it about guys driving with one hand that is so...

I brush the thought out of my mind. No. I will not go there. It already took me several days to get the chandelier incident out of my head, but even that didn't stop it coming into my dreams. Like the dream I had last night.

My stomach flutters, like a small animal is burrowing inside there. I quickly look away.

"So what made you want to become a director?" I ask, searching for a distraction.

"We're doing the getting-to-know-you car chats, are we?"

"You have a better idea to fill the next twenty minutes?"

He smirks. "Um... I don't know. I went with my dad when one of his novels got picked up by a studio. I was sold on the film industry straight away. I guess somewhere along the way I decided directing suited me best."

"I heard about your dad... seems like an important guy."

Adam nods. "Yep, pretty much a household name for book lovers."

I chew on my lip. Dee told me how he died a few months ago. "I'm sorry to hear that he passed."

Adam glances at me and smiles on the side of his mouth. "Thanks."

I think back to being in Adam's house, with all his dad's books lined up on the bookshelf.

"What's that like, having a famous author dad?"

"It's okay I guess," he says. "Got me a few extra connections in Hollywood. So I can't complain about that."

"It must be intimidating."

Adam looks at me properly now, frowning.

I go on. "Having a dad with such a legacy. Having all that pressure on you to live up to his name. It's big shoes to fill."

Adam is still frowning as his eyes flicker back to the road ahead of us. "Actually, yeah." He nods. "It's really intimidating."

I let the silence take over the car. One of those pensive, peaceful silences. We might be polar opposites, but there is something easy about being in Adam's company. Maybe because he is so blunt—it's easy to know where you stand with him so you're not left wondering if he hates you or not. But as he looks out at the open space in front of us, I have to admit, I have no idea what he's thinking now.

My phone ringing breaks through the quiet, and again, I'm so distracted with making the noise stop that I forget to check the number.

"Hello?"

"You're finally coming to see us?"

I look at the screen and see that Mom is calling from her office phone. "Um... huh?"

"A little notice would have been nice. But I guess we should just consider ourselves lucky that you're coming at all."

"Who told you I was coming to visit?"

"Your sister. She said you came up on her friend tracker or one of those young people things."

Ugh. I knew I should have hidden my location from Sarah a long time ago.

"Right. Well, actually, I'm here for work."

Adam keeps turning his head in my direction, trying to decipher my phone call.

"You would come all the way to San Diego and not visit your family?"

"It's not that, Mom. I'm here with the director as well." I look at Adam wide-eyed, like he can save me from this situation somehow. He just narrows his eyes in confusion.

"Well, bring him too. I'm making pork tenderloin."

I'm quiet while I search my brain for the appropriate excuse not to go. A dinner with my parents and my director seems like the exact last thing I want to do.

"We'd love to meet your work friends. Sometimes it seems like you're making this job up." She gives a fluttery laugh, and I glare out the windscreen.

"Fine."

"Great. We'll see you at seven." She hangs up.

I turn to Adam, chewing at my bottom lip.

"What was all that about?" he asks.

"That was my mom," I say, bunching my eyebrows together in anticipation. "How do you feel about pork tenderloin?"

The doorbell clangs, deep and ominous, as we wait outside the entrance of the Tuscan villa that is the Miller residence.

"Thank you for coming," I say to Adam. "I didn't mean to drag you into this."

"Believe it or not, I heard you the first seven times you thanked me."

I nod, exhaling into the thick wooden door.

"Hey, are you all right?" He places a hand on my shoulder and a quick shiver runs over me before the door swings open.

"Well, as I live and breathe."

Over the threshold stands my mother, her signature

cashmere cardigan draped over her slender shoulders. Her signature judgmental smile plastered across her face.

"Hi, Mom."

I close the distance between us and we share a brief hug with tiny tyrannosaurus arms.

"I feel like I could snap you," she says, taking my bicep in her vice grip. "I hope you're not starving yourself while you prove your point."

"You are skinnier than I am," I reply. It's nice to see she hasn't lost her touch in the unwelcome critiquing department. "This is Adam, the director of the film I'm working on."

He walks in awkwardly, hands in pockets. I get the idea Adam isn't a jump-through-hoops kind of guy when it comes to making a good first impression. I just have to hope my parents behave themselves until we can leave.

Mom gestures for us to walk with her. "Lovely to meet you. Evie's father is just through here. Sarah got called to the hospital, so it's just the four of us."

I look at Adam and mouth one final 'thank you' before we make our way to the dining room table, where my dad is waiting.

The rest of the introductions are made and within thirty minutes, we're sitting behind plates of pork tenderloin.

"So, you're the man running the show," my dad says to Adam between mouthfuls, touching a napkin to his mustache.

"I'm the director, yeah."

"I guess we have you to thank for our daughter flitting around in Los Angeles instead of coming home then," Mum laughs, like pretending it's a joke makes it less snarky.

"*Mom*," I say under my breath.

"Evie is doing really well," Adam answers. "She's a great asset to the team."

Mom seems mildly pleased with this answer, and then Dad chimes in. "I guess that comes as no surprise. Our Evie is a smart girl."

Three, two, one...

"Which is why she would've made an excellent doctor."

I breathe out as quietly as I can, tightening the grasp around my pork knife. Adam looks at me and smiles thinly before turning to my dad.

"I'm sure Evie will excel at whatever she decides to do after being a production assistant. She's great at managing people. In fact, the film might not have gone ahead if it wasn't for her." He gives me a knowing smirk. "I can see her producing one day."

"But it's all a bit vague, isn't it?" Mum says, interlacing her fingers.

Here we go.

"The thing with medicine is that there's a defined path set out for its graduates. Just look at Sarah." Mom turns to me now. "Your sister is already a resident and making a real splash."

"The other thing about medicine is that I have no interest in doing it," I snap.

The sound of cutlery against china takes over as we all fall silent.

After a few moments, Mom speaks again, her voice low and even. "One day, when you're a mother, you'll understand."

"Understand what?"

"That you just want the best for your children, and how disappointing it is to watch them just—"

"So I'm a disappointment, is that it?"

Dad reaches across the table, placing a pacifying hand over my wrist. "I think what your mother is trying to say is that we just want a bright future for you. We don't want to see you wasting your time."

I put my cutlery down. This fork is dangerously close to going through a hand.

"When I'm a mother, I'm going to support my children's ambitions." I whip my head toward my mom. "Even if they don't neatly align with my own."

She locks her gaze on mine before shaking her head and dropping her eyes to the table. "It's just a shame, that's all."

"*What's* a shame?"

"You just..." she looks at my dad, who nods with her in premature agreement. "... you had *so* much potential."

I feel a twisting in my stomach, like someone is reaching in and squeezing my organs with their fist. I'm here, scouting locations for a feature film, having *real, paid work* in the movie industry. And they still aren't satisfied with the path I've chosen. It doesn't matter if I'm a PA or a director or the fricking CEO of an entire production company, it will never be enough for them.

I will never be enough for them.

A hard lump settles at the back of my throat, and I stare at my unfinished pork tenderloin, wishing I could magic myself back to LA and the few people who actually support me.

"Evie has a huge amount of potential."

I'm startled when I realize it's Adam's turn to speak. All eyes focus on him.

"Not only is she a hard worker and always willing to help at the drop of a hat, but she has a great attitude. She is one of the nicest people you will ever meet, and everyone she comes into contact with has a brighter day for being around her. She is ambitious and confident and sweet, and the fact you're both sitting here telling her she's not living up to your expectations is complete horse shit."

My mouth hangs open in response, unable to form words.

"Now hang on just a second," my dad says, holding up his palm.

"No, *you* hang on." Adam holds up his own palm. "I've been in the film business for years and let me tell you, most people don't make it. The fact she has landed herself in a job with no connections is incredible in itself. And to hear you compare her to her sister is insane. I don't know your other daughter, but I can tell you now she has absolutely nothing on this girl."

Everyone has well and truly stopped eating at this point, and I'm sure if someone had an actual pin, you would be able to hear it drop.

Adam takes his napkin and drags it across his mouth. He doesn't make eye contact as he turns to address me, his voice quiet and raspy. "We have an early start in the morning. We should be getting to the hotel."

He pulls out his chair, standing up. "Mr. and Mrs. Miller, it was nice to meet you. Thank you for dinner. Evie, I'll meet you at the car."

And leaving us all there like a bunch of rabbits caught in the headlights, he walks out the door.

18

What the hell is wrong with me?

This has been my mantra for the last twelve hours. But I don't have an answer for it yet.

After my embarrassing outburst in front of the Millers, I bolted to the car and shut myself in, panting and trying to calm myself down for the five minutes it took Evie to join me.

Why did I lose my shit like that?

Evie's parents are assholes. There is no denying that. But it wasn't my job to stand up for her. I can only imagine what an idiot and/or psycho she thought I was, bringing me over for fancy pork circles only for me to have an insane fit at her mom's dinner table.

When she got in the car, neither of us said anything. Which made me realize how bad it was. Evie *always* has something to say. So the fact I rendered her speechless is a testament to what an ass I made of myself. There was nothing left to do but drive to the hotel as quick as I could and hide away in my separate room until the morning, when hopefully the shock of my outburst had worn off.

We meet in the parking lot just after sunrise, ready to hit the locations on today's list. The idea is to get them all done by the afternoon and make it back to LA before dark, and we have our work cut out for us.

At least it will keep us busy.

Meandering along the coast, we stop only for coffee, and eventually make our way to location one. The morning sky is clear and blue, and we check out the view from the top of the cliff first.

"I've been here before," Evie says, looking out at the ocean. "It's beautiful."

She's much quieter today, withdrawn. And I can't tell if it's because of all the things her parents said to her last night, or all the things *I* said. She is probably concerned I'll have another random meltdown and throw her over the edge.

"Let's go down to the shoreline," I say, leaving for the access path.

Down on the beach, it feels more isolated, enveloped with huge rock walls on either side and the never-ending expanse of blue water in front. The ocean is calm, with only small waves breaking and eventually making their way to the sand.

We split up to take photos and write notes—me about the shots we'd be filming here, Evie on where the departments could set up their sections—and before long we're onto the next location to do it all over again.

By early afternoon I'm tired, a little sunburned, and sick of looking at beautiful beaches. So when we meet at the next shoreline, I'm glad it's the last one. Evie, on the other hand, seems like she's still enjoying the views, staring out at the ocean like it's just as stunning as the first time she laid eyes on it hours ago.

"I wanted to say thank you."

Her words break through the silence and she turns to face me, her hand cupped over her brow to block out the sun. "For last night."

I make an awkward groaning sound.

We were so close to never bringing it up again.

"You don't have to thank me. It was nothing."

"It wasn't nothing to me."

Her eyes are fixed on mine as she smiles weakly. The breeze picks up behind her and sends her hair flying, shining auburn strands dancing in midair.

"I'm sorry you had to sit through it," she continues, attempting to tame her locks. "I'm so embarrassed. I didn't mean to air our family drama in front of you."

"It really wasn't a big deal," I say, relieved their quarrel is the part she finds embarrassing or inappropriate.

"They just drive me crazy sometimes."

"Really?" I cross my arms, staring out at the sea and frowning. "Can't imagine why."

She laughs and nudges me in the side. And just like that, the tension from last night is dissolved.

"But seriously, I hope you don't take to heart what they said," I say. "It's one of those weird career options that seems make believe. A lot of people just don't get it."

She smiles tightly. "Yeah, something like that."

I can tell she's still a little off, but I drop it. I don't have anything else valuable to contribute, anyway. And there's something about heart-to-hearts at the beach that makes me want to punch myself in the face.

Evie pulls out her phone, swiping and touching the screen. It occurs to me now that this is one of the few times I've seen her on it. Which is depressingly extraordinary. She is one of the few millennial girls I know who spends time looking at a beautiful ocean, not taking photos of it to upload on Instagram.

After a minute, she stashes it back in her pocket. She stares at me with a strange, cautious look on her face. Like she's already trying to guess my reaction to whatever she's about to say.

"Can I take you somewhere?"

"You don't want to head back to LA?" I furrow my brow.

Her confident grin returns. "Nope. There's something I want to show you first."

"Are you going to tell me what you're up to?" I say as she moves the stick into the next gear flawlessly.

"You'll see," she replies simply.

I sigh, watching as the world goes by out the window. All I can gather is that we're heading back into the hub of San Diego.

"I'm surprised you let me drive your car," she says, turning the corner. "Most guys don't like girls driving their cars."

"Most guys are wankers."

She laughs and turns another corner, driving alongside fields of green.

"Fancy a spot of golf, do you? Is that what you have in mind?" I ask.

"You really don't like being spontaneous, do you?" she laughs, turning away from the golf course.

"I don't like surprises. Especially when you don't know if they're going to be good or bad."

"You think I'd give you a bad surprise?"

I squint my eyes at her. "I'm still trying to figure that out, Miller."

"Well, you won't have to figure it out for much longer, because we're here."

She pulls into the parking lot, and I scrunch my forehead. "Fashion Valley?"

She goes to unbuckle her seat belt, and I put my hand over hers. "You've taken me to a *shopping mall*?"

"Come on, Thorne. Where's your sense of adventure?" She wiggles her hand free and bounces out of the car, leaving me no choice but to follow reluctantly. If this is the part of the movie where the bright, bubbly girl gives the moody grumpy guy a makeover, I need it to stop. Immediately.

She leads us through the mall like a woman on a mission. My mind is flicking through all the potential possibilities as to why she brought me here when she comes to a sudden halt.

"We're here!"

I look up.

"A movie theater?"

"Yep! And I know the girl who works behind the counter. She can sneak us in."

We walk inside, the smell of salty, buttery popcorn instantly wafting up my nostrils. "That's nice of you, but I think I can spring for a movie ticket."

"But that would ruin the surprise. Plus, it already started an hour ago."

"Why are we watching a movie that we've already missed the first hour of?" I protest as she waves to her friend near the soda machine.

"You'll see!"

We walk down the hall and come to a door, her friend ushering us in with a smile. "Enjoy."

As we creep into the back seats, I immediately know what movie it is.

"Oh... no."

"Yes!" she whispers.

"Why are we watching this crap?"

"You made it," she says, rolling her eyes.

"Exactly, which is how I know it's crap. I can't sit through this again!"

"Shhh!" she grabs my arm, stopping me from leaving my seat. "Just trust me, okay?"

Even in the dark, I can see her big brown eyes, imploring me to just go with it. And for some stupid reason, I do as I'm told.

It's my last movie that came out, released at the start of summer. The one I had sworn was going to be my last goofy action sci-fi when I watched it with a stomach ulcer at the premiere. Seeing it again now, I have the urge to do the old cover my eyes and peek through my fingers trick. It's awful.

I look around the cinema, still surprisingly full considering the movie came out months ago. People watch the screen, mindlessly shoveling popcorn into their mouths. Tossing in the odd Milk Dud. It is really a testament to how cheaply our attention can be bought these days.

I imagine the people who read my father's novels, sitting in silence and immersed in a complex world. Concentrating on the poetic words. Not gorging on snacks and walking away an hour later, only to forget the whole thing. My dad made art that stayed with people.

What is my work achieving?

No one understands what it's like to be in the shadow of a man like that. To have him come up in every conversation I have with important people. And a lot of heavy hitters know who I am, sure. But only because they know I can make this kind of nonsense. The kind that brings in the big bucks. There is nothing poetic about what I do. It has nothing on what my father gave to the world. And no one understands how hard it is to live up to that type of legacy.

Except maybe Evie.

I catch a glance at her sideways. Her face is lit up by the big screen, beaming and giggling at all the right places. Watching her watch the film doesn't bother me so much.

I think about what she said in the car, about it being intimidating to have a dad like mine. And I think it's the first time anyone has ever even noticed, let alone acknowledged that. After meeting her parents, it makes sense why she understands that kind of pressure.

What still doesn't make sense, though, is why she brought me here. We are close to the end now, thank God. But I still want some answers. If anything I want to talk to Evie to distract myself from the hot mess on the screen in front of me.

"Okay, I've trusted you long enough," I whisper, leaning closer to her. "Are you going to tell me what's going on?"

She giggles. "Sorry, I got carried away by the movie. But yes, there is a reason I brought you here."

She rotates her body and puts her hand on my arm, staring at me like she's about to impart some vital wisdom.

"I brought you here because I think you've lost sight of your passion."

I scoff. "You don't need to show me this garbage to tell me that."

"That's not what I mean." She shakes her head. "I mean, you've lost your grip on what you do, and the impact you have on people. You've become cynical." She faces the front again, but this time, she's looking around the room. "Look at everyone."

My eyes dart around and land back on Evie. "I don't get it."

"Look at them. Look at their faces, at the way they interact with each other. *Really* look."

I try again, taking time to settle on each person. For a while I still don't get it, but then it starts to register. People laughing, people smiling, people nudging the person next to them. One person throws their head back, letting a huge belly-laugh rip. Another whispers in the ear of their girlfriend, who squeals and nods and giggles. The guy in the row in front of us shouts "no way!", pointing at the screen and grinning to his buddy next to him.

"Do you see?" Evie grabs my arm again. "You said you wanted to make films that mattered, to do something important with your work."

She looks around the crowded room one more time.

"But you bring people joy. You make them *happy*." She tilts her head and smiles sweetly, her eyes rounded. "What could be more important than that?"

I look into her eyes and I can't even describe how I'm feeling. But suddenly my chest feels so full it could burst open.

The sun is dipping low in the sky by the time we leave the movie theater. Our work in San Diego is done and I should be exhausted. But I'm not ready to go home.

"Feel like a drink?"

Adam's eyebrows bounce up. "You don't want to head back?"

"It's nearly happy hour. I'm sure we can sneak one drink and still be back in LA at a reasonable hour."

Adam pulls out his phone, checking the time. Mr. Anti-Impulsive. There's a high chance I'll be heading back to LA without a cocktail in my system.

"You know what? A beer sounds great."

My mouth curls up at the edges and I take the keys from his hand. "Perfect. I know the best place."

I drive us to my favorite watering hole in San Diego—a tiki-themed speakeasy that makes delicious coconut-y cocktails and hands out leis at the door. I try to conceal my grin, watching Adam's face as the girl places the lei over his head.

"I should've known you'd take us to a place like this," he

says as we find a booth in the corner. "You take me as someone who's into this kitsch-y stuff."

"Um... this is not 'kitsch-y'," I say with air quotes. "Who doesn't love colorful paper lanterns and fake palm trees?"

"You're right. I'm an idiot."

I pick up the menu to peruse the happy hour specials just as the server comes to the table. "What can I get you guys?"

"Ooh, I'll take the Chi Chi," I say, already salivating over the tropical amazingness of the description.

"And I'll just get a beer."

I snap my head toward Adam. "You can't just get a beer at a place like this!"

"I don't do anything that comes in a novelty cup."

My eyes roll back in my head before I turn to the server. "He'll have the same as me."

"Coming right up."

When she leaves, I place the menu on the wooden table. "Now is not the time to stop trusting me. *Trust* me."

Adam smiles down at his hands, but nods. "Fine."

He didn't say much after the whole movie thing, but the look on his face, even though I couldn't see it properly in the dark, said that something struck a chord. Maybe I won't get him excited about *Primal Nature*, but I can at least try to lighten his Oscar-the-Grouch demeanor a tad.

The server returns with our drinks, placing them in front of us.

"Seriously?" Adam says, picking up the huge totem head tiki cup.

"You will drink it and you will love it. Cheers."

He grudgingly touches his cup to mine but refuses to drink through the bamboo straw, claiming it's like "sucking on a tiny penis".

"Jesus, how much rum is in this?" he asks, holding it out like the totem head might answer his question.

I shrug. "A tropical amount?"

"You do realize we have to drive home tonight?"

"Eh." I take another sip. It's pineapple and rum and coconut and magic. "We'll stop at one."

We did not stop at one.

"You look insane," Adam laughs.

"Do I?" I adjust the tiki mask on my face, and add a coconut bra over my chest. "How about now?"

"Jesus Christ."

I take off my props and go in for a large slurp from my cup—this time it's a giant coconut. "These drinks are stronger than I remember."

I have that fuzzy warm feeling. The one that envelopes you in a hug after you've had two to five cocktails. The place has really filled out, everyone drinking and having a good time. Including the man sitting across from me. In fact, I've never seen him so mellow, sitting back in the booth, people-watching with an easy smile on his face.

"This place suits you," I say, crossing my arms while I observe him.

"Shit, take that back."

"What! You just look happy is all."

"Well." He leans forward, bunching his shoulders. "I've had a good day."

"Me too."

We smile at each other for a second too long, and I tuck my hair behind my ear, ignoring that weird stomach thing again.

The truth is, I can't stop feeling the stomach thing.

I haven't been able to stop since dinner last night.

The way Adam stood up to my parents. The way he vouched for me. Defended me. I've never had anyone do that. Especially not some brooding, rugged man who is at this moment looking very attractive amongst the island paraphernalia.

A brooding, rugged man who is also basically my boss.

You need to stop.

I put the drink down on the table. Rum and a handsome male, and perhaps a touch of sunstroke, is a dangerous combination. That and the fact I haven't had sex in about a year. The most action I've had was Adam saving me from the candles. When his body was pressed on top of me...

I shiver just thinking about it.

I can't help but contemplate what he'd be like as a lover. Despite his blunt manner in everyday life, I expect he'd be more considerate in the bedroom. Deliberate and strategic to get the desired result. Directing the act the way he would direct a scene in a movie. Place hand here... put mouth there... a little softer... a little harder...

Why are you thinking about him and hard in the same sentence?

"Are you okay?" Adam stares at me, forehead bunched.

"Who? Me? I'm fine, I'm just..." I rack my brain for an appropriate response, "wondering where you and I are going to stay tonight?"

"What?" His eyes boggle.

"No! Not like that!" My cheeks burn warm. "That's your third cocktail. You won't be able to drive anywhere for a while."

"Oh... right. Well, I guess we'll just go back to the same place we went last night," he says.

I nod, trying to still the pesky butterflies. It seems like the only thing to do is drown them out. I take my drink and suck through the straw until the coconut runs dry. "In that case. Another round?"

Adam grins. "It would be rude not to. These themed cups are growing on me."

Two more drinks later, and things are getting silly.

"I'm not answering that."

"You have to answer, it's the rules of a game," I say.

"Choosing between having either a shark head and a human body, or a shark tail and a human torso and head, is never a decision I'll make in real life."

"It's a decision you have to make right now."

Adam sighs, sipping through his bamboo straw, which he succumbed to three cocktails ago. "Fine. I guess I'd pick a shark tail."

"But you would never be able to walk again?"

"Would you want to walk around with a shark *head*?" He balks.

I fall into a fit of giggles, barely able to talk. "Can you just imagine..."

"This game is ridiculous," Adam says, but he can't stop laughing either. We're wiping our eyes as the server comes back over.

"Can I get you another round?"

"Hey, would you rather—"

"DON'T answer her question," Adam jumps in and we crack up again.

"You seem to be having a good time here," the server smiles. "Can I get you anything?"

I look at my empty glass, trying to do the calculations in my head. At this rate, if I keep going, I'll definitely wake up with a hangover tomorrow.

"I think I need to cut myself off," I say, touching the corner of my eye with a fingertip.

"Just the check, please," Adam confirms.

As the server settles our bill, I'm overcome with that weird, end-of-date anticipation. Even though this isn't a date. Obviously.

But there's something about leaving the bar with Adam... the way he asks if I want to walk instead of get a cab... the way he puts his sweater over my shoulders when the breeze picks up...

It only takes us twenty minutes to walk to the hotel from the speakeasy, and we chat for most of the way. Now and then our eyes meet and linger for a moment, our reflex to look away compromised by rum.

I can't help but wonder if he's had the same thoughts I've had. This guy strolling next to me is miles away from the standoffish, abrupt man I met that first day on set. The person with me now is less guarded... relaxed...

... and he's still looking at me.

"I never showed my appreciation," he says, stopping just outside the hotel. "For earlier."

I smile. "I just wanted to help you... I don't know... find your joy again. Is that dumb?"

He laughs. "You are anything but dumb."

His stare is more intense now, and I'm not thinking straight. If I was, I wouldn't be having thoughts of grabbing his stubbly face in my hands and crushing my lips against his. The image floods my brain, and I inhale sharply to wake myself up.

"Should we go in?" I blurt.

He pushes open the door to the reception office, and a tiny lady with enormous glasses greets us. "You folks need a room?"

"Two rooms," Adam clarifies hastily.

"Oh gosh... I'm not sure we have two rooms left. Let me check."

She types on her keyboard and my heart pumps blood a million miles a second. This cannot be happening.

Sharing a room?

How the heck is that going to work? Would we ask for a cot? Make sure it had a couch? We couldn't possibly...

My mind wanders to the two of us, side by side, in bed next to each other...

"Ooh, you're in luck. I have two double rooms, just down the hall from each other."

"Great," Adam breathes, looking sideways at me.

My pulse resumes a normal pace, but for some reason, I feel almost disappointed. Sharing a room would be super weird, but this is the most fun I've had in ages. I don't want to say goodnight to him just yet.

The receptionist hands us our room keys and we pile into the elevator. I'm suddenly very aware of the four walls surrounding us.

"I had fun tonight," Adam says, filling the silence. "Maybe you've converted me into a tiki bar man after all."

"It's the best kind of man to be," I reply, rubbing at the goosebumps that have taken residence on my arm.

You need to chill out.

The doors open and we are back on unmoving land, making our way to our rooms. As we reach mine first, Adam stops and turns to face me.

If it didn't feel like a date before, it sure as heck does now.

This is that moment; that part after a first date that if all has gone well, is usually followed by a first kiss.

And maybe it's the rum talking, but I could reeaally kiss this guy.

I stare up at him, unable to breathe... dying in anticipation of what might happen next.

"So, I'll meet you downstairs in the morning? We can walk back to the car together."

"Sure," I say, exhaling, and feeling like a moron.

"Um, I'll text you to see when you're up?"

I nod.

He stands there, hesitating.

Is he going to kiss me?

"Well, goodnight then." He does a soldier salute before turning and continuing down the hall.

"Night," I call after him, watching as he gets further away.

I buzz myself into the room and close the door behind me, slumping back against it. Why am I being such an idiot? As if he was ever going to kiss me. And it would be a horrible idea, anyway. I'm his *assistant*. I'd have to see him every day at work. Make awkward eyes as I hand out gaffer tape and bottles of water.

No more lethal cocktails for Evie, I scold myself, walking toward the bathroom for a sobering shower.

But then there's a knock at the door.

Fuck.

What am I doing?

When we said goodnight, I felt my stomach sink. Disappointment eroded my entire body. Turning back around and heading for Evie's room felt natural—like gravity, or a human-sized magnet pulling me where I was supposed to be. But now that I'm standing here, rapping my knuckles on her door, I'm full of doubt.

What the fuck am I doing?

The door swings open, and she just stares at me. Like she knew it was going to be me.

Okay, say something.

"Um…" I mumble.

Say fucking more than that.

She probably thinks I'm a massive weirdo at this point, so I think as quickly as I can.

"My sweater," I finally manage. "I wanted to get my sweater back from you."

Ugh. Douchebag.

"Oh," she says, her eyebrows pinching at the middle.

She walks to the chair behind her and picks the sweater up. Which is just long enough for me to get a great view of her ass. Which is also great.

Jesus, I need to get a grip.

The entire night felt like foreplay. The smiling, the little touches, the prolonged eye contact. I tried ignoring it, but it's no use now. It's time to face the facts.

I want this girl.

And I had a feeling she wanted me too. The way her eyes flicked to mine at the bar. The way she bit her lip when I gave her my sweater.

But then, when we were outside the hotel, she couldn't get away from me fast enough. We were having a moment... at least I *thought* we were having a moment... and then she bolted inside. And the last thing I wanted to be was some creepy director trying to have it off with his PA.

I didn't want to be *that* guy.

So I don't know why I came back to her room. Call it a fool's errand. One last pathetic attempt to see if something was happening between us, or if it's all in my head.

But I can't do it. Watching her standing here, looking up at me with her gorgeous brown eyes I could just swim in... there's no way I'm risking taking a shot and finding out I've got the signs all wrong. I'm not exactly an expert when it comes to the female species.

"Thanks," I say, holding up the sweater lamely. I walk back toward the door, a second wave of disappointment clenching at my insides.

"Adam?"

I freeze.

Who knew my name on someone's lips could sound so perfect?

When I turn around, she's gazing at me intently. And there it is again.

That damn lip bite.

I don't let myself hesitate this time. Swinging the door closed and tossing the sweater on the floor, I close the distance between us in three steps, and take her face in my hands. Our mouths come together, and I'm filled with delicious, sweet relief as her hands slide around my back, pulling me close.

Her lips are as soft and smooth as they look, and as they massage against mine, I can't get enough of them. She tastes like coconut and pineapple and just when I think a kiss couldn't get any better, she slides her tongue into my mouth. It's delicate, yet playful... like she's testing how badly I want her.

Which is really fucking badly.

I move my hands around her waist, sliding them under her t-shirt and onto her warm skin. She weaves her fingers through my hair, tugging it lightly and pulling my mouth even harder onto hers. Our tongues dance together, meeting and retreating at all the right moments, and then her teeth graze over my bottom lip.

Fuck.

We break apart and she stares up at me daringly, letting me know she's not fooling around. "I want you."

I groan at the words, hoisting her up so she can wrap her legs around my waist. If she wasn't already aware that I want her too, she sure as hell will be now. I'm so hard, I feel like I'm going to combust.

We only make it as far as the wall. I press her against it as she pulls at my shirt, tugging it over my head. She drags her hands over my chest, stooping down to trace kisses across my collarbones. I have to stop myself from tearing her shirt right off her body, taking the time to slide it over her fair arms, tracing my fingers over the splatter of freckles across her shoulders. I unhook her bra with one hand, watching it fall to the side and reveal her perfect breasts. So perfect, I need to take one in my mouth before I can do anything else. She moans, clawing at my hair as I flick my tongue over her nipple.

I heave against her, our shorts the only barrier between me and what feels like the only thing I've ever wanted. Even through clothing, her body feels so good against my cock, and if I don't have her soon, I think I'm going to pass out.

"I want to fuck you," I growl.

She groans into my ear, sliding her hand between us and rubbing it against my crotch.

"So do it," she whispers, sending a current of electricity down my spine.

I hold my hands against her ass to pick her up again, this time making it all the way to the bed. Throwing her down on the mattress, I watch her hungrily as I unbutton my shorts, pushing them down so they fall on the floor.

Her gaze floats down until it meets its target. Which, at this point, could take an eye out. Her chest rises as she takes me in, before she does that lip bite thing again and...

Holy fucking shit.

I climb onto the bed, unzipping her shorts and pulling them down. Underneath, she's wearing pink underwear with *Simpsons* characters on them and honestly, nothing has ever been sexier.

I move over her, running a hand down her body until it rests on the space between her legs. And I begin to rub.

"I've been thinking about this all day," I say into her ear as she makes tiny little whimpering noises.

"I've been thinking about this all week," she breathes

And suddenly I'm a madman.

I move her underwear to the side and skim my fingers over her, relishing her moans before I slide my fingers inside. She feels like heaven and I'm done for.

I can't hold off any longer.

I lean up, hooking my fingers on either side of her underwear and dragging them over her legs. I'm on top of her again in a heartbeat, and as my face lines up with hers, she looks into my eyes, tenderly dragging her hands from my temple to the side of my head. I don't know how something so innocent can feel so sensual.

Without taking her eyes off mine, she moves her hand down and wraps it around my cock. As she strokes up and down, I touch my quivering lips to hers, and feel her put me where she wants me.

I press my forehead against hers as I push inside.

She arches her back, making a sound so appealing I'm worried I might finish then and there. But I hold off, moving my hips back and forth until I'm in deep.

"Holy shit," she gasps, and I do believe this is the first time I've heard her cuss. But I have to say, I share the same sentiment.

This. Feels. Fucking. Incredible.

I continue to rock my hips, feeling her legs wrap around me as I pick up the pace.

"Holy shit," she cries again, louder this time as I push in even deeper.

I get on my hands now, holding my body up so I can get the best angle and the best view. The position of her head tilted back, the O shape of her mouth, her breasts moving alongside the thrusts of my pelvis. It's like the best fucking film I've ever seen in my life.

And I can't hold it in much longer.

"I'm coming," I groan.

"Me too," she says, clasping her hands over my ass and moving them in time with my hips.

I push hard and fast until everything goes out of focus. The walls, the ceiling, the bed... everything is fuzzy, except for the gorgeous woman underneath me, who is making a sound that will make me hard for as long as I live.

The relief is intense and exquisite and surging in waves, making my entire body spasm on top of her while I try to hold myself up. I throw my head down, groaning into her ear as I jerk for the last time, and collapse on top of her. I don't want to crush her, but she doesn't seem to mind. She winds her legs more firmly around me, making it impossible for me to get off her even if I wanted to. But I don't want to. Her neck is hot and sweaty, but there's no place I'd rather be as I rest into it, breathing heavily into her chest.

"Holy shit," she says again, her fingers tracing lazy patterns onto my back. I stay there until my heart has stopped threatening to jump from my ribcage, and eventually crumble to the side, relishing the cool air on my chest.

As I lie there, staring up at the ceiling and listening to her breathe, it's gradually dawning on me.

Me and Evie just fucked.

What am I supposed to do now? I'm not going to get up and leave. That would be the jerk thing to do. And I don't want to leave, anyway. But does she want me to stay? Sleep next to her? Wake up in the morning and pretend it never happened?

I roll my head sideways to gauge how she might be feeling. She probably wants to talk about it, right? But when I find her eyes, they are closed, and her mouth is resting in a delicate smile.

As I watch her relax, I'm overcome with a definite, indisputable thought.

I don't want this to be a one-night stand.

In fact, I can see myself doing this with Evie again, and again, and again.

The talks we've had, the movie theater... the sex. The way I feel about her now leads to one inevitable conclusion.

I like this girl.

She mumbles something about the light and rolls onto my chest without opening an eye. The feeling of her against me now differs from before, but is just as incredible. I reach out with my free arm and flick the switch on the lamp, casting the room into darkness, save for the moonlight that shines through the open curtains.

Jesus. If anyone walked past earlier, they got quite the show.

As her breathing slows, I run my fingers over her back, drawing shapes and letting my own eyelids grow heavy.

And just as I'm drifting off, I'm wrapped in a contentment that I haven't felt in a really, really long time.

21

I'm awoken by a bright glare coming through the window.

Darn it, why didn't I close the blinds last night?

Last night.

Oh.

I roll over, and there he is. So, it wasn't a dream—or some elaborate hallucination brought on by rum and tiny paper umbrellas. And he stayed the whole night. In my bed.

Holy shit, I had sex with Adam.

As I cuss internally, I get a distinct feeling of déjà vu. Except, I'm remembering a much steamier point in time. One where I could feel the full weight of Adam's body on top of me... moving... gliding...

So, I had *really great* sex with Adam.

He's still sleeping and I seize the opportunity to take in his face. Every detail. I'm always so paranoid about him catching me staring, it's nice to have the chance to look over his features. His strong brow, the line of his nose, his relaxed mouth as he breathes through a narrow gap in his lips.

Those gorgeous lips...

While I'm looking at them, I have the sudden urge to

lean over and plant a soft kiss. The way they do in the fairy-tales. But it's occurring to me now that I don't know how he'd react.

And he's my director.

Good God.

What have I done?

Delicately lifting the sheets, I slide my legs out of bed, trying my best not to disturb him. When my feet hit the floor, I see the proof of last night's antics. Clothes are strewn around the room—a shirt here, a pair of shorts there—and scrunched up near the bathroom are my favorite *Simpson* undies.

They probably wouldn't have been my first choice if I knew I'd be getting primal.

Oh geez.

Talk about Primal Nature.

I'll never be able to say the name of the film again without blushing.

Trying to make zero sound, I pad across the carpeted floor, making my way to the bathroom where I shut myself in and turn the lock as gently as possible.

I look at my reflection in the mirror, taking in the girl staring back at me. Wild hair, naked body, maybe a little pink cheeked from the day in the sun. Or maybe it was because of the memory of his pen—

No. I will not let myself think about it.

Not yet. Not until I know what it meant.

I reach into the shower, turning on the faucet. The pipes clang to life with the loudest, most obnoxious sound and I groan under my breath. Well, if Adam wasn't awake before, he sure will be now. But at least the shower gives me some time to think. I always do my best pondering under a stream of almost boiling water.

I step in and turn my face up toward the shower head, relishing the feeling of getting clean. I never got to bathe last night. As I lather myself up with some harsh-smelling hotel soap, I get to thinking.

What the heck are we supposed to do now?

It's not like we're dating or even *talking* about dating. We hadn't even shared a *kiss* before last night. I have no idea how Adam feels, or how I feel, for that matter. Will he wake up and have crippling regret? Will the rest of production be awful and awkward?

And then I have a wave of nausea. One that I wish I could blame on a hangover.

What will everyone at work think?

Oh God.

I'm going to be *that* girl.

That young PA who sleeps with the director to get ahead in her career.

Who knows what Kylie will do with information like this. She is probably going to have a field day, for crying out loud.

How could I have been so careless?

I hear footsteps beyond the bathroom door and immediately feel queasy. I can't just stay in here forever, can I? At the very least, I'll have to go out to fetch my *Simpsons* undies and clothes from yesterday because I have nothing else to wear.

I remind myself that I am a strong, intelligent woman, who isn't scared of grown-up conversations, and I wrap myself in a towel. When I push the door open, Adam is standing there, in his shorts from yesterday, picking his shirt up off the floor. My traitorous eyes gravitate to his chest.

"Morning," I say with as much cheeriness as I can muster, snapping my stare back up to his face.

"Hey," he says with a smile that doesn't reach his eyes.

Great. He *does* regret it.

"So... last night," he begins.

"I think it's best if we just keep it to ourselves," I jump in.

I don't need to hear the vague reasons he doesn't want this to happen again, or the insulting discouragement I've had from men too many times before. In fact, I'm going to beat him to the punch. Because I don't think this was a good idea, either.

"I wasn't going to tell anyone," he says, frowning.

Oh right, because that would be so humiliating for you.

"Good."

I busy myself collecting my clothes, trying to bend over without giving him an eyeful. Not that it's anything he hasn't seen before.

"Are you okay?" he asks, taking a step toward me.

"I'm fine, why?"

"I just thought that..." his eyes flicker up to mine, like he's trying to communicate telepathically "... that we—"

The phone on the bedside table rings sharply, making me jump.

"Yes?" Adam answers, pausing to listen. "We're coming down now."

He hangs up and turns back to me. "That was just reception. They want to know if we're checking out yet." He pulls his shirt over his head and collects the sweater he threw on the floor last night. "I'll meet you out the front."

And with a tight smile, I'm left in the room alone.

It's a quiet drive back to LA, but not the easy silence it was yesterday and the day before.

Before we decided to change everything.

And we were really getting somewhere, too. Getting closer. I started to think we were actually *friends*. Now we're in this weird no-mans-land, not speaking and not acknowledging the elephant in the room.

"Should we talk about last night properly?" Adam asks, reading my mind.

"I didn't think you were particularly into conversing with other humans," I quip.

Ugh. I meant it to sound joking, but it comes out snarky and sarcastic.

"Sorry, that wasn't an insult."

"It's fine," Adam says, keeping his eyes firmly on the road ahead.

Another awkward silence follows, but I just can't bear it this time.

"Yes, let's talk about it," I say, rolling my window up so I can hear him easier. "We're adults. We can talk about sex and not make it weird."

The corners of Adam's mouth twitch, and I realize I have most definitely already made it weird.

"We did it with each other, so what?" I continue to dig my own grave. "It doesn't have to be awkward that we've seen each other's genitals."

For the love of God, stop speaking.

Adam bites down on his lip, like he's trying not to laugh. But then glances over at me. "I just wanted to make sure you were okay."

"Okay?"

"Yeah. You just seemed kind of... mad earlier."

"I'm not mad," I say, shuffling in my seat. "I guess I'm just worried."

"About me?"

"About what people might say. What they might think."

Adam draws his eyebrows together.

"I'm the PA who slept with her director. We both know how that looks," I explain.

"No, how does it look?"

"Like I'm trying to sleep my way to the top."

"Hang on. We both know that's not what's happening here," Adam says. He reaches over, almost like he's about to grab my hand, but then settles his fingers around the stick shift.

"I know." I look at his hand, wondering if it would feel nice curled around my own. "But other people will jump to conclusions."

"Who cares what other people think?"

"I do," I say, suddenly feeling very defensive. "It's okay for you. You're already respected and have a high position in the industry. It won't reflect badly on you that we've been together."

A pause.

"I'm sorry," he replies, his voice growing quiet. "I didn't realize being with me would cause you such issues."

His tone isn't sarcastic, it's more... deflated.

"It didn't, it won't. I'd just... like to keep this between us."

He looks over at me and attempts a smile. "As it was always going to be."

I nod, turning my attention to the window. If Adam says he won't tell anyone, I believe him. But there's still an uneasy feeling in the pit of my stomach.

I watch the coastline go by outside and try to push away the thing that's glaring right in my face. Because the truth is, I don't regret my night with Adam.

It's been so long since I felt a man's arms around me,

since I felt warm lips kissing my neck. Every second together was incredible, and more than that.

Every second together felt *right*.

Part of me wishes this movie was already done, and we had the option to explore whatever happened between us. But there is no use fantasizing about that, partly because it isn't the case. And partly because I don't even know if Adam feels the same way. He hasn't made any indication that last night actually meant something to him.

Whatever happened between us in that bed, it was amplified by the fact I hadn't dated anyone in about five hundred years. My defenses were down, and I was vulnerable to falling victim to it.

The feels.

And I can't have feelings for Adam. Not when we have the rest of the movie to get through. There is only one logical thing left to do, and the sooner I get a start on it, the better.

I have to start dating again.

That's it. I have to put myself out there, because a year of celibacy is dangerous—especially when you're drinking tropical cocktails with your funny, cute, sexy—

Okay, enough.

It's settled. I will make a profile on the best app when I get home. No, not just the best app. On *all* the apps. Better to cast a wide net. And then I can forget all about the night I had with Adam, and we can go back to just being colleagues. Or whatever you call people who work on a film together.

We're nearly back in LA, and I'm glad that I at least have a plan of attack for moving forward. I roll the window down again, soaking in the midday sun.

But as the breeze hits my shoulders, I'm taken by a

memory... the feeling of Adam tenderly stroking my hair as I fell asleep on his chest. And suddenly I'm overcome with emotion—a weird combination of loneliness and sadness, and pining for a time that was only mere hours ago.

Yet feels so out of reach.

22

ADAM

I never thought I'd see the day that I'd be happy to meet up with Eric and Simon. Yet here I am, with a script on the table in front of me, waiting for them to meet me for coffee. I'm *actually excited* to tell them a few extra ideas I have for the rest of the shoot.

Something has changed. Ever since that day at the movie theater, it's like a load has been taken off my mind. Like I'm allowed to embrace this film for the fun, stupid, lighthearted adventure that it is.

Why did I let myself get so bogged down?

For too long, I've been comparing myself to my father. Measuring any success against his insane legacy, and beating myself up every time I come up short. I let myself get so wrapped up in his highbrow literacy achievements that I forgot why I fell in love with film in the first place.

The spectacle of it all. The sheer boyish joy. The huge sets and the magic and the storytelling, drawing people into a new world where they can explore and laugh and experience life through a character's eyes.

No, my movies aren't the same as my dad's books. But

the truth is, we are apples and oranges. And comparing my work to his is irrelevant. Maybe my films aren't pensive or complex or get discussed at wanky pretentious parties, but that doesn't mean my work is any less important.

"I was surprised you wanted to do this," Simon says, accepting a coffee from the server. "If I can be frank, you haven't seemed all that invested in the film. Not since Nolan came to set."

I smile at my coffee cup. "Let's just say I had a change of heart."

I think back to sitting in the theater with Evie, her big excited eyes looking into mine, and my smile fades.

"Well, I'm glad to hear it, because I think we have a hit on our hands. We should all be happy!" Eric says, sharing a fist bump with Simon.

Oh geez.

I go over my plan for the rest of the film, which is the same as we've been doing, just with even more commercial oomph. More action, more goofs, more special effects in post. Eric and Simon look so excited, it almost makes me want to leave. But I can't say I blame them. Eric is right, whether you regard it as lowbrow or highbrow, this film is going to be a hit.

But there's still something in the back of my mind, putting a cloud over my newfound enthusiasm.

Evie.

We've barely spoken since we got back from San Diego, and honestly, I have no idea where I stand with her.

The morning after our night together went nothing like I thought it would.

For starters, she wasn't even there when I woke up. I didn't want to begrudge her the right to have a shower, but how quick did she want to get her body away from mine?

Was I that repulsive? I was kind of hoping she'd come out of the bathroom and give me a kiss, share even an iota of the happiness I'd been feeling. But she was completely distant.

I understood why she wanted to keep it a secret and her concerns about how it would look if it got out. But what I didn't understand was why she couldn't get away from me fast enough.

Did she wake up and regret sleeping with me? Or was it just that she didn't want it to happen again?

I'm not above one-night stands, but I didn't get the sense that was what happened between us. We'd gotten to know each other, we were friends, even. It was something a bit more.

At least, I thought it was.

Thank God I didn't tell her how I felt, because I'd be looking like a real jackass. It was bad enough getting rejected while I scavenged my clothes off the floor.

"Earth to Adam?" Eric waves a hand in front of my face.

Do people still say that?

"Err, yes, I think if we use creature performers for that scene, it will look more realistic," I say, pushing thoughts of Evie to the back of my mind. "If there's room in the budget."

"I don't think Nolan will be worried about that." Eric smirks.

We go over a few more details, and by the end of the meeting, I feel prepared to keep shooting the next day.

Prepared to see everyone on set, however, is another thing.

"Cut!"

I walk to the video tent to play back the last take.

"Okay, we got it. Let's move on," I say, sliding my headphones off my ears.

"Really?" Dee asks.

"Yep, it was great."

She looks at me like I just told her I joined a pole dancing class. "It was great?" she says with air quotes, reminding me of somebody else.

"Yes, great. Like, better than good. Ring any bells?"

"Okay, smart ass. You've just never given this film or anyone on it a compliment in like... ever."

"That's not true," I say, bunching my eyebrows while I go over the details of the next scene. "I give compliments."

"Mmm hmm..."

I sense her watching me, but I don't have time for a Dee inquisition right now. The crew packs the camera equipment to transport it to the set on the other side of the sound stage, and while I follow them, I can feel someone at my heels.

"So how did the location scout go?" Dee is back at my side.

"Why? Who's asking?"

"Um... I am? Because you didn't reply to like any of my texts while you were there."

It suddenly feels a bit warm in my t-shirt and shorts.

"I never reply to your texts," I say, trying to act normal as I read the shot list. Instead, I drop my pen on the floor, pick it up, and drop it again.

Nice.

"Are you okay?" She pinches her eyebrows together.

"Yes, I'm okay. Why wouldn't I be okay?"

"I don't know. You're just acting really weird."

"Your mom's really weird."

"Dude." She scrunches her face up like she smells a dead rat. "Did you just 'your mom' me?"

"I'm fine, okay? I'm fine, the scout was fine, we got what we needed..." my mind trails to a dangerous place "... we're all set to shoot the cliff scene down there. Everything is and was fine."

"Okay, okay. Please stop saying fine."

We're at the new set now and the crew is setting up lights.

"Dee for Evie. Can you swap out with Jackson?" She says into her shoulder mic.

"You're swapping out Jackson for Evie in here?" I ask, watching Jackson head toward the door of the sound stage.

"Yeah, he keeps telling me random film facts. He's driving me nuts. I'm putting him on door duty."

I nod, looking back toward the door as Evie comes through to take her position on set.

"Is that a problem?" Dee continues.

"Of course not," I reply quickly. "I'm just eager to get started on this scene."

"Okay, seriously, what happened in San Diego?"

As Dee rounds on me, I break out in a cold sweat. How could she have figured it out by the few pathetic sentences I'd given her? Evie steps up into the set and my stomach lurches. She'll hate me if it gets around and it's my fault.

"Nothing happened in San Diego," I blurt, scratching the back of my head. "Why would you even think that?"

"Ever since you got back, you've been all Mr. Positive about the film. It's wigging me the fuck out."

My body unclenches as I realize she's not talking about Evie. Who appears by Dee's side about three seconds later.

"What's the four-one-one?"

"You're such a dork," Dee scoffs and drapes her arm

around Evie. "I was just asking Adam why he's been so weird since you guys got back from San Diego."

Evie's eyes widen as she gives me an anxious glance.

"He's all excited and shit about the film," Dee goes on. "Did you give him a lobotomy while you were away?"

"Oh," Evie laughs. "Well, you know, I tried. But I couldn't hold him down."

As the words come out of her mouth, I'm filled with the image of Evie on top of me, her delicate hands holding me by the wrists, and I goddam near get an erection. By the look on her face, it seems she's drawn a similar parallel and her cheeks flush a warm shade of pink.

Suddenly I'm back at the tiki bar, looking at her across the table, her cheeks glowing from one too many cocktails. God, she was so gorgeous that night. Even now, in her spotty shorts-and-top suit thing, she might be the most magnificent creature I've ever seen.

"Well, whatever you did, well done girl." Dee pats Evie on the back and leaves us for Joel.

We both look intensely at the floor, like it's the most interesting thing in the world. If only Dee knew how profoundly awkward she is making life for both of us.

When I look back up, Evie is staring at me, a sweet smile on her face.

"I'm glad you got your mojo back," she says. "It's nice to see you enjoying the job."

Seeing her beaming face, I can't help but question if we would've been better stopping the trip after the movie theater. I've never had someone go to such lengths to help me. I've had friends tell me I am a grumpy shit, ex-girlfriends telling me to cheer up, but never anyone going to the source of the problem and genuinely helping. I've never had someone care about me enough to go that far. I would've been happy just having a friend like that in my life.

But then we had sex.

Okay, we'd only done it once, and clearly, Evie isn't interested in doing it again. Surely, after a while, we can be normal again. Just go back to being friends. Rewind to before the tiki bar when we were just two people who understood each other.

"I'm going to get some hot bricks before we get started," Evie says, hopping down the steps of the set toward the tent where we keep the extra batteries on charge.

Maybe if we just give it some time... Eventually, I'll be able to look at her without that feeling in my stomach, like going over the first dip of a rollercoaster.

But when she looks back at me from the tent, sliding a piece of hair over her ear and smiling, I'm reminded of the feeling of stroking her head as she fell asleep on my chest.

And I know that forgetting is only a pipe dream.

"Wow, even I'm getting hot and bothered," Sylvia says, fanning her décolletage with her hand.

I'm sitting on her bed, filling her in on my trip to San Diego with Adam.

"Sounds like he put on quite the performance."

I feel giddy at the memory. "It was… something."

"Or maybe more than something." Sylvia arches an eyebrow. "Are you really telling me that didn't leave an impression on you? Sticking up to your parents like that?"

I haven't told her *all* the details.

"He probably just felt he ought to vouch for me, you know, because I basically work for him," I reply, taking one of her long hair extensions and winding it around my arm. "It's like how employers are required to give you a good recommendation."

"And you're telling me you didn't immediately picture him naked when he started yelling in your defense?"

An actual memory of Adam naked invades my mind, and I hold the hair extension up over my face to shield my bushing cheeks. "I don't know what you mean."

"You're a horrible liar," she says, snatching the extension out of my hands.

I bite the corner of my lip, inspecting my nails. I can see Sylvia watching me in my peripheral vision, but I don't meet her eye. I'm scared the whole sordid sex fest will play in my mind and she'll see it reflected out my pupils.

"Remember the time I was dating that DJ guy, the one with the long hair?" she asks.

"Ugh, yes. How could I forget," I grunt, glad for the change in topic.

"He was a jerk, and you knew it. Remember how you saw him kissing that goth girl in the corner while I was at the bar, but you didn't want to say anything to me because you knew it would break my heart?"

"He was so beneath you," I say, scrunching my face.

"He was," she confirms. "And remember how I asked you what was wrong, and you said nothing?"

"Why are we talking about that long-haired douche clown?"

"Because you have the same face now as you did that night." Sylvia crosses her arms and stares me down. "What aren't you telling me?"

She's right. I am an awful liar. If I ever got caught up in a gang, I'd probably snitch at the first point of questioning and would be sleeping with the fishes.

I take a deep breath in and out.

"I slept with Adam."

"Holy shit!" She slaps my ankle. "I *knew* you guys were into each other. I saw it the first time I was on set. *You had sex!*"

"Yes, I just told you that."

"Why aren't you more excited about it? He's hot! And

well… it's been a minute." She pulls a face and darts her eyes in the direction of my vagina.

"Thank you for the reminder. But you don't get it. I'm the PA and he's the director. If it gets out, everyone will get the wrong idea."

"Oh sweetie, who cares what people think? Everyone sleeps with everyone, it's LA. No one cares."

"Well I care. My career is important to me. I want to get ahead on merit."

"You *will* get ahead on merit."

"That's not what everyone will think."

Sylvia tilts her head. "Since when do you care so much about what people think?"

I grab one of her pillows and lie down, squeezing it to my chest. I never care what people think. But this is different. If it gets out… I just have a bad feeling about it.

"So how was it?" She has an evil glint in her eye now.

I sigh. "Incredible."

"Like how incredible? I need details!"

I sit up. "Like body earthquake, toe curling, made me cuss out loud incredible."

My body clenches up just thinking about it. The truth is, no one has ever made me feel like Adam did. And I'm not sure anyone ever will again. You get to a point where if you haven't experienced unbelievable passion in your life, you just think it's a fantasy. Something that only happens in Nicholas Sparks movies. But Adam blew that theory wide open.

"He made *you* cuss?" Sylvia sits back, her eyes wide. "Damn."

I hit the pillow. "Yes, he made me cuss. And he's sweet. And he lets me be a dork. And he stuck up to my parents for me. And he's really fricking cute. But there's no point in talking about it. It can't happen again."

I dangle my legs over the edge of the bed so my feet can touch solid ground. I need to just forget about the whole thing. Take my head off, shake out all the memories, and then screw it back on straight.

Sylvia is giving me that judgy look.

"Are you trying to convince me it can't happen again, or yourself?"

~

We are taking a break from shooting while the actors rehearse a scene on set. And I've finally given in to Dee's questioning.

"So you just... took him to the movies?"

Luckily, her radar isn't as good as Sylvia's, but I had to give her something.

"That's why he's been acting different since you guys got back?"

"I just wanted to remind him how much people love his work," I say, shrugging. "It was no big deal. I'm sure spending the day at different beaches contributed just as much to his change in attitude."

"If I had known a ticket and a bucket of popcorn could lighten him up, I would've tried that earlier," Dee says. "Good job."

"It really was nothing."

We keep watching the rehearsal—today the creature performers are various animals escaped from the zoo.

"I think we need another script," Dee says. "Do you mind getting one from the side office?"

"Sure."

I head over to the corner of the sound stage where a tiny office stands, holding extra scripts, shot lists, and call sheets. Only when I open the door, someone is already in there.

"Oh, sorry... I..."

When Adam looks up, I turn around, but see Kylie coming. What if she sees me leave and thinks something is going on in here?

I quickly step into the office and shut the door, locking it behind me.

"Um... what are you doing?"

"Shh!" I wave my hand behind me while I peek out the tiny window.

"Why did you lock the door?" Adam is looking at me like I might pull out a prop knife.

"Because Kylie is out there. And if I walk out now, she'd see me and think we were in here together... alone."

"So your solution was to come back in and shut the door?"

I pull the little curtains across, satisfied that she is gone. And it's only now that I realize I've locked myself in a tiny room. With Adam. The man that I boned only days ago. The conversation I had with Sylvia is still fresh in my brain, which also plays snippets from my night with Adam like a highlights reel.

He ruffles a hand through his messy hair, taking a step closer. "Are you okay?"

I finally understand the expression of feeling weak at the knees, because I literally cannot stand straight being in such close proximity to him. I reach behind me, grabbing hold of the desk for support.

"I'm fine."

I lean against the desk casually. "So, how have you been?"

His face twitches. "Um... okay, I guess? The shoot's been going well."

"Good, good." I nod my head.

"But I've been thinking about you."

Oh no, the stomach flutters.

"And the night in San Diego."

Oh no, the other kind of flutters.

"Is that so?" I say, trying to keep my voice steady as he takes another step toward me. "And what do you think about it?"

He's only two feet away now. So close I can smell that man shampoo that is stupidly arousing for some reason.

"That it was the best night of my life."

His voice is deep and husky, and I'm brought back to the hotel... him whispering that he wanted to f-word me...

Our mouths collide and I weave my hands into his hair. There is no warming up like last time. Our tongues caress each other's, sending immediate sparks downstairs. I can taste the soda he's been drinking, sweet and warm, and I need more... *more*...

"We can't do this." I break apart from him, catching my breath. "We can't have sex again."

His dark brown eyes are stormy... ravenous, even. I can feel his desire radiating into my own body. The reflection of how I look in his eyes is an insane turn on. I've always been the sweet girl, the goofy girl. But staring at Adam, I've never felt so *sexy*. And I don't want that feeling to end.

Our mouths come together again, but this time his hand moves down from my waist and under my skirt. As soon as he touches me, my body is alert. Alive. I'm hyper aware of every hair on my skin, standing on its end... his thumb moving in tiny circles...

And then he moves his hand, and I think I might cry. He

looks at me like maybe he's come to his senses, but then he lifts me onto the desk and dips down, getting onto his knees.

"Oh my God," I say, watching him crouch in front of me, trailing kisses up my thigh.

He pushes my skirt up around my hips, continuing the journey with his mouth until he reaches my underwear. He kisses me over the top, sending tiny chills down my legs. Before he goes on, he looks up at me, daring me to tell him to stop.

Which I have no intention of doing.

With one finger, he slides my underwear to the side and skims his hands around my backside, hoisting my legs over his shoulders. I can feel his breath as he hovers excruciatingly close... closer... closer...

And then I feel his tongue. Flicking and tickling and teasing.

"Oh my God," I say again, leaning back on my hands and looking up at the ceiling. He is going down on me in the side office. I repeat, he is going down on me in the side office.

I'd heard about this before, but I can't say I'd ever... experienced it quite like this. The delicious pressure, the tingling through my legs. Every circle of his tongue is building toward something implausible... and the anticipation is killing me.

Then he changes speed. Instead of delicate flicks, he is devouring me. Like I'm a tropical fruit, and he's savoring it until the end. His tongue is warm as it laps over me.

The pressure becomes more intense, and my entire body tingles.

"Oh my God, I think I'm..."

And the next sound I hear is my own cry, which I have to muffle with my hand. I grab hold of his hair as he continues to lick and kiss. My legs stiffen as waves of exquisite electricity funnel through me. It courses on and on until finally, it settles in my stomach, like the embers of a burning fire.

I feel like melting into a pool on the floor. I think I'd be pretty happy down there, actually. I'm so content, I could just slide off the desk and into a pile and take a nap. Preferably on Adam's chest.

He takes his finger, sliding my underwear back into place, before straightening up. My legs are still spread so he stands in between them, placing a hand on either knee.

I'm still catching my breath, staring into his eyes while my heart resumes a healthy pace. Once I've calmed down, I hop off the desk, adjusting my skirt so it looks normal.

It's official. I cannot trust myself around this man.

I push past him and head toward the door.

"We didn't have sex," he says, prompting me to turn around and face him. "It doesn't count."

I laugh out my nose, shaking my head and smiling at the floor. Now this, I'm not going to forget any time soon.

"Trust me. It counts."

24

It's a warm night, so instead of going home when we wrap, I grab a couple of cold beers and meet Bob. This isn't our usual routine, but ever since Kimberly took Rufus back, the shine has been taken off going home. Stupid cat. He is proof that you shouldn't let yourself get attached. To anyone.

"What's this?" Bob grumbles, sniffing inside a container.

"A spicy noodle thing."

"I'm not so hot on the spicy foods," he says, patting his stomach.

"Here, I'll have it. Try the baked chicken."

We swap containers and dig in. A couple of friends sharing leftovers and beers on the sidewalk. Now and then someone drops shrapnel or a dollar bill into his trucker cap, and I wonder if I can sneak in some extra without him noticing.

He grabs the hat and looks inside. "I shouldn't let you sit with me. You're bad for business."

"I wish you would just let me give you some cash."

"I'm not your paid escort."

I laugh. "Thank fuck for that. You're really not my type."

Bob laughs, shoveling chicken into his mouth and chasing it with some beer.

"How's that girl of yours going?" he asks between mouthfuls.

"Kimberly?"

"No, not her," he growls, like her name offends him. "The one you brought to meet me."

"Evie?" I lean back on my elbow. "She's not my girl. I was just walking her to her car." I know this is the truth. But that doesn't stop the warm and fuzzy feeling I get when Bob calls her *my* girl.

Ugh, I'm a moron.

"She seemed like a good girl," Bob goes on.

"How do you know that? You talked to her for like two seconds."

"I have about three decades on you, boy. I'm an excellent judge of character."

I sniff and take the beer to my lips. The fact is, I am dying to tell someone how I feel about Evie. Anyone. But she made her feelings about our *interactions* reaching the rumor mill very clear.

But that didn't stop me from replaying them in my head on repeat. Especially the last time in the side office... I curl my fingers around the neck of my bottle as I remember her delicate moans.

Fuck me. It was hot.

I sit upright, shaking the thought from my head. I have a feeling Bob won't tolerate me sprouting a random erection in the middle of our hang out. He would probably never speak to me again.

"Your wrist looks better," I say, noticing the swelling in his arm is almost gone. "Did you end up seeing somebody about it?"

"Course not. I told you it was nothing to get in a tizzy over." He reaches for the container that holds the pudding, lifting the lid and taking a whiff as he always does. "Things in life have a way of sorting themselves out."

"I don't think that always applies to medical issues," I say, suppressing an eye roll as I take a swig of beer.

"It's the best advice I can give you. Let the chips fall as they may."

I watch Bob as he spoons pudding into his mouth, reclining back and looking at the cars and people going by. For someone who has many issues from the outside, he doesn't seem to have a care in the world.

Maybe he is on to something.

I replay Bob's words in my head for the entire walk home. Perhaps I don't need to know where I stand with Evie. I just have to sit back and see how it all pans out.

As I walk through the front door, the first thing I see is the humongous portrait of Rufus leaning against the wall. I still haven't got around to hanging it—partly because I'm lazy, and partly because I'm not sure I even want it up. It's an absolute eyesore. Me a few months ago wouldn't have dreamt of having that thing on my wall. But a lot has happened.

I pull open the drawer with all the bits and pieces that don't have a proper home and scramble through it until I find a wall hook. After some measuring and some dodgy hammering, the hook is installed, and the painting is up, in all its absurdity.

I stand back and look at Rufus's face, all colorful and artistic.

Here is the thing about letting the chips fall: I don't know if I'm ready to just give it all up to fate. I've had a taste of life with Evie Miller in it, and I'm not sure I'm ready to let it go, or chalk it up to a couple of fun hookups. And don't get me wrong, they were really fun. But they were more than just fun. She is a breath of fresh air, and looking at the painting she made for me, I can't help but imagine what her bright colors would look like against my bare white walls.

What would my life be like with a girl like Evie in it full time?

I'm good at being alone. Maybe *too* good. But it wasn't until I let her sunshine in that I realized how damn dark my world is. She busted in and lit up shady corners I forgot even existed; reminded me of feelings I'd forgotten I could have.

And I don't know if I *want* to go back.

I settle in on the couch and flick on the TV, but in my periphery is the portrait, the rest of my blank walls, and the thoughts that linger in the back of my mind.

"Oh my God. I can't do this," Emma says, backing away from the open set window.

"Did we know this was an issue when they cast her?" I mutter to Dee out the side of my mouth. She shrugs me off.

"I promise you'll be fine," Dee says to Emma, walking to the window. "You can't fall."

"Why can't the stand-in sit here while they set the lights up?" Emma asks, looking at me with rounded eyes. "My agent knows I'm scared of heights."

"The stand-in is sick today." Do second floors count as heights?

"Can't you do it?" Emma looks at Dee, who laughs in her throat.

"Honey, my skin is a bit darker than yours. We need

someone with the same complexion, otherwise the lighting will be all wrong."

"This is the worst. I said I would get the take done, not sit around next to a hole in the set while they mess around with filters." Emma shoots her eyes to the lighting technicians, who are working at a very efficient pace. I go to defend them, but Dee holds up her hand to stop me.

"I know you're uncomfortable, but we need to set up and rehearse the scene so the camera guys know what they're doing."

Emma's strained face searches the room until her eyes stop on something. "She can do it."

"Me?" Evie perks up, looking between Dee and Emma. I'm surprised our leading lady even wants Evie's help, given the last time Evie helped she dumped a bucket of water on Emma's head. It's still one of the greatest things I've ever seen in my life.

"You have a similar complexion to me," Emma says. "You can stand-in for me until they're ready to shoot."

Evie looks at me and shrugs.

"If it'll hurry this along—and Evie's okay with it—whatever." I look at Evie to make sure she is okay with it, but my view is cut off by Damon stepping between us.

"Great, let's get this show on the road." He grins at Evie.

My stomach churns at his leering face. I know Damon hits on any attractive young thing with a pulse, but the face he's giving her makes my shackles stand up.

Can he just fucking *not*?

"Okay, let's block the scene from the top," I say to draw the attention back to myself. "Evie, you know what's happening here. You're standing next to the open window, peering out so we can get the shot from ground level. Then you see a swarm of birds coming in the distance. You don't know what they're doing at first, and then realize they're coming straight for you." I scratch the back of my head, grimacing at this next part. "Damon charges in and scoops you up, slamming the window closed as the birds smash against the glass. Then you just have to pause while he holds you up. The rest takes place away from the window, so Emma can take over from there."

"Roger that," she says with an adorable salute. I smile before forgetting the company we're in.

I walk back to George, keeping a side eye on Damon as he goes over the choreography with Evie, scooping her up in slow motion. He directs her on arm placement, and consoles her in the most douchebag-y way—"don't worry, you're not too heavy for me. I bench press three hundred."

"Let's rehearse," I bark. "Damon, can you get out of the frame? Evie, you're at the window."

She nods and goes to her position.

"Okay, action."

Theatrics are unnecessary while the camera blocks out the scene, but that doesn't stop Evie's wide-eyed expression as she gazes at the invisible, murderous birds. I watch her face on the monitor, wishing I could swoop in and pick her up myself.

"Cue Damon."

Damon flies through the set door and lunges for Evie. It's clunky, hardly a smooth romantic moment. But just the vision of his arms around her body gives me the creeps. They stumble away from the window, and pause to look into each other's eyes.

"Cut. Okay, let's reset and rehearse again."

"Whew, talk about sweeping a gal off her feet," Evie says, finding her footing on the floor as he puts her down. I know this is just her goofy way, but the glint in Damon's eyes says he actually thinks she's into him. Guys like him don't need any extra encouragement.

"You ain't seen nothin' yet," he says with a wink.

"RESET," I say, a fraction too intensely. Dee scrunches her face at me like I might be losing it. To be fair, I think I might be.

Whose idea was Evie standing in with Damon again?

It takes me right back to high school, when I had a crush on Cindy Broker. We sat together in math, and would rewrite amusing lyrics to our favorite songs, usually to include our drone of a teacher. Cindy was my favorite person in the world. Of course, I could never *tell* her how I felt. And for the most part, it didn't matter. I was happy just spending time with her. Plus, I could bide my time—all the other guys were chasing the blonde girls who rolled up their skirts at the waist, not Cindy. I felt like she was my goofy, cute as hell, little secret. No one else knew how great she was—at least not until our senior year. Then everything went to shit. The star of the basketball team *also* noticed she was cute as hell, and I had to watch her blush as he started giving her attention. But I still didn't say anything. What chance did I have over a guy like that? Girls didn't choose the reserved film geek. Not when they could have one of the most popular guys in school.

I still remember watching them at prom, her arms around his neck... his face dipping low to kiss her...

Yet somehow, this is even worse.

Maybe I haven't told Evie how I feel about her, but I like to think I have shown her in more ways than one. Does she think I go down on every girl who walks into the side office? I'm not a caveman—I don't think Evie is *mine* just because we had sex—but we had started something together. And seeing Damon work his sleazy charm on her gives me a stomach ulcer.

She's a smart girl. Surely she knows he's full of shit.

Right?

"Action," I call, pulling my focus back to her face on the screen.

Right on cue, Damon makes his grand entrance. Only this time, after he scoops her up, he leans his face toward hers... closer... closer... their lips only an inch apart...

"Cut!" I all but scream. "Damon, what are you doing?"

"I think this scene could benefit from a kiss, don't you think?"

"Absolutely not," I say, all too aware of my heart pounding in my chest as he sets her back on the floor. "The first kiss doesn't come till later in the film."

"I guess I was just feeling the chemistry," Damon says, bashfully running a hand through his hair and smiling crookedly at Evie.

"I think we can bring in Emma now," I say, hooking my headphones next to the monitor. "But first, let's take five."

As I stalk off set, I try to ignore the sounds of Evie's giggles.

25

I was happy to see Emma's stand in return to set early on Wednesday morning, bleary-eyed and ready to be scooped. Not that being held between Damon's biceps was the worst thing I've experienced (I'm only human), but I'm much more comfortable with my walkie talkie and sharpies on standby. Being the object of Damon's affection is kind of like being at a male strip show. The oily person flexing in front of you is sexy, objectively, but it just isn't my *thing*.

"He might be an idiot, but he sure is fine," Dee had muttered to me when we took a break after rehearsing the scene. But I was too distracted watching Adam walk off set. He seemed to be getting stressed out again, and I was starting to worry that my whole trip-to-the-movies ruse wasn't as effective as I'd thought.

I haven't really seen him today either, because I've been on door duty all morning. It's not until I'm lining up to get lunch that I see him across the tent. Our eyes meet for the briefest of seconds before his fall down to the table, his mouth in a hard line.

"What's this shit?"

I turn around and see Gus, flicking through sloppy joe mix with a big spoon.

"You put it in a hamburger bun."

"It looks rank," he says, ditching the meaty sludge for some Asian greens.

"I don't understand half of what you say," I laugh. "Shall we dine together?"

"After you, mate." He swoops his arm sideways for me to lead the way. I find a space next to one of the runners and Jackson, who are, thankfully, deep in conversation. I'm not in the mood for a pop quiz on films from the 1970s.

When I compare my plate to Gus's, it's obvious why he's a lean ninja man and I am not. Everything in front of him is either lean protein or green or a strange wholegrain I can't identify.

"Shredding for bikini season?" I ask, stabbing a chunk of crispy pork and shoveling it into my mouth.

"Gotta watch those macros," he replies, pulling up his shirt and slapping his six-pack.

"Oh no, you didn't just do that."

He laughs and spears a piece of broccoli. "Can you believe we only have a couple of weeks left?"

"Don't remind me."

I'm not ready for this job to be over. For more reasons than one.

"What do you have lined up after this?" he asks.

I shrug. "Your guess is as good as mine."

"You'll be fine," he says, moving onto his weird grainy salad. "You've basically made it through an Adam Thorne film. You'll get work on any set now."

I can see Adam through the lunch crowd, flicking through his food. His thick brown hair looks extra messy today. I want to run my fingers through it. "I don't see what the fuss is. He's not that bad."

"Reputations are a bit like Instagram in Hollywood. The truth doesn't matter, it's what people assume about you that counts."

I think about this for a moment. I haven't been in LA long enough to get to know many people, especially before *Primal Nature*. Adam is one of the few people who sees me for me, the real me. Not just the bubbly, quirky girl that everyone else sees. And I have a feeling it goes both ways. Everyone thinks Adam is the grumpy, sarcastic film director. But I know him as the guy who is actually very sweet. The guy who stood up to my parents.

The guy who went down on me in the side office.

A fire stirs in my stomach and I toss my fork on the table. Suddenly, food is the last thing I feel like devouring. I have other things in mind...

"Are you okay?" Gus asks.

"Easy breezy." I squash any thoughts of Adam's face near my thigh before I dissolve into a puddle of lust. "So what are your plans for after the film wraps?"

He drags his napkin across his mouth. "I think I'll take a break. Reevaluate what I want to do."

"That's very existential twenty-something of you."

He laughs. "Well, I've been thinking about our conversation the other week. And I don't know, maybe it's time I refocus on what I originally came here to do."

"You're going to try acting again?" I grab his wrist.

"Jesus, calm your farm," he chuckles, looking to the side at the few people who have tuned into our conversation. "I'm just mulling it over."

"I think it's an amazing idea! Why shouldn't you follow your dreams?"

"Because I might fail again." He gives me a wry smile. "Because I'm only getting older, and because I might be an idiot to walk away from consistent stunt work while I'm getting it. Maybe something reliable isn't so bad."

"You can be consistent and reliable when you're dead. Now is the time to go for it!" I turn to face him, the way I like to when I'm giving one of my pep talks. "You're young, talented, and very handsome. Which should make you incredibly annoying, but you're super modest and friendly too."

He laughs.

"Why shouldn't you be successful? I think you should just give it all you've got, and don't let anything get in the way."

"I feel like you're about to break into song."

I pinch his arm skin, which is very difficult because he has zero fat on his muscles.

"I'm kidding," he grins. "But seriously, I appreciate the vote of confidence. You're a good egg, Eve."

No one has ever called me Eve before. Mainly because it isn't my name. But Gus likes to abbreviate everything.

"Any time," I say in my favorite wise old man voice, and we go on eating.

But I'm still distracted by Adam sitting on the other side of the tent. As I evoke the memory of my fingertips grazing his temples, I question how long I can ignore the thoughts in the back of my mind. And whether I can squelch my feelings for long enough to reach my own dreams.

By late afternoon, I still haven't spoken to Adam, and something tells me I need to. We haven't talked properly since the day in the side office, and I'm dying to be alone with him again.

No, not for that reason.

Okay, *maybe* for that reason.

The truth is, I'm seriously questioning my ability to keep my hands off him. It's almost been a blessing to miss out on private time together. Sex only makes things more complicated. Especially when I need to be focusing on my career.

But I really want to know where his head's at. Gus is right—it's time to figure out life after the film is done. It isn't just a movie set fling that's at stake for me. It's my whole future.

What I need is to catch Adam for a quiet conversation, but not somewhere private enough where we can get to each other's privates. When I see him turn down the side of the sound stage toward the art department, I take the opportunity to intercept him.

"Hi!"

"Fuck!" He jumps away and holds up his hands like I'm about to mug him. "Why are you creeping in the corner?"

"I wasn't creeping, I was just waiting to catch you alone."

"That is literally the definition of creeping."

I roll my eyes and pull him behind the classroom set so we are out of view. "You're such a drama queen. I just wanted to chat... away from everyone else."

Adam narrows his eyes like he's trying to decipher my motive.

"No funny business, just talking," I confirm.

All I can think about is the funny business. Or rather, Adam pushing me up against the set and pulling my underwear to the side.

No, Evie. Bad thoughts.

Focus.

"What did you want to talk about?" he asks.

"I just thought we should touch base... you know, check in with each other. We haven't really talked since..."

He watches me carefully, waiting for me to finish the sentence.

"Since..."

Is he really going to make me say it?

"...when..."

"When I went down on you in the side office?"

"Shh!" I press my hand to his lips and I can feel them curl up under my fingertips. His smile is still there when I move my hand down, and for a minute I wonder if public intercourse is something I might consider. Why is stubble so sexy?

"I wanted to talk to you as well," he says, breaking the tension.

"You did?"

"Well, more like warn you."

I pull a face. "That sounds somewhat foreboding."

He laughs, scratching his head. "It's no big deal. I just wanted to make sure you were being careful... around Damon."

"Does he have a shady criminal record I'm not aware of?"

"More like a womanizer record."

I draw my eyebrows together. "Okay, not sure what that has to do with me, but thanks for the heads up, I guess?"

Adam sighs, looking uncomfortably at the ground. "I just saw how you were together on set and... I don't want you to get caught up in his whole act."

"Wait... are you *jealous*?"

I've never had anyone be jealous over me before. Judgmental of my zany outfits, maybe. But never jealous.

It's kind of nice.

"I'm not jealous. I'm just looking out for you." He frowns before looking up at me and smiles out the side of his mouth. "You're too good for him."

I return his smile, tilting my head to the side. "If I was going to get involved with anyone from set, I think you know who my first choice would be."

His chest rises under his t-shirt as he takes a step toward me. Tucked away behind the set, no one can see us.

Just one kiss?

What's the harm in that?

"Oh, sorry. I heard voices."

Both of our heads snap to the side, and standing there watching is no other than Kylie.

Of course.

"I didn't mean to interrupt."

"You're not interrupting," I say at warp speed. "We were just discussing the props for the next scene."

"Right." Kylie nods her head slowly, an unmistakable smirk on her lips. It's not like she *saw* anything. We were only talking.

A couple of inches apart.

Kylie turns to Adam. "Dee is looking for you," she says, before bringing her walkie to her mouth. "I have eyes on Adam."

"Tell them I'm coming."

"He's on his way," she says into the walkie, before shooting me another smug look and sauntering away. I wait until the sound of her footsteps has disappeared.

"That was way too close," I say, breathing for what feels like the first time in minutes. "She's probably already onto us."

"I'm sorry," Adam says, and he looks it. "I know you're worried about people talking.

I nod, preparing to pull the trigger I know needs to be pulled.

"I think we just need to keep our distance until we wrap. I mean, it's just a couple of weeks. And then maybe..." I shrug, looking at Adam with wide eyes.

"And then what? You'd want to maybe pick up where we left off?"

"I mean, if you'd be interested in th—"

"I'm in," he says, that gorgeous carefree grin spreading across his face that I love so much.

"Okay, great. So we'll revisit the idea of you and me in a couple of weeks," I reply, holding out my pinky with a smile. "Friends until then?"

He laughs and shakes his head before linking his pinky with mine.

"Friends until then."

26

This is going to be the longest two weeks of my life.

Every time I see Evie, I want to wrap my arms around her; kiss the gorgeous freckles right off her face. But we are playing it strictly platonic. Those are the rules. The important thing is now I know she's at least open to the idea of there being an 'us'. I just have to keep it cool until we wrap.

This is no easy feat, seeing her bounce into the studio every day with all her colors and ribbons and hair ropes. But just knowing Evie Miller might be in my life after *Primal Nature* keeps the smile on my face. Which gets even wider when she sidles up next to me to make coffee.

"Lovely day, isn't it?"

"It just got significantly lovelier," I say quietly. Her cheeks flush red and she looks down at her cup, adding a teaspoon of sugar.

"How's my artwork going in your house?"

"Well I've stopped playing dead whenever I pass it, so that's something."

"Hey." She playfully slaps my arm. "I know you secretly love it."

"You know, I actually do."

We share another lingering smile before moving on.

"I've been meaning to ask you. How are things going with your parents? I haven't heard you mention them ever since—"

"Ever since you gave them the verbal dressing down of the century?"

"Was I really that bad?" I stir in some cream, frowning.

"Bad, no. It was epic." She grins. "And to be honest, I haven't spoken to them."

"At all?" My stomach lurches. "I'm sorry... I didn't mean to make things worse for you guys."

"All you did was expose some realities that we were all very aware of, and chose not to confront. I think I just need to move on... I'm never going to get their support, let alone praise."

I exhale forcefully. It's crazy that any parent would withhold admiration for such a great girl. How could anyone not be proud of Evie? It pains me to see that their lack of approval affects her so much... even if she pretends it doesn't.

I just wish I could help.

"Hey kids," Dee says, joining the coffee crew. "Talkin' shit about me over here?"

Evie laughs, throwing an arm over her shoulder. "Dee, I am way too smart to ever cross you."

Dee winks and wraps her arm around Evie's waist. There's something satisfying about seeing them get along so well. Like seeing a sister approve of your girlfriend. Not that Evie is my girlfriend.

Ugh, I have to get a grip.

Evie pauses and looks into space, holding a hand up to her earpiece. "Copy," she says into her shoulder mic. "I have to go help set up some props. A PA's job is never done." She waves to us like the queen and disappears into the sound stage.

"You know, not to toot my own horn, but I did an excellent job at finding the production assistants for this film," Dee says.

"I've never known you not to toot your own horn," I reply. "And some might be too sharp for their own good. You know Kylie almost caught me and Evie—"

I come to a halt just before the last words tumble out of my stupid mouth.

This is what happens when you lose your grip. You get sloppy.

"Almost caught you and Evie what?" Dee's eyebrows come together in suspicion.

"Um… talking," I say lamely. It's not a complete lie.

"Why would it matter if Kylie caught you and Evie talking?"

"I guess it wouldn't," I say, picking up my coffee. "I'll see you in there."

I march toward the sound stage but am brought to a stop when my arm is yanked. Dee pulls me behind the catering truck and rounds to face me.

"Do you think I'm a damn fool?"

"Is that a rhetorical question?" I say, avoiding her eyes.

"Adam, my bullshit radar is honed to perfection, and it just blew up back there. Now, I can get it out of you, or I can get it out of Evie."

"Don't go to Evie," I blurt. I can only imagine how panicked she'd be if Dee started questioning her about us.

"Well." She raises her eyebrows. "Spill."

It's impossible to keep anything from Dee, especially

when she suspects you are hiding something. I groan, knowing full well she isn't going to drop this any time soon.

"We kind of slept together in San Diego."

"I fucking knew it!" She punches her fist into her palm. "I knew she would be a good influence on you, and I was hoping you guys would click on your trip together. Though I've got to say, I didn't think you would *bang*." Her eyes are lit up like a Christmas tree. "You've exceeded even my expectations."

"Bang, seriously?" I look around to make sure there are no eavesdroppers. "Just calm down about it. Evie doesn't want it to get out."

"Is she embarrassed about boning an old grizzly bear?"

My face drops.

"You know I'm kidding," she laughs. "I think this is great! You guys balance each other out. Why don't you seem more excited?"

"Because we've decided to keep it platonic until the film wraps. Evie doesn't want it getting out and people making assumptions about her. Career climbing and shit like that."

Dee nods, pressing her lips together. "People are the worst."

"And speaking of which, Kylie saw us having an... intimate conversation. So if you hear any gossip, can you handle it?"

"I'll deal with Kylie," she says, before leaning back and crossing her arms. "So you two love birds, huh? I don't know why I haven't called you Adam and Eve before."

"Because it's the worst joke I've ever heard?"

Dee just laughs and shakes her head. "Little Miss Sunshine found a way to tame the angry beast."

"Can you stop comparing us to fictional characters and biblical figures?"

"I'm just excited!" She grabs my arm. "Kimberly was all wrong for you. I'm just glad you've found a keeper."

"I would have to *have* her to keep her."

"Mm..." Dee's smile fades. "I get why she wants to keep in under wraps, though. Being a woman in this industry sucks dick sometimes. The last thing you need is assholes talking shit about you."

I sigh, knowing she must be right. She always is.

"Just give her space. She'll still be the same Evie in two weeks. Cooling it for a while won't kill you."

She scruffs up my hair before leaving for the sound stage. And as I follow her, I hope she's right.

If it's even possible, Damon is being even more obnoxious this afternoon.

"Let's reset and go again," I say to Joel, rubbing my eyes. We're shooting a chase scene involving wires, stunts, and creature performers. There are many moving parts to keep track of as it is, but Damon has decided he needs to make it more difficult.

"These shoes feel wrong," he says, flicking his foot around like he's trying to kick the combat boots off his feet.

"They're the same size you tried on when they were fitting you," Dee replies, and I can tell she's getting just as tired as I am.

"It's not the size, it's that they're rubbing against my ankle when I run."

"We can fly in Gus and have him shoot this scene if it's too hard." I'm trying my best to be patient. "You were the one who wanted to do more of your own stunts."

"I do," Damon mumbles, returning to his starting position.

He'd read somewhere that Christian Bale did his own stunt work while playing Batman, and is now insisting he do his own as well. The only problem is, Damon is crap at doing stunt work. He's always complaining about being uncomfortable, and unfortunately, the bulk of the shots for the rest of production are stunt scenes. His request to take on his stunt work also means Gus has fewer hours on set. Which is sad for everyone, as people actually like Gus.

"Action."

Damon runs to his mark, and I'm surprised he doesn't stop to have a cry about his boots halfway through. He darts between creature performers, running down the green screen corridor that will transform into a New York City street in post-production. He reaches the part where he runs up and over a car (with the help of wires and cables) and is lifted into the air. By the time he's on the car roof I can see his face grimacing, but we almost have the take done. So close...

And then he reaches down and pulls at his crotch.

"Cut!" I call, hearing Evie's voice echo after mine.

I walk over to Damon, burying the heels of my palms into my eye sockets.

"This harness is so uncomfortable," Damon says, shifting his junk around again for those who missed it the first time.

"You can't grab your balls in the middle of a take," I say. It's ridiculous I even have to point that out.

Damon's face turns sulky. "You try getting lifted in this thing."

"The stunt doubles manage just fine. If you have an issue with it, then you should've left it to the professionals."

His face goes hard. "Excuse me? Professionals?"

"Yes, professionals. As in the people who are trained to be lifted in harnesses without pulling at their junk when I'm trying to shoot a film."

"Maybe if they harnessed me up properly, we wouldn't have this problem."

"I don't think the harness is the issue." I turn and see George, who shares my tired expression. We don't have time for this shit. "Let's try again. From the top."

"I need a drink," Damon announces. "Water?"

Right on cue, Evie comes bouncing onto the set, passing Damon a bottle of water.

"Thanks, gorgeous," he says, downing the entire thing like he's crushing a beer. I glower as he wipes his mouth with the back of his hand and passes the empty bottle back to her with a grin. For someone in severe discomfort, he seems pretty happy about himself.

The crew reset for their starting positions, but Damon takes his sweet time, chatting with Evie so she's unable to leave.

"Did you get cuter since yesterday?" he says, running a hand through his hair and prompting someone from the hair department to come and fix it. "I think I see a few extra freckles."

Evie chuckles and shakes her head.

Now he's commenting on her freckles?

Damon Reeves could have any girl in this room. Why does he have to set his sights on Evie? I've seen the women he brings to industry parties—Evie isn't even his type. He's not genuine about her. It's all just a big show for everyone. He wants to prove he's a big shot by flirting with any female within a five-foot radius. Sweet talking women is just another way to flex his muscles and prove he is a big man. And I've had enough of the performance.

"Can we get back to work, Damon?"

He rolls his eyes dramatically, shaking his head at Evie. "No rest for the wicked." He winks at her. "Come by my trailer again so we can keep chatting."

Come by my trailer?

Again?

I'm saved from responding to Damon by Adam stalking over to us.

"Action!"

"I'm not at my starting spot?" Damon bunches his eyebrows at him.

"We don't have all fucking day to wait for you, Reeves. Can't you see I'm trying to shoot a film here?"

"What's your problem?" Damon says, bringing his hands to his hips.

"*You're* my problem. You're whining and complaining and holding up the shoot, even though you're not supposed to be here. I knew it was a mistake letting you do your own stunts."

"I'm sorry, *letting* me?"

Adam holds out his hands, like 'yeah, so?'.

"*Letting* me do my own stunts, like I'm a fucking child?"

"If the shoe fits." Adam snorts. "Wah, my feet hurt. I'm thirsty. Let's all stop production while I play with myself!" he mocks. "Sounds like a child to me."

There are a few noises around the set. Dee's eyes are

wide as saucers and she lifts a clipboard over her mouth to conceal a smile.

Damon's chest rises indignantly. "You want to come a little closer and say that?"

"Whoa, whoa, let's take it down a notch," I say, stepping between them. "There's no need to get worked up. And if you need to have it out with each other, I say dance battle." I do the beginning steps of a break dance move, which earns me nothing in the response department. Out of the corner of my eye I see a makeup assistant pull out her phone and point it toward us. I take that as my cue to step away. The last thing I need is to go viral in some scandalous backstage testosterone scuffle before my career even gets started.

"Don't you know who I am?" Damon booms.

"Yes. You're a pain in my ass!" Adam yells back.

"I'm the only reason people will watch this pathetic film! You think you're some great director? You are not what the audience is interested in. It's me! Do you know how many followers I have on TikTok?"

"None with any brain cells," Adam retorts. "Now get back to your position and do your fucking job."

"You can't speak to me like that! I'm Damon fucking Reeves. I'm the reason you have a job! People actually want to *be* me. Can you say the same? Can any of you say the same?" He turns to address the entire crew. "I see you whispering. You're all just fucking jealous!"

Wow.

Adam has really poked the sleeping bear.

"My career is just getting started and there's nothing but bright lights ahead for me, baby. I'm a fucking star! I don't need this shit. Especially from you!" He points a finger at Adam. "Let's see how your film does without its leading man."

He fumbles with the cables attached to his harness, trying to set himself free. "Can somebody get me out of this thing?!"

The stunt assistant comes over and unclips him in one effortless motion. Damon kicks off the harness, followed by the boots, but they get caught on the balls of his feet. He loses his stepping and falls over, growling like an angry little Labrador. "Mother fucker!"

When he is finally free of his boots and harness, he throws them across the room and stands triumphantly, before setting off toward the stage door and disappearing through it with a loud bang.

It's a lot.

"What did you do that for?" Dee hisses, marching over to Adam as the sound stage breaks out in whispering and the odd giggle.

"Do what?"

"Set him off like that! You do realize we need him for the rest of the film?"

"I didn't say anything that wasn't true. He was being impossible!"

"Damon has always been a diva. Why are you deciding to go all caveman on him now?"

Adam opens his mouth to respond and his eyes dart to mine before he just shrugs. "I guess I've had enough."

"We've all had enough. But we don't just go pissing off our lead actor a couple weeks before wrapping."

Adam drags his palm down the surface of his face. "I knew he was a mistake for the lead. We should've got Grant Bradley," he mumbles. "He's a professional."

"Maybe I should go talk to Damon?" I suggest meekly. I can't help feeling responsible somehow. I was part of the reason he wasn't getting into his starting position.

"No, I'll go," Adam says.

"No, Evie will go." Dee puts her foot down. "You will only make him angrier. Evie will calm him down, won't you?" She looks at me with genuine concern in her eyes. This film is important to Dee, too.

"I won't let you down."

As I turn to leave, I just catch the strained expression on Adam's face.

"Damon?" I knock lightly on his trailer door.

"Go away."

Suddenly I'm brought back to the start of production, the last time I was standing at this door. About to get duped by Kylie.

It's crazy how much has happened since then.

"It's Evie, can I come in?"

An audible groan passes through the door that suggests he doesn't want me to come in, but I open it anyway. He's sitting in a chair, aggressively typing on his phone.

"I just wanted to see if you were okay."

I'm not usually the lying type. But I have a feeling 'I just wanted to coax you back onto set so we can all get on with our jobs' won't be as effective.

"Did you hear the way he spoke to me?" Damon says, looking up.

"Yes."

We all heard it. And to be honest, I'm still trying to digest it. Adam was right. He didn't say anything that wasn't true. But I still don't know why he got *so* mad *so* quickly. Damon is a lot to handle, sure. But why the colossal blow up now?

"Everyone treats me like an idiot, and I'm tired of it," he

says, throwing his phone on the table. "Do you think he would speak to Ryan Reynolds that way?"

To be fair, I don't see Ryan Reynolds carrying on the way Damon does. But that's another thing I choose not to be honest about. Instead I go with, "you're under a lot of pressure."

"Damn straight I am. And no one else gets it. I'm the main character. Everyone is counting on me getting it right. And I don't need some washed up director getting in my face when I'm trying to work on my craft."

A weird pang jolts through my stomach as he insults Adam. I chew on my lip to keep my expression sympathetic.

"I'm sure he'll be apologetic if you just come back to set."

Adam is absolutely not going to be apologetic.

"Let's just take a big breath and go back. What do you say?"

"I'm not going back in there." He glowers.

Okay, so I need a different approach. Maybe he just wants to be coddled? I could do that. I cross the trailer and sit in the chair opposite him.

"I don't even know how you've made it through the film this far. Coming here day in, day out? You must be exhausted."

"It's been a lot," he says, ruffling his hair. "This is my first role where it's just me and a few creature performers. Not many people to bounce off."

"And you've been handling it so well. Like a pro."

If you discount the endless complaining, the tardiness, the inappropriate comments to members of the crew...

"Well... it's nice someone finally noticed," he says, half defiantly, half softening.

So he does want to be coddled...

"I don't know how you actors do it," I go on. "Me? I just

have to hand out tape and water and pick up the trash. But to show up and perform every day?" I smile, shaking my head. "It's impressive."

The side of his mouth curls up, so I keep going.

"You've had a grueling schedule the last few months, and I think you need to just give yourself a pat on the back."

He's nodding now.

"And remind yourself there's less than two weeks to go."

At this, he stops nodding. "No. I don't think I can go back in there. I don't think I can tolerate being treated like that a day longer."

Ugh.

I lean forward and put my hand on his shoulder. "I think you're underestimating yourself. You're *Damon Reeves*. You're a superstar. And look where you are, you made it to Hollywood! If you can do that, you can do anything."

He frowns for a second, and then as if something is dawning on him, his mouth spreads out in a smirk.

"You know what, Evie?"

He takes the hand I had on his shoulder and places it in his own.

"You're something else."

"No, *you're* something else. Which is why I know that you're going to go back in there and kill it. It's just a few more days, really. You've got this in the bag."

His demeanor has changed now. His skin color has cooled down from the beet red, and his shoulders are no longer bunched up around his ears. I don't want to praise myself too quickly, but I think I've totally turned him around.

I give his hand a squeeze and sit back to release myself, but his grasp is firm. His eyes are fixed on mine, and it's a look I've definitely seen before. The one he gives Emma when they're shooting a love scene—soulful and intense.

Uh oh.

There's something bewitching about being on the receiving end of it. Like a sunset, or Jafar's snake staff from *Aladdin*. I can't look away, but at the same time, I'm deeply uncomfortable with the direction this has taken.

His hand comes up to the side of my jaw and I'm like a wild duck caught with a hunter—thinking that maybe if I stay really, *really* still, he will disappear.

But he isn't going anywhere. In fact, he's leaning so close that his fancy man perfume is invading my nostrils, and his face is going out of focus.

His lips connect with mine, and it all happens so fast I can barely think straight, let alone react.

A – a very attractive Hollywood film star is kissing me.

B – I have no interest in this Hollywood film star who is kissing me, and

C – someone is standing in the doorway.

Adam.

I push against Damon's chest, but I know it's too late.

Adam doesn't speak a word, but then again, he doesn't have to. His expression says everything. His eyes are dark and intense, and his mouth is in a straight line. But there's also something vulnerable about his appearance—a slight shudder in the way he draws in breath.

"We were just coming back in," I say, standing up. Our eyes meet and I try to hold his gaze; make him stop thinking all the things he's thinking. But his stare is cold.

He drops his eyes to the floor and shakes his head.

Damon goes to walk past, but Adam stops him with his hand. "I don't want any more of your shit on my set for the rest of the shoot, got it?"

Damon's eyes turn wild. "My *shit*?"

"Yeah, your shit."

They stare each other down before Damon laughs bitterly.

"I don't have to deal with this." He grabs his jacket and car keys from the counter. "I'm out of here."

And just like that, Damon is marching toward his Porsche, leaving Adam and I alone in his trailer.

28

I want to rewind to before this day. To when my only grievance was waiting a lousy two weeks to have a shot with the girl I like.

With the girl I *love*.

Because if I didn't know it before, I know it now. My feelings for Evie aren't fleeting or shallow. I love her. Which is made all the clearer by the sinking, twisting feeling in my stomach at the sight of her lips on another man.

On Damon fucking Reeves.

Watching him leave was satisfying. On a professional level, I should be freaking out. But the only thing I want right now is to never see his arrogant face again. I hear the engine if his Porsche come to life; the only sound that can be heard in the motionless innards of his trailer where me and Evie stand. Unmoving. Unspeaking.

"Adam... I know you're weirded out right now. But it wasn't what it looked like."

"It looked like you were kissing."

"I know." She tucks her hair behind her ear, and if I

didn't know better, I'd think she was blushing. "But that's not how it was."

"How was it then?" I ask, shrugging. "Were you choking on something? Was this a mouth-to-mouth situation I wasn't aware of?"

She frowns. "He kissed me."

"Ahh, of course."

"He did." Her tone is sharper now.

"And you tried to ward him off, obviously."

She flinches at my sarcasm, but I can't imagine how she's acting hard done by in this scenario. For weeks she's trailed me along, dangling the potential for us in front of me like a carrot, claiming her only hesitation came from not wanting to get involved with someone from the set. And then she does this.

Making out with the lead fucking actor?

I should have known. This is my own stupid fault, really. How could I have thought a girl like Evie Miller would still be interested in me when she had the option of some hunky douchebag? Same LA story, different version. People in this city claim to be more, to want more. But at the end of the day, they are only interested in one thing. Appearances. Having the best of the best and showing it off to the world, like it even matters. No one is sincere or deep. When it comes down to the punch, girls around here want the Damon Reeves of the world. And guys like me get cast aside —left to watch at the door like a fucking moron.

I turn to leave, but Evie stops me.

"You can't go. We have to talk about this."

"What's there to talk about?" I face her. "Damon made a pass at you, and you just let it happen. I'm sure it was awful, by the way."

Her eyes fall to the floor

"And by the sound of it, this wasn't the first time you've been in his trailer, alone."

"Excuse me?" Her eyes shoot to mine.

"Earlier, he said 'come by my trailer again'. It doesn't take a rocket scientist."

"You've got to be joking." She's smiling, but not her usual bubbly smile that brings out her freckles. This one is acidic, and it's honed right at me. "The last time I was here was when I was sent to fly him to set. I'm a PA for God's sake, I've been everywhere on this fricking lot."

I huff out my nostrils. Even if that's true, it doesn't change what I saw here tonight.

"Is that what you really think of me? That I'm some shallow idiot lusting after movie stars?"

"You were kissing!"

"He kissed me! I was trying to sweet talk him to come back to set, and he got the wrong idea. I didn't want to make him more upset!"

"Jesus, Evie. There's nice, and then there's too fucking nice. You didn't need to let him maul you because you didn't want to hurt his feelings."

"And you didn't need to chase him off set. Why are you acting like a Neanderthal? You do realize we're all up the creek without a paddle without him. Did you think of that before you lost your head?"

I almost have to stop myself from smiling. Even in a scenario when 'we're all fucked' is the appropriate response, Evie finds a sugary sweet way to describe it. The only time I've heard her curse was that night... in bed together...

But I can't let myself think of that. The memory is tainted now that we're here.

"I don't have to put up with his shit," I say. "Why does

everyone feel like they have to appease that idiot? This is my film!"

"Actually, you're wrong. This is all of our film. And now we don't have one to finish, because of you. What made you so angry?"

"Well seeing the girl I like tongue tied with an obnoxious asshole for a start."

"For the last time, it wasn't like that!"

"Maybe you were right about what people will think. Maybe you are just trying to hitch your wagon to the best horse. It just turned out you had a better option."

Her lips part, but she doesn't speak. I can tell by the strain in her eyes I've hit a nerve, and probably one I shouldn't have. But I can't stomach what's gone on here. Evie has confirmed all my worst fears about people in this fake, sorry excuse for a city. She is the one person I thought was above all that stuff; all the status and money. I thought she was *real*. But when it came down to it, she was just as susceptible to the flashy lights as anyone else.

And it's a good thing I've come to this realization, because it looks like I've lost her anyway.

"I think we're done here," she says, her voice just above a whisper.

She pushes past me and disappears into the darkness of the studio lot.

As I open my bleary eyes the next morning, reality hits me like a truck. It feels unnatural, lying in my bed after nine, when I would've normally been on set for three hours.

I texted Joel from Damon's trailer and told him to wrap the crew for the night. I didn't have the energy to go back into the sound stage and face everyone, so I snuck off to my car and drove away.

I'm still seething about Damon—his stupid face made appearances in my dreams all night. But deep down, I know I've let the team down by pissing him off. At least they made it through most of production with a paycheck though.

So far, I've successfully dodged calls from Dee, Eric and Simon, but I knew my luck could only last so long. Which is why I reluctantly agreed to a meeting with Eric and Simon when their tenth email came through.

Dee, I will face later.

I throw on a t-shirt and shorts and make my way to the coffee shop near my house. It's the only one I agreed to meet them at because it's close, and it also means I don't have to pass Bob. He would know straight away that something is up, and I don't want to talk about it. The 'it' being the fact lurking in the back of my mind.

There will never be a me and Evie.

I sat with the idea all night, tossing and turning. A couple of times I thought about texting her, checking in to apologize for what I'd said. But then the image would flood my brain again. Her lips. On Damon's.

She was so fast to shut down anything between us at the fear of getting caught, but then she happily let him be all over her like that? It didn't make sense to me. Which left me with one obvious conclusion.

Evie isn't the girl I thought she was.

I walk through the doorway and Eric and Simon are already sitting at a round table, with looks on their faces as dark as their espressos.

"Well, the shit has hit the fan," Eric says by way of a greeting. I sit down in my chair, exhaling. "You have to go talk to Damon."

"I'm not doing that," I say, pointing to Eric's cup of coffee when the server comes by.

"You have to," Simon exclaims. "We have no film otherwise."

I press my lips together. I do feel bad for him. Many scripts never make it to production, and his is so close to being actualized on screen. But I have to stand by my code.

Don't let assholes walk all over you.

"Damon is out," I say. "He made that clear last night. If he's going to throw a tantrum and leave, that is a problem for his manager, not me."

"Look, we all know Damon is a dickhead," Eric cuts in. "But this is for the greater good. We've already tried talking to him. He's still too furious to even consider coming back. At this point, the only hope we have is some good old fashioned groveling, and there's only one person he'll want it from."

"You're delusional if you think I'm going to get on my knees and beg that idiot to come back."

Eric and Simon share a look before Eric leans back in his seat.

"Then you can tell that to Nolan tomorrow at the studio."

For the walk home, I reflect on the dismal turn of events. I'd finally come around to the film, finally found my joy in directing again, finally found someone genuine that I might've had a future with...

And now look at everything.

The film we've all been working on for nearly three

months is circling the drain, and the girl I want isn't interested in me.

Not once in her entire defense did Evie say she wanted to be with me. Maybe she didn't pursue Damon. But she also didn't care about me enough to reject him.

I walk up the driveway and remember another dampener on my day: I'm going to have to face up to my crew and my friends.

Sooner than I expected.

"You didn't think you could avoid me forever, did you?" Dee is leaning against the side of my house, arms crossed over her chest.

"I'm not that lucky."

I unlock the door and she pushes past me, marching into my house.

"Please, come in," I say flatly, holding my arm out.

She takes a few steps inside before whipping around to face me.

"Would you like to tell me what the fuck is going on?"

"I'm assuming you heard the gist of it. Damon is out and the rest of production is on hold. Indefinitely."

"I don't want the gist of it," she barks. "I want to know what happened in that trailer. The last I knew, you were going to help Evie persuade Damon to come back, and next minute he is driving out of the lot, you disappear into thin air, and Evie looks like someone has died."

My stomach knots at the thought of her being upset. Because of me.

Or maybe it was because of her guilt.

I don't have the energy to beat around the bush, so I just come out with it. "I saw them kissing."

Dee's eyes widen. "You saw them kissing?"

"Yes."

"Damon and Evie?"

"No, Damon and the catering guy. Yes, Damon and Evie." I throw my house keys on the counter. "In his trailer."

"And did you ask her what happened, or did you just fly off the handle?"

"Of course I did. She said he kissed her. But honestly, it didn't look like she was trying to get away. Not till she realized I was there." I walk to my comfy chair and slump into it, rubbing my forehead.

"That's just your cynicism talking," Dee says, sitting on the couch. "If Evie says there was nothing to it, there was nothing to it."

"Right. Because making out with one of Hollywood's most lusted after actors was an accident."

Dee's eyebrows come together. "When did you get like this?"

"Like what?"

"So defensive. So sure that everyone and everything is out to screw you over."

"It's called life experience."

"No, it's called being a bitter old man. Seriously Adam, I've known you for a while now, and I thought you were getting better." She shakes her head. "It baffles me that a young man with so much opportunity can be so damn pessimistic."

I feel a heat swelling in my chest. Now Dee is making this my fault, too?

"I don't get why I'm getting the dressing down here. Evie went to great lengths to keep us separated as some noble attempt to protect her reputation. Yet she skulks around in trailers having secret make out sessions with film stars."

Dee's eyes round as she watches me. "Why do you insist on seeing the worst in people?"

I lean forward, staring at the floor.

"Because life isn't a fucking movie, Dee. And when someone shows you who they really are, you should pay attention."

Dee nods, her lips in a firm line.

"Wow, Adam... I'm sorry."

"Yeah, I know. It fucking sucks."

She stands up, folding her arms together. "No, I'm sorry because up until now, I thought your attitude was a fun quirk. But now I'm realizing it's the only thing stopping you from being happy."

I inhale sharply as she walks toward the door and disappears down the driveway, leaving me with a sinking feeling in my gut, and the giant cat portrait hanging on the wall.

"And I thought the stunt you pulled last time was bad enough. Now you're bullying the main cast off my set?"

I lean my ear closer to the door, careful to remain out of sight.

"I was hardly bullying him. He was being a little bitch," Adam retorts.

Production is back on with scenes that don't include Damon, but that can only last so long. Especially if he is never coming back. I snuck over to the production office when I saw Nolan and Adam go inside. Adam and I aren't even speaking, but I need to know what's going on.

Like if I have a job to come to tomorrow.

They've been arguing for the best part of five minutes, but so far, they are mainly shouting in circles.

"We all know Damon is a snowflake," Nolan says. "But as professionals, it's our job to appease talent like that. You think you're the first director who's had to deal with a diva?"

"I've dealt with divas. But Damon is a whole other level of entitled."

Adam's voice is low, and I can't help but draw my own parallels to his comment.

"What's going on here, Thorne? Do the two of you have personal beef or something?"

"Of course not."

"Well there has to be something going on. Otherwise you wouldn't be intent on destroying my film two weeks away from wrapping!"

"He was disrespecting me!" Adam roars. "He was disrespecting the whole crew! Wasting everyone's time! Guys like that don't deserve to be in the limelight if they won't do their fucking job."

"And *your* job is to work with people like him. For God's sake, suck it up!"

Adam growls and they go silent. I'm tempted to take a peek inside, but I can't risk getting caught.

I haven't seen or spoken to Adam since we argued in Damon's trailer. Also known as 'the worst night of all time'. I'd thought about reaching out to him, but every time I picked up my phone, his words rang in my head.

Maybe you're just trying to hitch your wagon to the best horse.

How could he even think that about me? Let alone say it. I get he was upset about Damon, but he knew me better than that.

At least, I thought he did.

I can't get the vision out of my mind. That crushed shock in his eyes. The way he looked straight through me, like I was a stranger. But he wouldn't even let me explain, wouldn't even listen to me properly. It was like he *wanted* to believe I was being shady.

"You have to go to him. You have to apologize; say whatever you have to say to make him come back," Nolan continues.

"Over my dead body."

"Does it look like I'm playing around? I swear to God, Thorne. You better make this right."

Nolan's tone is cutting, sharp as glass.

"Or what?"

I don't like where this is going, and I'm desperate to help. I do think that Adam overreacted, but it's obvious now that Damon bothered him even more than I realized. And I feel bad for my part in fueling the rivalry.

"Or I'll blacklist you across the entire industry." Nolan's voice is deep and menacing. "Every production company, every studio. Nobody will touch you. You can consider your career over."

"Kiss my—"

"Wait!"

I come through the door, making Nolan flinch.

"Miss, we're in the middle of a private conversation," he says.

"I know. And I have an idea that could make everything better."

I let my eyes drift to Adam. He looks tense, like the sight of me is causing him physical pain. I take a deep breath, trying to compose myself. I will have to deal with that later —one issue at a time.

Nolan raises his eyebrows at me. "This issue is a little above your pay grade."

"Let her speak," Adam says, holding up his hand.

I give him a weak smile before turning to Nolan.

"Gus."

"My name is Nolan."

"I know. But the idea . . . it's Gus."

"Who the hell is Gus?"

"Damon's stunt double," Adam cuts in, frowning.

"And he's the spitting image. Honestly, you wouldn't believe it," I say quickly, worried Nolan's going to boot me out of the office at any moment. "We've already shot all the scenes with dialogue. Now it's just some actions scenes and second unit won't be filming with Damon's character at all. It's perfect."

"Except for that stunt doubles aren't actors," Nolan says, sighing like I'm a little kid wasting his time.

"Except he is! That's the whole reason he came to LA."

"How do you know that?" Adam asks me.

"He told me."

Nolan drags his hand over his shaved head. "We can't just swap out actors with other actors for different parts of the film. I'm not producing a soap opera."

"The audience will hardly notice," I reply. "Seriously, you need to look at this guy."

Adam is still frowning, but nods his head. "She's right. We could get away with it for the final shots."

"Or, you could go and talk to Damon like I'm telling you to."

Adam exhales, burying his hands in the pockets of his shorts. "Honestly Nolan, it's this, or it's the end of *Primal Nature*."

Nolan glares at him, but I can tell by the way he swallows he knows it's his best option. He turns to me and puffs out his chest.

"Get this stunt double in here immediately. And tell him to bring his showreel."

∾

In all my talking him up, it didn't dawn on me that Gus may not actually want this. And I am realizing this now as he steps into the production office with sheer panic in his eyes.

"This is Gus," I say lamely, presenting him to the room. Which now includes Eric, Simon, and a woman from the casting department. Gus smiles nervously and holds his hand out to Nolan, who regards him with a crease between his eyes.

"What did I tell you? Uncanny, right?" I look up at our executive producer with a hopeful smile.

Nolan inhales and accepts Gus's hand. "Well, I guess you weren't lying."

"I'll take that as a compliment. Damon's a good looking bloke," Gus says.

Nolan smirks. "That accent is a giveaway. It's a good thing there's no dialogue left to shoot."

"Nothing that we can't bluff in post," Adam says. "Did you bring your showreel?"

Gus presents a USB with a tight smile and hands it to Adam, who plugs it into the Mac on the desk. I give Gus the double thumbs up, on account of he looks like he's about to pass out or pee his pants. Or both.

I just hope I haven't made it worse for everyone. It's only occurring to me now that maybe Gus didn't make it for a reason—maybe acting *isn't* his strong suit, and maybe we're all about to be deeply, deeply uncomfortable.

As his showreel plays, I slowly let the breath escape from my chest.

There is no reason to be worried.

Each clip is better than the next—mainly student films and tiny parts in features—but it's easy to see the guy has talent. There's a snippet from a short drama, a comedy, and a gritty crime pilot that never continued. When it comes to an end, the production office falls into silence. Gus looks at me through the side of his eyes, and I can tell he hasn't breathed in several seconds.

"Well..." Nolan says after the longest pause ever. "I don't see why we can't use him."

Adam nods. "I think it's our best option—"

"—if, you can stick to the current schedule."

Adam's jaw twitches.

"I mean it, Thorne. Not another day over schedule. And it's going to be clunky, working in a replacement. So you better find a way to whip the crew into gear, and fast."

Nolan turns to Gus. "Good luck. You're going to need it."

Gus returns his foreboding well wishes with a tight nod, and Nolan leaves the office. Eric and Simon scurry after him.

"Let's get you to hair and makeup. Make sure your cut is still consistent with Damon's," the casting director says to Gus.

As he steps out the front door he turns and flashes me with a grin, mouthing 'thank you'. And with that, everything is worth it. I beam as he walks to the hair trailer. But when I turn around, I'm reminded of the issue I haven't resolved. Which is standing awkwardly, not looking me in the eye.

So this is how it's going to be.

Rather than torture myself, I leave for the door.

"Evie?"

When I turn, Adam is finally looking at me. And dare I say, there is almost a smile on his face.

"I just wanted to say thank you for helping with Nolan," he says. "You didn't have to."

I shrug. "It's important to me that this film gets made. I'm happy to help where I can."

Adam nods, and it seems those are the only words I'm going to get out of him. I go to leave again, but stop myself.

"Do you think we could just call a cease fire? We don't have long to go. Can we just be civil and try to enjoy the last days of filming?"

He has his poker face on. The one he perpetually wore when I first met him, when it was impossible to tell what he was thinking.

"Sure," he says. "Call it a cease fire."

I smile on the side of my mouth and leave him in the office. I want so much more than a cease fire with Adam, but maybe this will have to do.

The gravel crunches under my feet, and I walk across the grounds to the sound stage. It's such a bright day, I don't see Kylie until she is two feet away from me.

"There are quite the rumors going around about you."

I frown and look back to see Adam step out of the office and look back to Kylie. "We were just watching Gus's showreel."

Kylie smirks. "You and Damon?"

Ugh. Of course. She's talking about me and Damon in his trailer.

I should have never gone after him.

"That was just a misunderstanding," I say, walking past her.

"You don't need to defend yourself to me. He's a handsome Hollywood star. Any girl would like to lock lips with that." She walks after me. "I guess I was just surprised, that's all."

"And why is that?"

"Because I thought you had a thing with Adam."

I stop and face her.

"Hey, you don't need to worry. I can keep a secret." She winks.

"I don't have a thing with Adam," I say. "And I would appreciate it if you wouldn't gossip about me."

She laughs, and heads toward the sound stage. "This is showbiz, honey. The sooner you accept that gossip is inevitable, the sooner you realize that your actions have consequences."

As I stand there squinting into the sun, I can't shake the feeling her words aren't pearls of wisdom.

They are a threat.

In all my years of directing, I've never felt so out of my depth.

The crew are gathered in the sound stage, but instead of setting up for our first shot of the day, they're waiting for me to tell them what the hell is going on. Morale is low, and you can see it in everyone's tired faces. It's not unusual to be exhausted this far into filming. But it's usually the light at the end of the tunnel that motivates the team for the home stretch. The promise of a great film, the chance to see your name scroll up in the credits at the first screening. Now, they have no idea what the fate of *Primal Nature* is.

But I have a deadline to meet, and an angry producer's promise that I will be blacklisted across the industry if I don't pull this off. I need my crew in top shape. And the group in front of me look like they've just witnessed a puppy getting flattened by an army tank.

I climb up to the second level of the set so I can see everyone and clear my throat.

"I know you're all wondering what's going on."

A few grumbles roll around the room. I suspect the news

about our leading man has gotten around by now, but I know I still need to make it official.

"I'm sure a few of you have already heard, and I'm sorry to confirm the rumors are true. Damon has left *Primal Nature*, and he isn't coming back."

Heads drop to the floor, a few people gasp, and a couple of younger female staff look like they might cry. I ignore the gnawing feeling in my stomach and move on.

"I know this comes as a shock to the production, especially being so close to wrapping."

"Wasn't he under contract?" Brian asks.

I rub my eyebrows. "Apparently his agent found a loophole. Damon is claiming abuse on set."

And this is the first time I see it—the resentment for me. Whether or not they think Damon is a tool, they know it was me who set him off. They blame me for this mess. And the worst part is, I can't even say they're wrong. I let my anger and jealousy get the better of me, and now my crew—the people who have worked hard for me for months—are paying the price. It's now my job to get them on board again, to ask them to have faith in me and help me pull this off. But that's eons out of my comfort zone.

Directing camera movements and dialogue delivery, I can do.

But this?

I search the room, looking for an answer, a sign, anything to help me with the task. And then my eyes settle on the face I need.

Evie.

I think back to our time in the movie theatre, the way she dug deep and helped me see the merit in my work. I think about the easy way she connects with people, not just me, but the whole damn crew. I think about how she knew

Gus's talents before I did, simply because she was curious enough to ask. She has a genuine interest in people; an understanding and enthusiasm that's intoxicating. Hell, she should be the one up here giving the speech. But I'm the director. I have to find a way to go from grumpy boss to motivational speaker.

I have to find a way to be inspiring.

Fuck.

"I know some of you might not be happy with me about the whole Damon thing," I go on. "And I'm here to tell you..."

Some of their faces flinch, like they're about to cop an earful.

"... you're right."

The demeanors around the room shift.

"Damon was a pain in my ass, but I could've dealt with him better. And I'm sorry I've stalled production. Especially after you've all been working so hard. I know I don't say this enough—or ever—but I appreciate you."

I catch Dee's eyes, and for the first time in days, she's smiling at me.

"The thing is, I need to ask you to keep up the hard work. As they say, the show must go on."

"So it's true then? You've found a replacement for Damon?" Jackson asks from the back of the crowd.

"We have." I shield my eyes from the lights on the ceiling so I can spot the person I need. "Gus, can you come up here?"

In a couple of limber movements, Gus is next to me on the second level, a coy smile on his face. I grab his shoulder, giving it a squeeze. "Team, you know Gus. He's our new leading man."

If I was concerned about the reaction to this news, I

didn't need to be. The crew greets Gus with cheers and grins. It appears he has more people in his corner than just Evie.

"We're going to shoot the rest of the film with Gus. With some clever camera work and a bit of CGI, we're confident we can pull it off. But we need your help."

I take a step closer to the edge of the set.

"We're still working to the same deadline, so we need to muster all our energy to get this done. I know I've let you down, and I know some of you don't even like me. I haven't always been the best leader, and I'm sorry."

I make eye contact with a few people, hoping they can see my sincerity.

"But I'm asking you now to trust me, to help me. If we're going to do this, we need all hands on deck. Each and every one of you has a job to do, and each of those jobs is important. You're all important. I know it's a big ask, but we can do this. I know we can do this. They say the sequel is never as good as the original, but..." I turn to Gus and pat him on the back. "I think they're wrong this time. The next week of shooting is not only going to be a success, but it's going to be great, for all of us."

I look back at the crowd, taking a deep breath in.

"So let's take *Primal Nature* out with a bang. Let's work our asses off and make this film something we can all be proud of. Who's with me?"

The crowd is quiet, and for a split second, I think this might be the most humiliating moment of my life. But then a gruff voice breaks through the silence.

"Fuck yeah. You can count on us, boss."

Everyone looks at Joel, taken aback by his sudden show of extroversion, and then they erupt. The crew cheers and claps, some people punching the air, some people nodding.

I'd usually be dying from the cheesiness of it all, if I wasn't so fucking relieved.

Just as I'm about to step down from the set, I catch a pair of big brown eyes on me. Evie, at the side of the group. Grinning at me from ear to ear.

Our first few shots with Gus are like a damn dream. It's almost comical how much more efficient he is than Damon. I'm wishing we had of just cast him from the very beginning as the lead role. Even his American accent isn't half bad.

I don't know if it's his talent, my speech, or the fact everyone already knows Gus, but the clunkiness Nolan was worried about feels nonexistent. The crew and Gus work together like sugar and water, dissolving into one. And I know exactly who to thank for all of it.

I'm sitting in the side office when I see her face peeking through the open door.

"Hey, I saw you come in here," Evie says, stepping tentatively inside. "Have a minute?"

"For the girl who saved the show?"

I point my hand toward the chair on the other side of the desk, and she takes a seat. "I'm not sure I'd go that far."

"I would."

We share a brief smile, but then it's like the cloud that's been following us around finds its position—directly over our heads.

So much has happened the last few days. And although it seems the film is back on track, the whole debacle has had its consequences. We may have made it out the other side, but we are battered. Bruised. I don't know if we are being civil, if we are friends. I don't know how I feel about us... or if the concept of us is just a distant memory.

She looks at the desk, biting her lip, and I wonder if she's remembering our last time alone in here together. Geez, to think we had problems then. I would give anything to go back to that time together, before everything got so... complicated.

"I wanted to say something to you," she says. "Now that we're back on speaking terms."

"Oh?"

I brace for it. What I'm bracing for, I can't be certain. An earful about my behavior? Another apology? I hold my breath, waiting for her to speak.

"I wanted to say I'm so proud of you."

A warmth creeps into the hollows of my body. "Of me?"

"The way you've turned this all around, what you said to the crew earlier. Adam, it's incredible. And I know how hard it must've been to stand up there and face everyone." She looks down at the desk. "And I know your dad isn't around anymore, so I thought someone should say it. I'm proud of you. You did great."

My chest swells and surges, like my heart has received a fresh influx of blood, rejuvenating and revitalizing my barren insides. Like I've been dormant and have just woken up. I look at the girl sitting across from me, staring at me with such sincerity in her eyes that I actually believe it. I've done a good job. I should be proud.

Everything is going to work out.

Having Evie in my life under any capacity is like a breath of fresh air. I don't know what the future holds for us, but I know I just want her around.

"Thank you," I say. And I hope she understands the depths of my gratitude.

She stands to leave, but stops at the door.

"And for what it's worth, I was never interested in Damon. It's you. It's always been you."

She steps out and I have the overwhelming urge to chase after her. To wrap my arms around her and kiss her soft lips. But I know that professionally, nothing has changed. She still needs us to keep our space, so I need to express my feelings in another way.

I pick up my phone to make a call but am sent to voicemail, so I keep it short.

"Eric. We need to meet about changing the credit for a member of the crew. I think they deserve more recognition. Call me."

"Someone getting a promotion?"

I jump at the voice, for a moment thinking Evie came back.

But it's Kylie.

"Hey, ahh... yeah, kind of."

She steps into the office and closes the door. I've barely spoken to this PA, but usually the closed door is a sign that someone wants to have a serious chat. She's probably disgruntled—I suppose there has to be some fallout for this whole fiasco.

"Who's it for?" she asks.

"Well... they don't actually know yet, so I probably shouldn't say."

"Is it for Evie?" She looks at me, smiling. "Don't worry, I can keep a secret."

I know I should wait until it's official, but she seems sincere. And it will get out, eventually. "Um... yeah. She's been instrumental in replacing Damon, and I think she deserves a production coordinator credit."

"Wow." Kylie nods. "I guess her hard work paid off then."

She stands from the chair, heading toward the door. I guess she's not disgruntled after all.

"Yep. She's definitely been a great member of the team."

Kylie laughs, her hand on the door knob. "That's not what I mean."

I walk around the desk. "What are you talking about?"

Kylie sighs, dropping her arms beside her. "Look, I respect Evie as a colleague, and I can't fault her for wanting to progress her career. But... I know she's been... *involved*, with members of the crew."

"If this is about Damon, that was just a misunderstanding."

And for the first time, I actually believe that.

"I know she wasn't interested in Damon," Kylie says. "She's just very good at making the rounds. Haven't you seen her rubbing shoulders with everyone?"

I frown.

"I guess she bit off more than she could chew with Damon," Kylie laughs. "Not that she would've been mad about it. I mean, who would be? A guy like that kissing you?"

She touches the sides of her short hair.

"I guess some people are easily fooled by her sunny exterior," she goes on. "But that's the thing about sunshine. It can be blinding."

I know she's talking about Damon, but her words sink into my stomach like lead.

"Not that I'm judging her or anything. I admire her ambition. Making everyone love her? She probably already has a job lined up for after this is over. And this industry needs that—more women with drive. And a girl who will stop at nothing to get what she wants? That's a force to be reckoned with."

She opens the door and steps out to the sound stage.

"I just hope she doesn't hurt anybody on her way to the top."

31

EVIE

Gus is a superstar. His timing is perfect. He picks up every direction with ease, and not once does he complain about harnesses or shoes or balls in his face.

He lands on his mark stuck to the floor, snapping his head up to the camera.

"Cut!" Adam calls. "That was great, let's move on."

The crew set up for the next shot, and I follow Adam to the other side of the set.

"He's doing so well, isn't he?!"

Adam's eyebrows bunch down, and he doesn't meet my eyes. "Yeah, he's a natural."

I expect a bit more enthusiasm, seeing as we made this whole change-up happen together. But it seems like ever since I stepped onto set today, Adam has been frosty. It's like we've been catapulted right back to after he saw Damon kissing me.

But we sorted through all that.

Didn't we?

Someone nudges me in the side and I turn to see Gus.

"Well look who it is. I'm surprised you still have time for me now that you're on your way to an Oscar."

He laughs. "For the girl who got me the gig? I have endless time."

"Well... at least one person likes me." I watch Adam sit in another chair, many feet away, despite the fact his director's chair is right next to me.

"Adam?" Gus follows my eyes. "He's just like that. I wouldn't worry too much about it."

I know there is no point talking to Gus about this. There's no way I could spill my secrets to him. And without knowing the full story, he can't understand.

But maybe there is someone I can talk to.

I look across the room and spot Dee, and without a second to reconsider, I march over to her.

"I need to talk to you."

She doesn't look up from her clipboard. "Shoot?"

"About Adam."

She looks up and appraises me carefully. Her expression tells me she may be a few steps ahead already.

"You know, don't you?"

"Come again?"

"Seriously, Dee... I know you know. About everything."

She stalls for a second, and then sighs. "I basically beat it out of Adam. Please don't be mad at him."

"I knew he would end up telling someone, and you're his best friend. I told mine." I can't begrudge Adam for confiding in someone he trusts. He is only human.

She nods. "He knew how important it was for it not to get out, and your secret is safe with me. I promise."

"I'm glad to hear, but actually... that's not what I wanted to talk about."

I pull her further to the side, away from prying ears

"Have you spoken to him since yesterday? I feel like he's mad at me... again."

"About the Damon thing?" She rolls her eyes. "He better not be. He filled me in on that too and I told him he had it all wrong. If you said nothing was in it, then nothing was in it."

"Right. And I thought we'd moved past it, but I don't know."

I look over to where Adam is sitting. I feel like he's purposefully stopping his eyes from drifting toward me. I always catch him staring, but this morning it's like he would rather look at Brian's butt crack than my face.

"He hasn't really talked to me in a few days. You know how he is... he doesn't exactly wear his heart on his sleeve," Dee says, raising an eyebrow.

This is the understatement of the century. I didn't even know Adam liked me until his penis was inside me.

"Here's the thing about Adam," she continues. "I've known him a few years now, and he's one of the most stubborn people I've ever met. He's bitter, he's cynical... he's got some proper angry old man energy going on."

I snort. "No kidding."

"But the truth is, it seemed like he was evolving since you've been around." She smiles. "You're a good influence on him, Evie. But I don't know... people get stuck in their ways, I guess. And no one changes overnight."

Could that really be all it is? He is just holding a grudge?

Seeing him sitting there with his shot list, I feel a deep, unrequited yearning in my stomach. I miss the man I went to San Diego with, the man who stuck up to my parents, the man I made love to in that hotel room. Adam was the first person to make me feel valued, to really see me for who I am.

Now he is acting like I don't exist.

Maybe Dee is right, maybe there once was something between us. But being around him now hurts. And still wanting him when he obviously doesn't want me anymore breaks my heart.

Maybe what they say is right—you can't have it all. I can chase my career and I can make new friends, but asking for love is too much. Wanting Adam at the end of all this is just me being greedy. And it's too late.

So there's only one option left. I can be like Dee, climb the ladder to success, and put my heart on the back burner. But what I realize now is that I can't do it around Adam, not for the rest of the shoot, not even for another day.

I sit down for lunch next to George and Joel, and I'm glad that Adam is nowhere to be seen. The less I see him, the better. Especially until I decide how I'm going to keep my distance while seeing through the rest of the film.

"Did you get what I left last night, George?" I ask, flicking through a noodle salad. "I was worried a raccoon might get to it first."

He laughs. "We sure did, sweetheart. Elsa loved it."

"Good, good." I smile down at my plate, still not putting anything in my mouth.

"Do you have any plans for work after we wrap?" he asks, sending a jolt of anxiety through me. With everything that has been going on, I've had no time to line up another job.

"No, not yet."

"Ah, not to worry. You'll pick up something in no time,

lovely girl like you." He shovels a forkful of pasta into his mouth.

Jackson sets his plate down opposite mine and digs in. It appears everyone has a healthy appetite except me.

"We may not see you kids around much, starting tomorrow," George goes on.

"Oh no, why not?" I look at him with rounded eyes. I'm already getting sad about saying goodbye to everyone. I'm not ready to start the farewells early.

"Moving over to second unit with Joel, so we'll be working in another sound stage."

Jackson leans closer to me. "Second unit film shots that don't include the principal actors. Establishing shots, exteriors, crowd scenes, that sort of thing."

I nod to appease him. I know what second unit do.

"So you guys won't be with the main crew for the rest of the shoot, huh?" I say, even less hungry now. George is one of my favorite people.

"Sadly, no," George says. "But don't worry, sweetheart, you'll get to have all the fun on the main stage. Gus is a dream to work with. Your last week will be great."

I wish he was right.

But at this point, I can't wait for production to be over. And I didn't think I could ever feel that way. Everything is a huge mess, and if I didn't know any better, I would say that mixing business with pleasure was a big mistake. But I do know better.

I know I could never regret my time with Adam.

No matter how sad I feel it's over, or how sick it makes me when he treats me like a stranger, I can't bring myself to take it all back. Adam gave me a taste of what it could feel like.

Love.

But it's done. Adam's done. And I can't bring myself to have one more conversation with him to try to make things right. He's made up his mind about me. That stupid incident with Damon has changed everything, and I can't change it back.

And not only that, but something has shifted in him. I saw it the day he made his speech to the crew. Adam's found his passion again, and he's finding a way to inspire others. I care about him way too much to let him lose it again… especially if it's my presence that drags him back down.

Maybe that's all we were ever meant to be—a catalyst for each other to get on the right path. Me, into a film career, and Adam to find his mojo. I did my job that day in the movie theater, and now it's done. Maybe we were always meant to help each other, and then go our separate ways.

I don't say this often—but fate is a real bitch.

The only thing I can try to control now is my job, and making the most out of the last week I have left. And as Joel gathers his plate and cutlery, I have an idea.

"Hey Joel?"

He looks across to me, wiping a napkin across his beard.

"You're the director for second unit, yeah?"

He nods. "Affirmative."

There is only one way to go.

"Need an extra PA?"

32

ADAM

The one benefit of this whole fuck up is that I can arrive to work and not want to shoot myself in the face. Gus is a professional; I don't know why his acting career hasn't taken off already. But don't even get me started on the biases of Hollywood. I would snub the whole industry if I could—if I didn't have to kiss its ass to make my living.

Getting Damon off the set was like the last piece of the puzzle falling into place. I remember what it's like to come to work filled with inspiration, and share it with people who want to work just as hard as I do. Working with the crew and Gus now fills me with hope of what my career might look like once this film is done.

What my personal life will look like is another story.

I can't ignore what Kylie said in the side office. Ever since she insinuated Evie was a ladder-climbing mastermind, I can't bring my guard down.

I'm a private kind of guy, and I like to play things close to the chest. But that doesn't mean I'm not in tune with what's going on around me. I like to consider things carefully, gather all the information I need, and act accordingly. And I can't help but acknowledge that what Kylie said rings true. Evie *is* a social butterfly among the crew, always chatting and being friendly with people. And there is no crime in being likeable in the hope that it might score you more jobs. It's actually a great tactic. But Kylie doesn't realize what she shed light on. Maybe Evie isn't just working the crew, maybe she was manipulating *me*, too. After all, it's not like Kylie knows what was going on between us. She didn't know she was inadvertently sticking Evie in the shit.

But I need time. Time to figure out what Evie's deal is.

"Okay, again from the top."

Unfortunately, I also have a film to direct and a producer breathing down my neck.

"Does anyone have a sharpie? I need to mark something," I ask.

A few members of the crew pat their pockets, shaking their heads. Maybe she is using me to climb the ladder, but I know I can count on Evie now. She is like an extra bubbly Inspector Gadget, ready with any plausible device I might need. "Evie?"

"Evie's not here," Dee says, frowning. "Don't you know?"

"What do you mean? Where is she?"

"She's working with second unit for the rest of the shoot," Brian cuts in.

"Oh." Well that was... abrupt. And what am I, the last person to know?

She just left the main crew without saying anything to me?

"Here," Jackson says, panting and holding out a sharpie. "I just got this from the production office."

"Thanks."

I go on with the shot, but can't shake the feeling of Dee's eyes on the back of me the whole time, watching me like I'm about to spontaneously combust. So Evie has left the main crew without saying anything to me. No big deal. And maybe it's good she's not here. Maybe a bit of space is what we need.

Eventually we wrap for lunch, but I decide to stay back on set. I've been avoiding the lunch tent lately. Partly to get some extra work done, and partly to avoid seeing those big brown eyes. It's hard enough to keep my head straight without seeing Evie's face.

Yes, Evie leaving the main crew is definitely a good thing.

"You seemed surprised earlier."

Dee walks around the corner, finding my hiding spot.

"Of?"

"Don't play dumb. Of Evie transferring to second unit."

I shrug. "If she'd rather be over there, I don't have a problem with it."

"Oh cut the shit," Dee snaps. "I know you've been freezing her out. Are you seriously still hung up on that Damon bullshit?"

"I'm not hung up on anything, especially fucking Damon. And who said anything about freezing her out?"

"She did."

A pause. So I guess they are chummy now...

I sigh. "I'm just trying to figure a couple things out."

"What's there to figure out?" Dee throws her arms out. "You like her and she likes you. What the hell are you dragging your feet for?"

"But she may not like me for the right reasons."

Dee pulls a face, prompting an explanation.

"She's an ambitious girl," I continue.

"So?"

"So, maybe her motives aren't as pure as they seem. And

before you get all up in my face, I'm not just making this up."

"Okay, then where are you getting this stupid idea from?"

I stand up defiantly, putting my hands on my hips. "Kylie."

"*Kylie?*"

Someone talks through Dee's earpiece and she huffs, listening in for a moment and then talking into her shoulder. "I don't know. Come to set. He's here."

She looks back at me and shakes her head. "Men are so fucking dumb."

"Excuse me?"

"Kylie *hates* Evie. Why would you believe anything she has to say? And better yet, why would you believe her over Evie, the girl you've actually spoken to for more than five minutes?"

She keeps shaking her head, muttering under her breath. "Kylie told you... stupid ass..."

I bury my brow in my nose.

Kylie hates Evie?

While my brain tries to play catch up, Jackson appears in front of us.

"Sorry to interrupt. The Millers just called the production office. They want to confirm their visit tomorrow?" He looks at me, puzzled.

The Millers. I totally forgot.

"Tell them it's confirmed, and when they arrive, send them to the second unit sound stage. Tell Joel they have my approval."

Jackson disappears and Dee is again distracted by her shoulder mic. She rounds me up before she leaves, pointing a finger at my chest.

"I have to go, but you need to sort your head out. Before it's too late."

I do need to sort my head out. But what I need more is a beer. I was glad when George accepted my invitation to grab a drink after work, so I didn't have to be that sad loser, sitting at the bar alone.

My mind is swimming.

I want to go with what Dee said, just forget my conversation with Kylie. But there is more going on than just that. It seems like every new turn we take, some other issue pops up, like some fucked up monster re-growing heads every time we cut one off. The need to keep us a secret, the need to stay just friends, a sleazy actor, a conniving opponent.

Are relationships supposed to be this fucking difficult?

"Cheers," George says, holding his beer in the air.

"Cheers."

We both take a long gulp, mine longer. I just want to take my mind off everything.

"How are things going, George?"

"Ahh, you know, I'm still trucking along," he says, appraising the label on his beer.

I nod. "And Elsa?"

"She's responding well to her new treatment, so that's something."

"Sure."

"Her pain still isn't great though, she has trouble with her hands." He extends his fingers, then balls them into a fist. "Gets in the way of her crafts."

"I'm sorry to hear that." I press my mouth into a line. "We don't have to talk about it if you don't want."

Surprisingly, George smiles. "I'm learning that talking about it is better than keeping it all bottled up." He faces me. "A little birdie taught me that."

I frown, and take another swig of my beer, unsure if I'm meant to understand who he's referring to.

"It's funny how different couples are together," he goes on. "Me, I'm the practical one. When Els got sick the first time, I said don't worry, we'll sort out a treatment plan. Everything will be okay. And it was... for a while."

He takes another swig of beer.

"When it came back the second time, I was straight back to the treatment plan. If it worked the first time, it would work now. And do you know what she said to me?"

I shake my head once.

"She said George, I want to go skinny dipping."

I nearly choke on my beer.

"And we did!"

He roars with laughter, and I try to squash the visual of a naked George frolicking in the waves.

"She sounds like she has spirit," I chuckle.

"Oh, she does, in spades. She thinks we spend too much time trying to control everything, that sometimes you just need to let life take over."

His smile fades.

"I know she's only getting treatment now because I want her to."

I watch as he scratches at the label on the bottle. Happily married for so many years, they'd made it through thick and thin.

"Can I ask you a question?"

"Sure?" He looks across at me.

"How did you know you and Elsa were right for each other?"

He laughs, the smile returning to his mouth. "That's easy. I married my best friend."

"And it hasn't been hard?"

"Every marriage has its ups and downs." He looks up at the beach painting on the wall, like he's watching the waves roll in for real. "But being with Elsa is as easy as breathing. It just feels natural to be together."

He pulls out his phone, grinning at the screen.

"She's a sweet girl, isn't she?"

"Elsa?" I ask, bunching my eyebrows.

"Evie." He waves his phone in the air. "Elsa just texted saying she's dropped around another lasagna for dinner, so I don't need to pick something up on my way home."

"Evie dropped around dinner for you guys?"

"Sure. She's been dropping stuff off for weeks. Main meals, cookies." He stuffs his phone in his pocket. "She's something, isn't she? Not many people think to do that... it's those little things that help in tough times."

As George drains his bottle, I know it's no longer a question. Evie is that girl, the sweet, considerate, bubbly girl she always seemed to be. Damon made me question it, and so did Kylie, but I saw through it... eventually. My feelings for her are based on truth. She *is* being real with me.

But is it easy?

I bring the bottle to my lips, knowing that my deliberation has to come to an end, just like this beer will. And maybe my answer is right there; maybe you shouldn't have to deliberate in these situations. Maybe being with the right person should be natural, a choice that's as straightforward as choosing to brush your teeth in the morning.

I have real feelings for Evie, feelings that developed because she is genuine and quirky and amazing.

But easy?
It is not.

I've done it. I'm officially a member of the second unit, and it feels...

Weird.

It's less pressure; no principal actors, no complicated action scenes. And I don't have to weather Adam's cold shoulder. I can just show up, do my job, and go home. Simple. Uncomplicated.

But it's not the same.

Call me crazy, but I miss Adam's grouchy voice. The way he sarcastically snaps at people when they make a dumb mistake. I miss Brian being a creep and Dee shutting him down. I miss Jackson's annoying 'fun film facts'. I miss the excitement and not knowing what's going to happen every day. But I have to stop crying about it. That's not what being in this industry is about. It's about being able to pay your rent doing something you love, and I can. I should be grateful.

We're setting up for an establishing shot of the exterior of the vet clinic. Joel glides through the shots easily. He and

Adam are similar in some ways—both men of few words—but Joel has a gentle giant nature about him.

Having a smaller crew in second unit means I get more hands-on experience. I walk next to the camera during dolly shots, making sure the cables are out of the way, help out with props. Today the clapper is sick, so I get to handle the slate. It's sounds dumb, but I've always wanted a shot at this. Clapping the slate feels like a rite of passage when breaking into the film industry, no matter what your specialty is.

I try to focus on these little novelties, rather than let my head get caught up elsewhere. The film will be over in a few days, and I'll wish I hadn't been sitting around pining over a guy.

"Evie?"

I turn around and am surprised to see Jackson in the sound stage and not with the main crew.

"You have some visitors."

I look past him and the breath catches in my throat.

"What are you doing here?" I blurt.

"Adam said it's fine," Jackson continues. "They were invited."

He turns and walks away, leaving us alone.

Me.

And my parents.

"What...? How...?"

"This is quite the setup, isn't it?" my dad says, brushing past my utter shock. "These buildings look even bigger inside than they do outside."

He looks up at the bright lights connected to the ceiling.

"Sound stage," I manage to speak.

"Huh?"

"The building, it's called a sound stage."

"Ahh." He smiles. "Very good,"

I look at Mom, who still hasn't made a peep. She clutches her handbag like one of the creature performers might scamper past and snatch it out of her hands.

"Why are you here?"

"We were invited," she says, like I'm insinuating they would just show up out of the blue. "Your friend called us."

"My friend?"

"The chap you brought over for dinner," my dad says. "Aaron."

"*Adam*?"

Adam invited my parents to the set?

Why?

"Yes, Adam. It's not like you've brought any other men to meet us." Mom does her fluttery laugh.

"Evie, we're going to run through the fire hydrant shot," Joel calls.

"Okay, I was just..." I look at my parents, wondering what to do with them, half hoping they'll disappear as quickly as they showed up.

"They can watch from the sides. Adam okayed it," Joel confirms.

Adam okayed it?

What the heck is going on?

I stumble over to the camera, picking up the slate as I go, and stand in position in front of the lens.

"Twenty-five, beta, take one."

I clap the slate down and walk out of shot, looking over to my parents and biting the insides of my mouth. A creature performer runs into the frame, screeching and making ape-like sounds. He grabs the fire hydrant and tries to shake it, beating and swatting at it aggressively. On cue, it falls to the side, sending a spray of water into the air. The camera dollies to the side with me in front, gathering the cables as it tracks. We stop right in front of the creature performer, who stands on his bent legs, screaming triumphantly, before Joel yells, "Cut! That was perfect everyone, no need to go again. Let's get this water cleaned up and move on."

We go through several more shots, and the whole time my mind is hyper aware of the pair sitting in the corner, watching... waiting...

They probably think this is all ridiculous, playing with cameras and fake monkeys and water explosions. I don't know why Adam invited them—he doesn't seem like the kind of person who would force a reunion between estranged family members.

Especially with how the last one went.

An hour later, we're ready to break for lunch, and I drag my feet to the chairs where my parents are sitting. I can only imagine how they'll compare me helping people with their costumes and picking up empty water bottles to being a doctor.

I guess I'm about to find out.

As I approach, they stand up, my mom still clutching her handbag. "Well... I'm not sure what to say," she says.

"Whatever it is, you might as well be out with it."

"That was..." Dad looks around the sound stage. "Incredible."

"I *know* you don't approve and you think this is all stupid, but... wait, what?"

"It's wonderful, Evie," he says, holding the outside of my shoulders. "Really."

My mouth drops open as I look at Mom.

"I had no idea..." she gazes into my eyes, shaking her head "... what goes on here, the people involved. It really is special."

"I'm sorry, I think I need to sit down." I rub my head

Dad laughs. "Darling, we owe you an apology. We thought you were lost, confused... making a mistake when you walked away from medicine."

"Yes, I've heard."

"But we were wrong." Mom grabs my hand. "Seeing you here today, in your element... we get it now." She smiles. "It's not easy to get on board when your brilliant daughter says she's up and leaving her life for Hollywood. But your friend was right, we just had to see it."

"That's why Adam invited you? So you could watch me do my job?"

"He called a couple of weeks ago to apologize for how the dinner turned out, but said we ought to see what you'd been up to out here," Dad says. "Organized a driver, a fancy hotel, all of it."

My vision goes out of focus.

Adam orchestrated this whole thing.

"I'm sorry it's taken us so long to say but," Mom wraps her arms around me. "We're so proud of you, Evie."

"You've done great." Dad puts his hand on my head, fuzzing the top of my hair.

I swallow past the lump in my throat and slowly unfold my arms from my chest. I reach out for Dad, wrapping one arm around him, one around my mom.

"Thank you."

"Why are you not racing to his house and jumping him right now?"

Sylvia was nearly hyperventilating when I filled her in.

"Because he organized it a couple of weeks ago, before everything turned upside down."

"So? The man called your parents—who are intimidating as hell, by the way—and arranged this whole thing so you could have a shot at a relationship with them again. Who cares what's happened since then? The writing's on the wall."

"Oh yeah? And what writing's that?"

"That he's in love with you, obviously."

I swallow my wine. "You don't know that."

My phone pings on the floor and I open my emails.

Sylvia rolls her eyes. "Are you seriously going to let the fear of people talking about you get in the way of this?"

"Holy cow."

"What?"

I look up at Sylvia and pass my phone to her. She reads off the screen. "Hey Evie. Not sure what your plans are for after we wrap, but I've got a directing gig on an indie film. Not as big as PN, but decent pay. I've put you forward for a PA position. They said they'd be happy to have you. Joel." She looks at me. "You got a job?"

"I got a job," I parrot, my eyes wide.

They said it would happen like this... that I'd meet people, get more work through connections. It's happening. I'm not just going to be a one hit wonder.

It's actually going to work out.

"If that's not a sign, I don't know what is," Sylvia says.

"A sign for what?"

"To go after Adam! What's holding you back now? You've found more work which has nothing to do with him. You can be together, and no one can say anything about it!"

I sit back, grabbing my wine glass and swishing the contents. She's right. My work with Joel I got on my own merit, and the film is basically done. There's nothing stopping me and Adam from picking up where we left off.

Except everything.

"There's just too much water under the bridge."

I tip the glass toward my mouth, letting the wine soak into my tongue. And I keep tipping until the glass is empty.

"We had our chance. I think it's time to move on. This is the right thing to do, for everyone."

Sylvia leans back on her hand, watching me with creases in her perfect forehead.

"Then why do you look so sad?"

34

The last week of shooting always goes the fastest. It seems like only a second ago that Gus stepped in to take Damon's place, but the next thing I know we are wrapping on our second last day of filming and I'm on my way home.

The air has turned cooler, but it's not cold. It never gets cold in LA, and anyone who thinks it does is an idiot. As I reach my condo, I'm overcome with that same feeling I've been having the last couple of months—that I don't want to go in there and spend the rest of my night. Alone.

I go inside, just long enough to go to the refrigerator and grab a carry bag.

The houses along the street have swapped their Halloween decorations for Thanksgiving ones—clusters of pumpkin and squash, maple leaves, turkey statues. I don't get the showiness of it all. Why do you need to decorate the outside of your house, only to see it for two seconds when you walk through the door? But that's LA for you. The 'look at me' culture is as free flowing as the Botox injections.

"Great, I'm starving," is all Bob says as I approach him, passing him a stack of containers.

"Tomorrow's the last day of leftovers. Maybe you'll finally take me up on the offer of pizza at my place."

Bob grunts. "You've never invited me over."

I crease my forehead. He's right. I've never invited him over. Probably because I know the invitation would just make us both feel uncomfortable. But it's getting harder to accept Bob's rejections of help, except for boxes of leftovers and the odd ten dollars to buy a sandwich. I haven't cared about many people in my life, but the thought of Bob out here throughout the night bothers me.

"But you know where I live, right?" I say, twisting the top of my bottle.

"I've walked past it, once or twice."

I nod, taking the beer to my lips.

A couple of disheveled youths walk by, yelling and swearing. One of them barks something incoherent at Bob and the youths both laugh, stumbling down the path, off their heads.

"You must get tired of being around all that," I say.

"Eh, they're harmless."

"Yet they chased you away from your original spot."

He leans forward, scratching at his bare ankle. "Better here than in the trenches."

I snort. "I don't think war and homelessness should be your only two options."

"Yeah? What do you know about it?"

I normally wouldn't push him this far, but a voice in my head tells me I shouldn't back down. A voice that isn't mine. A female voice that says when you care about someone, you help them with their problems.

"I know you're an old fart who shouldn't be sleeping on the sidewalk."

A laugh rumbles out of Bob's chest, deep and crackly. "I'm Burt Reynolds compared to you."

"There's a reference with a little dust on it." I laugh with him. "I bet those youths that give you grief don't even know who Burt Reynolds is."

With the tension dissolved, I reach into my shirt pocket.

"The thing is, I have this squirrel problem."

"Get a pellet gun."

"I was thinking it would be easier if I had someone around to scare them off." I place a key on the blanket next to him. "See, they're in my granny flat out in the yard."

Bob looks at the key and up to my face. "And do I look like a granny to you?"

"Kind of."

We both laugh.

"It's empty in there, a stupid waste of space." I take a swig of beer. "You'd basically be doing me a favor."

"I know what you're doing," Bob grumbles.

"Yeah? And is it working?"

He chuckles and scratches at his beard before answering. "I'll think about it."

I wonder if he actually will think about it, but then his hand moves over the key, and he puts it in the little zippered pouch he keeps attached to his belt. The one that contains all his important possessions. I smile into my bottle.

"Whatever happened to your girl?" he says, changing the subject.

I've filled Bob in on bits and pieces of the Evie saga. I couldn't talk to anyone from the film—Dee gave me a lecture whenever her name was brought up—and Bob is basically the only other person I spend time with.

"I think it's done."

As I say the words, they drift down my core and settle at

the pit of my stomach, hard like cement.

"Why?"

I exhale hard out of my nose.

That's the million-dollar question. Why throw away a connection like ours? The thing is, I've thought a lot about my conversation with George, and everything that's happened the last few months. My feelings for Evie haven't changed—she is the most incredible woman I've ever met. But it's always complicated with us, and relationships aren't meant to be like that. As easy as breathing... that's what George said.

I sigh, leaning back on my forearm and tapping the side of the bottle with my fingertips.

"It just got too hard. And we're done with filming after tomorrow. I might not even see her again. Maybe once at a screening. I just feel like... maybe there's a reason it fell apart. Why push it, ya know?"

I take a long sip, looking out at the street in front of us.

"I think of your life, and how it's simple. And I want that too... straightforward, no dramas." I look at Bob with a half-smile. "Let the chips fall as they may."

Bob finishes his beer and tosses the bottle to the side. He picks up a fork to dig in to his dinner. But then he points it at me.

"Now listen here, you little shit."

His tone is so stern that I sit up, my eyes honed on him and the fork pointed at my chest.

"For years I've known you now. You come here after a long day, grumbling about the stupid people you work with, annoyed at the posers and phonies in this town. And then you meet a beautiful girl who makes you happy, and you're running away like a scared little boy."

"Hang on a second," I say, putting my beer down. "No

one is running anywhere."

"You talk about how people suck, about how you'd rather be by yourself, but I know you're a lonely old bastard in that house all alone. Why else would you hang out with an old codger like me on the street?"

"Because we're friends," I say, but his words pinch a nerve in my chest.

"Then as your *friend*, I'm telling you to stop being a moron. You need to go to that girl and tell her how you feel."

"I can't do that."

"Why the hell not?!"

"Because I'm scared!"

Our sudden outbursts send us into an awkward silence. I pick at the grass and Bob shakes his head, reaching for the satay noodles.

But it's true.

I'm scared shitless.

Ever since I saw Evie with Damon in his trailer, I've been terrified. Even after I found out it was a misunderstanding, it was too late. It triggered something in me. That feeling of not being good enough, of not measuring up. That fear of failing... of opening myself up to someone who actually had the power to break my heart.

Kimberly was right. I never made myself vulnerable to her. Not once. Not to anyone I've ever been with. Evie was the first girl to make me *want* to give in... to consider the idea of giving my heart away. She was the first person to see right into my soul, and not only that, but she liked what she saw. The way she smiled at me, the way she held me in that hotel room. I knew I could be hers... if I just let myself.

But then I saw her with Damon, and my walls went up... iron strong and twelve feet high. Even the idea that I could let her down, that I wouldn't be enough, that she would look elsewhere... it scares the shit out of me. Because I don't know how I could recover if I had her for real... and lost her.

"Listen, boy," Bob says after a long pause. "I never had any kids of my own, but let me give you some fatherly advice."

He puts the container down, wiping his hands against each other.

"I know you pretend to be fine alone, but it's a long old life. Take it from someone who's been alone for most of his."

He removes his trucker cap, so I can see his full face properly. Deep wrinkles line his skin from countless life experiences, many he went through on his own.

"When you get to my age, it's not the things you said or the risks you took that you regret. It's the things you didn't say, and the chances you didn't take. Now I know you have what you need... a job, a home. But it don't mean squat without someone to share it with. It's time to find your balls and go tell her how you feel."

I look at his icy blue eyes.

"What if it's too late?"

"That's what being brave is all about! You don't know what the outcome will be, you just have to jump, and hope for the best. That's what letting the chips fall really means. Giving it your best shot and then letting it be."

My heart is thudding away in my chest. Bob is right. I don't want to end up bitter and alone. Maybe it's complicated between me and Evie, but it's worth a shot. And fuck easy.

Some things are worth fighting for.

"I need to make a call," I say, standing up.

"Eh, go on." Bob waves me off, returning his attention to the next container.

I walk a few feet away and pull out my phone, bringing

up the number I need. And all the while, my mind is racing.

I've been playing it safe in my personal life, and look how far it's got me. I'm always the guy who doesn't say how he feels, who shies away from anything cheesy, or extra, or over the top. I hate showiness. But finally convincing Bob to accept help and move into my granny flat has showed me something; that sometimes you just need to push a little harder, be assertive, put your cards on the table.

Sometimes you need to come out, guns blazing. And if you get shot down?

At least you damn well tried.

I bring the phone to my ear and hold my breath as it rings.

"Well, look who it is."

Dee's signature sassy voice emits through the speaker.

"Hey, I need to talk to you."

"We're all on track for tomorrow, right?"

"This isn't about the film."

Dee is quiet on the end for a moment, before she says "Ahhh... I think I know what this is about." She chuckles. "Go on, you can say it."

I sigh. I knew I wasn't going to get through this without a little punishment. "You were right, Dee. About everything."

"That a boy," she says, and I can almost see her smug smile through the phone. "And?"

I roll my eyes. "And... I need your help."

"That's what I like to hear," she says, a grin in her voice. "All right. What's the game plan?"

The sun is barely in the sky when I arrive at the studio for my last day. I got a message last night to come an hour earlier to help with a last-minute set problem, but it appears I'm the only lucky one recruited, as there are hardly any cars here yet.

I step out into the parking lot, adjusting my sunglasses. It's not bright enough for shades, but that's not why I need them. I haven't slept a wink, and my eyes are tired and puffy, exhausted from the last twelve hours.

Sylvia was right. I'm sad. And not because it's my last day on this set.

It's my last day with Adam.

In the last three months, we've gone from strangers, to colleagues, to friends... lovers... to fighters, to friends again, and now we are here. No-man's-land. Too much history to be strangers again, but not friends either. I obviously hurt him more than I knew with Damon, and there is no going back. I've weathered his frostiness and given us space, and now it's over.

But then there was the thing with my parents.

I pull out my phone, looking at the last text my mom sent me. It's a picture of the three of us; her, me, and my dad, arms around each other and smiling, standing out the front of the sound stage. George took it for us before they left for San Diego.

I can never thank Adam enough for what he did for me. He reached out to my parents, basically strangers, and made them understand my passion. He brought us together again.

How could he do that for me, but still treat me with such indifference?

I head toward sound stage five, where I'm helping out this morning. I just need to not think about it. Maybe Adam cared about me once, but things are different now. His feelings have changed, and there is nothing I can do about it. If I've learned anything in my years of being friendly and bouncy and positive, it's this.

You can't make someone love you.

I push through the door and close it behind me.

And I'm enveloped in darkness.

"Hello?" I call out. Did Dee send me the wrong sound stage number? I thought it strange at the time. We haven't used number five the whole time we've been shooting. I actually thought they were shooting a fantasy film in this space.

"Is anyone in here?"

There's a clunking sound and the room comes to life, but it's difficult to see at first, because of the haze floating in the air.

"Did someone leave a smoke machine on?" I say, stumbling through the mist and batting it away with my hands. And then I see the set.

There's just one set in the whole sound stage, and it's sitting right in the middle.

It's a wonderland.

Enormous trees come up from the floor, covered in moss and entwined with sparkling lights. Vines dip and drape between them, zigzagging up to the ceiling which is covered by the mossy canopy, drops of tiny crystals and twinkling beams suspended in the air. The fake forest floor expands all the way to a waterfall, trickling with actual water and surrounded by boulders almost bigger than me. There are toadstools, exotic looking flowers, all illuminated by the most beautiful filtered light, coming from all different directions. In the background, there is even music... a delicate harp and chirping birds. The smoke settles around my ankles and the scene is so beautiful, it takes my breath away.

But it's not a scene from *Primal Nature*.

What the heck is going on?

I look around, trying to find another human. "Am I being punked? Is this a prank?"

I hear a chuckle from the side of the room, and someone walks out of the darkness.

Adam.

"I was thinking of more an apology."

His flannel shirt is rolled up around his forearms, the way it always is. And as the day goes on, he will realize it's too hot for flannel and take it off, wearing only the white t-shirt he wears underneath. If I got close enough, I would be able to smell his man shampoo, and see the creases at the corners of his eyes, the ones that become more pronounced on the chance I make him smile. If I extend my hand to his face, it will be scratchy around his jaw, the same kind of scratchy I felt against my forehead as I nuzzled into his chest that night.

I know every inch of this man, and I've been spending the last week trying to forget it all.

But that was before he was looking at me.

Like *this*.

"Hi," he says.

"Howdy."

I'm too overwhelmed to think of a more appropriate response.

He laughs. And there are those eye crinkles. "Will you come with me?" He holds out his hand, and I take it. It's like a magnet, there is no use refusing. We walk onto the set, which only becomes more amazing inside. I almost feel like I'm in a real forest.

It's a fricking fairytale.

"What's going on?" I finally say, turning to face him. "What is all this?"

"It's my way of saying sorry."

"This is how you say sorry?" I snort. "Wait, what are you sorry for?"

Adam smiles and grabs my hands, and that's when I know he's nervous. He's trembling.

"Are you okay?"

He grins at me. "Classic Evie, always concerned about everyone else."

"Well, your paws are a bit clammy there, son," I say, wiping one of my hands on my shorts. "What, did you join a gang since we last spoke? Shoot a man and throw him with the fishes?"

"Will you just let me talk?" he laughs. "I wanted to say sorry... for everything. I'm sorry for not believing you straight away with Damon, I'm sorry for listening to Kylie, I'm sorry for freezing you out—"

"Kylie? What—"

"—it doesn't matter now. Just... I'm sorry. I'm not good at

this... interpersonal stuff. I don't know how to react, and I don't know how to talk about my feelings."

"Okay..." I say, frowning, and still very confused. "So, you brought me to fairyland?"

Adam drops one of my hands, but keeps the other one entwined in his. We walk like that through the set, the fake moss soft under our feet.

"I wanted to show you I can do this. All this... *expression* stuff. Maybe cheesy isn't so bad." He picks a tulip, which is pulled from the fake ground, almost like a real flower. "Maybe it's time I tell you how I really feel."

He turns and faces me, holding out the flower.

"Evie Miller, you're incredible. You're crazy and goofy and smart and beautiful, and I think you might be the kindest, most real person I know. I genuinely didn't think humans like you existed, but here you are."

He drops his head to the floor, but then smiles.

"Wearing your bright yellow rain boots in Los Angeles where it literally never rains."

"They're cute," I squeak, which is all I can manage right now.

He inhales, his chest rising underneath his flannel.

"I'm sorry for being an idiot these past couple of weeks. I should've known you better... but to be honest, I think it's *because* I knew you better I made excuses to put a wedge between us."

He looks at me with pain in his eyes.

"Why?" I whisper, my chest heavy with trapped air.

"Because I think you're perfect. And getting a chance with you and then losing you... I think it would kill me." His deep brown eyes bore into mine. "But I don't care about that anymore, because I know I'd be a moron to risk never knowing how it might've turned out. I can see myself spending my life with you, Evie. I can see you living in my empty condo, with all your colors and your terrifying cat portrait."

I laugh, wiping a tear from the corner of my eye.

"I love you. I've *been* in love with you. And I think you should know."

"Well..." I clear my throat, taking a deep breath "... I appreciate you telling me."

I drop his hand.

And walk across the set.

"What?"

I turn back and see the look on his face, and burst out laughing.

"I'm only kidding, you goofus!"

I run back to him and jump into his arms, wrapping my legs around his waist to get as close to him as physically possible. Our mouths crush together, and his hands tighten around my waist. I break my lips away, just long enough to say what I need to say.

"I love you too, you big old grump."

He laughs and I see a tear roll down his cheek, and I kiss him again. And somewhere inside me, I know I would be happy kissing him every day for the rest of my life.

8 months later

I look up at the big square archway and have to pinch myself.

Holy cow, I'm actually here.

Everywhere I turn, I see a new celebrity, smiling at the paparazzi and making their way inside to watch the film.

Our film.

A huge banner hangs under the arches, a flaming depiction of our leading man and a bunch of CGI animals. It's Gus in the picture, and he looks every bit the shining star. Damon has dropped off the face of the earth since his meltdown, which was uploaded by one of the makeup assistants and went viral. I don't blame him for hiding.

Iron fencing blocks the area off, guarded by muscle men who watch the screaming, cheering fans on the other side.

This is it. We worked hard and stayed overtime on set and now we are here, enjoying the glitz and the glamor of showbiz. People are finally going to see what we made, and

I. Can. Not. Deal. I'm so happy, I want to freak out right here on the red carpet.

But I can't do that.

Because I'm a professional.

"You're doing that goofy break dance move in your head, aren't you?" Adam says, giving me the side eye.

"With level-ten energy and jazz hands." I grin at him. "How could you have ever been not keen on doing this film? This is epic!"

"It all worked out considerably better than I thought it would." His lips curl up in a soft smile, and he tenderly squeezes my hand.

"Hey lovers!" Brian appears beside us. "Wow, you're actually here. Surprised you made it out of the love nest!"

Adam's smile immediately fades. "Brian, get away from us."

"What he means to say" I hold up my hand "is love the support for us. Hate the creepy undertones."

"Ha!" Brian pats us both on the shoulder. "I love you guys. And hey, I hear congratulations are in order?" He looks at me with raised eyebrows. "Getting recruited by Nolan Smith himself, very impressive!"

"Impeccable problem-solving skills and dedication to the project, were his exact words when he made the offer, I believe," Adam says, smiling down at me. "And they couldn't be truer."

"Well, what can I say." I swish my hair over my shoulder. "But I might make him sweat a while longer. I feel like he has a better offer up his sleeve."

Brian grins. "Playing hardball, I like it."

"A girl after my own heart."

We all turn and see Dee, looking like a movie star in a

floor-length green dress. It makes her eyes sparkle like emeralds.

"You're one to talk," Adam says. "Mrs. First AD."

"That's *Miss* First AD to you," she says with a smirk. "This rising star isn't tied down by no one. But the contracts aren't final yet, let's hope the film goes through. Just what we need, right? Another pirate movie."

"Word on the street is you're in luck," Adam replies with a knowing nod.

Brian looks like he's seen the ghost of Marilyn Monroe, resurrected from her hand prints. "Whoa, Dee... can I just say..."

She turns and puts her hand on her hip, raising her eyebrow.

"... that you're incredibly talented, and any production would be lucky to have you on their team."

Dee downturns her mouth in surprise. "Thank you, Brian."

"And you look smoking hot in that dress."

"Brian!" the three of us chorus in unison, before all bursting into laughter.

"Shall we do this shit?" Dee says, motioning towards the grand entrance.

We file through the monumental building and find our seats and my insides are buzzing. Maybe Adam didn't give me an unfair leg up professionally, but it *is* a nice bonus that being his girlfriend means a ticket to the premiere. Usually PAs don't get to go, though I'm surprised Kylie didn't scheme her way in. Not that she even made it till the end of production. Dee made sure of that. While trying to destroy my reputation and career, Kylie flushed hers right down the toilet.

Isn't life funny like that?

Once we're settled, I find a few friendly faces around the room. Gus is in the center, next to the strapping man he came with. He looks at me and grins, doing the shaka symbol with his hand. A couple rows away from him is George and Elsa, both, I'm warmed to see, are looking very well. Walking in, wearing a very expensive looking suit, is Nolan. He and Adam exchange cordial nods as he passes with a supermodel on his arm.

I feel my phone buzz in my pocket and take a peek before it starts.

Mom: Enjoy tonight, sweetheart. You earned it x

I smile while I read it. My parents are almost as excited for the premiere as I am. We told them all about it last week at dinner. I'm happy to say Adam's subsequent dinners with them have gone better than the first.

"It's starting!" Dee stage whispers behind me and I stash my phone away, biting my lip. Adam squeezes my hand and we share a long, tender look before fixing our eyes on the big screen.

It's difficult to describe; the feeling of all our hard work playing out before our eyes in one polished piece. Seeing it here in high definition, it makes it *really* real.

I did it.

I've been waiting for this feeling forever, and it's made all the more special by the man sitting next to me. This dream, I couldn't have dreamt up even if I tried. We faced complications and misunderstandings, and maybe it took us until the last take, but we figured it all out, and we are even better for it. And now, the only drama left is the one playing out on the big screen in front of us, and it's quite an entertaining show.

I discreetly watch Adam. Every time the audience laughs or cheers or claps, his face glows with that smile. That darn smile I love so much. When the film ends, I'm filled with a new excitement as the credits start to roll. And much sooner than I expected, there it is.

Evie Miller – Production Coordinator

"I never did thank you for that little promotion," I whisper to Adam.

"Don't worry… you can thank me later." He grins.

I nudge him in the ribs, but know that I definitely will. I can barely keep my hands off the man.

Our eyes stay on each other, and his grin settles into a pensive smile. "You know this wouldn't have happened without you, right?" he says, holding my hand between his. "You changed my life."

I lean forward and press my lips against his, ignoring the catcalls from Brian and Dee behind us. But I have to admit, it's lovely not to hide this from anyone anymore. In fact, I want to shout it from the rooftops.

I'm in love, I'm in love, and I don't care who knows it.

I break away, but keep my face only a couple of inches from his.

"We're only just getting started."

ACKNOWLEDGMENTS

It's always scary releasing a new book, especially a new series. So if you've made it this far, thank you for reading *The Last Take* and jumping on this new adventure with me! I'm really excited to introduce you to some new, fun, sweet and wacky characters.

Creating a new world isn't glamorous business, so thank you to Rishton for accepting me in all my unwashed hair, dressing gown, haven't moved from my laptop all week glory. And also for pretending to be excited when I hit my word targets for the day.

And finally, for all my readers, old and new, for taking a chance on a new author. This is book five, but I still feel like a rookie most of the time. So thank you for reading my silly words and reaching out on social media. I love connecting with you all!

Printed in Great Britain
by Amazon